Cursed by Chemistry

by

Kasey Mark

Cursed by Chemistry

COPYRIGHT © 2015 by Kacey Mark

Contact Information: info@thewildrosepress.com

Cover Art by *Diana Carlile*

The Wild Rose Press, Inc.
PO Box 708
Adams Basin, NY 14410-0708

Visit us at www.thewilderroses.com

Publishing History
First Scarlet Rose Edition, 2015
Print ISBN 978-1-5092-0412-0
Digital ISBN 978-1-5092-0413-7

Published in the United States of America

Scorching hot chemistry's one thing; third degree burns are something else entirely…

Shauna ducked her head and tugged in a deep breath. She could do this. She'd been practicing for years. All those evenings spent seducing her own reflection, hoping that one day Adrian would see her.

But to tempt her body with someone like him?

Not like him. It was him. The flesh-and-bone infatuation to end all others.

Giving herself over to a lust that strong could put them both in danger. She looked up through a fringe of moist lashes. But would she ever get a chance again?

Starting in the corner of her mouth, Shauna used the point of her tongue to follow along the sharp bow of her upper lip. She continued her painstaking circular path to trace her mouth's full outline.

Adrian's lips parted as his attention followed her. A feral, hungry sound seemed to drag behind his breath.

Shauna's gaze fled to the silent rise and fall of his winged tattoo. A persistent reminder of how far Adrian had traveled into the world of sex and a mysterious omen of where he was about to lead her. She stalled her approach and shifted her weight slowly from one foot to the other. What if she didn't know enough to please him?

"Closer." Adrian's word ebbed with challenge.

Shauna's eyes squeezed shut, and she stole the remaining distance between them before her body roped him off with more excuses.

She cracked an eye open. Adrian hadn't moved. The most peculiar look of mirth formed in the sensual curve of his mouth. He dipped his head, mouth angling toward hers. The heat of his breath fanned her mouth just before he meshed his lips against hers.

Dedication

Many thanks to
Doree Anderson, Sandy Rowland, Clancy Metzger, and
Keith Hale for their undying support!

Chapter One

Oh, great. Him again.

Shauna eyed the lone, pale SUV as it sloshed through a dark puddle and jostled into the parking lot. The streetlight's beams glanced off the golden emblem painted on the vehicle's door.

Her heart rate sped to a gallop.

She tossed the large stone cradled in her hand. It jumped and skittered away into the shadows.

Shauna's glossy, white rain boots clicked over wet asphalt. Caught in the open with no place to hide, she fought the panic crawling through her and the urge to increase her pace.

She could have lost something—her wallet, maybe? That's a time sensitive issue and a perfect excuse to be there after hours. Or she could have taken a job throwing boxes on the night crew. Her contact, Samuel, would have to cover for her.

She glanced to her berry-pink trench coat. Not really dressed to pull off manual labor. Better go with the wallet story instead.

Shauna shielded her eyes from the SUV's blinding beams as she continued on her path to the mall's vacant loading dock. The vehicle slowed to a crawl beside her as if trolling for an explanation. The window planed down with an electric hum.

Shauna swallowed hard, lifted her chin a notch,

1

and continued marching. She might not be able to explain it aloud, but she *did* have every right to be there. She'd been invited. So what if the invitation had come with a three-hundred dollar price tag…

"Good evening."

Her vision narrowed on the cement staircase ahead. She hated that sharp, full of purpose, tone—like she was in trouble. She cast the agent a brief glance before returning her focus to the twin metal doors of bay 215. She tried to steady her voice. "Huh—hi." *Yeah. Keep trying.*

His voice took on a note of intrigue. Almost delight. "We've got to stop meeting like this."

She slid her gaze in his direction again and managed a weak laugh. Utah might be the Shakespearian mecca for romance and destiny, but not this encounter. This seemed more like stalking.

"This is two nights in a row, and I told you before, the mall closes at eleven."

Shauna blinked. "Isn't mall security a little out of your jurisdiction? Detective?"

His thin lips pressed together in pause. "Agent." His tone hardened as he matched her accusation. "Is there some reason why you're out here? Again?"

"I'm meeting someone."

"The someone without a name?" he quipped.

Heat crept over her face. She stopped, tossed a help-me smile to the blanketed sky, and then pivoted to the driver's side window. She could just make out the occupant's shadowed features in the dashboard's glow. What was his name again? Squid-linski? With a bulbous head and a nose like that, he could certainly pass for a squid.

"Mall's had a rash of break-ins lately. I'm not so sure you should be out here by yourself."

Shauna tipped her head. "But I'm not by myself." She coated her voice with sticky-sweet sarcasm. "I have you."

She set her shoulders and headed for the bay doors again. Just fifteen feet from the paint-crusted steps. *Almost there.*

The car's engine persisted. The grit of tires on pavement followed alongside her.

"Well, that's true...but see, here's the problem." His voice elevated because, apparently, Shauna had nothing better to do than listen to him all night. "I did a little checking. The mall association thinks these burglaries are an inside job."

Shauna gripped the cold, metal railing. Her tone matched her pace as she crept up each step of the loading platform. Anxiety nipped at her ankles. "Uh-huh. Inside job. That's great. Very interesting. Good sleuthing there. But I don't see how that has anything to do with me. You see, I'm...*outside.*"

The vehicle eked to a stop. The detective—agent—whatever, threw open the door and stepped out. His tone elevated as he followed her up the stairs. "Bottom line, the dock is off limits to unauthorized visitors, especially after dark. Let's see some ID."

She stopped short of the door. "Like you don't already know who I am." With a sigh of indignation, Shauna rifled through her patent-leather billfold. "Seriously. This is borderline harassment."

"It's also borderline trespassing."

She dealt him her driver's license. "The FBI must not be paying you new guys enough these days if you're moonlighting as a mall cop." She hammered three short knocks on the metal door.

Nothing.

"Very funny." He frowned at the plastic card. The moment of silence stretched out for what seemed like a week. "Is your friend *invisible*, Miss Tamson?"

The dopey swagger of each passing second continued, and the pressure built until Shauna had few options between dashing off like an escaped mental patient and appealing to his better nature. Neither option sounded good.

Why hadn't Samuel answered yet? He gave strict instructions to only knock once but maybe he didn't hear it.

"It is *Miss*, Right?" Squidlinski persisted. "You're not married?"

"No." *Not yet, anyway.*

"Boyfriend?"

The contents of her stomach churned with unease. "Geez, don't they brief you people anymore? Read your freakin' paperwork."

The feds had been lurking in the shadows of her life long enough for at least one lead agent to retire. Never thought she'd miss Special Agent Oaks. She even sent him flowers on his big day. The guy was old. Slow. She could outrun that one.

"You didn't answer my question."

"Yes. I have a boyfriend," she exclaimed.

His gaze lowered to her mouth, where she had apparently been trying to gnaw her way free. "You paused there. Are you lying to me?" He tipped his head. "Do you know where liars go?"

Shauna stuffed both hands into her trench coat. She

jerked them out again the moment her hand touched yet another stone seeking woolen refuge in her pocket. "I'm not lying. And since when do people get taken to jail for lying?"

"I didn't say I'd take you in. Is that what you want?" His crooked grin widened. "There's got to be a reason why you keep coming back here." His heavy-lidded gaze took its time invading every curve and crevice from her mouth to knee-high boots. "Dressed like that. During my shift."

She didn't respond.

"Shauna." He drew out her name as if urging her to admit to…whatever the hell he was trying to get at. He tucked both thumbs in his belt and widened his stance, her card anchored tight between his pudgy first and middle finger. "You can't give me any other valid excuse for being here."

"What's wrong with the way I dress?" she asked, hoping to steer him off subject.

His Muppet-worthy unibrow peaked with feigned innocence. "Not a darn thing."

"It's perfectly modest."

"A little too modest."

She blinked. "What's that supposed to mean?"

The agent leaned back. "Well, for a girl in your line of work…you must be pretty high priced to dress that way."

Shawna's mouth flapped open in offense.

He shrugged. "Give me another reason why you're here. Who you meeting with?"

Did he just label her a prostitute? "I work at a *make-up counter*. Clinique, actually." She couldn't help the pissed-off superiority that laced into her tone.

Sixteen months of cosmetology school and for what? To be labeled a streetwalker? Don't think so.

"Clinique? Like here at the mall?"

Shauna clamped her lips between her teeth. Did she really want this federal creeper to know where she worked?

His lips curved into a victorious smile. "Uh-huh. Then why use the back door—and why would your so-called boyfriend let you wander around this late without him?"

"You know, your badge isn't a stalking license. Why don't you save the harassment for traditional business hours?"

The agent didn't move.

Shauna pushed out a sigh of irritation. "My boyfriend's busy. And besides, he doesn't own me. He likes that I'm independent." She cast a wistful smile heavenward in an attempt to blow off her little white lie. In reality, no way in hell would she tell Richard where she'd gone. Or why she was here.

West Valley wasn't the safest place after dark. It wasn't that big either, and with a name as prominent as Tenerelli, she couldn't utter it aloud without people making the connection. Word might get back to him, and he would freak. Out.

"Look. I appreciate your mission to serve and protect the lamp posts out here," she nodded to the pole above door 215, "and that one's out by the way."

"What—"

She stole another quick rap on the door when the agent looked to the marred light pole and the pixie sprinkle of broken glass below it. The light's shell held one gaping cavity where a bulb had been, and another

6

light that buzzed and flickered in self-defense.

Lucky he hadn't shown up earlier. Then he'd have a vandalism charge on her too.

"See. You have a stone-throwing, light-buster person to catch, and I need to be on my way." She searched the door for some kind of knob or lever to grant her access, but a thin metal plate was welded where the doorknob should've been. The one way through the door was from the inside.

The agent menaced over her. "That light was fine an hour ago."

Shauna dipped her gaze to evade him. "Wow, and I was only joking about the mall cop job. You really are working here?"

He angled his head low, denying any escape. "There are easier ways to get my attention, you know."

"I don't want your attention—"

The muggy heat of his arm pressed against her shoulder when he braced one hand on the door. "Now you have it."

Yippee. Frustration itched up her sides. Another setback. She'd have to bail, contact Samuel, and hope to try again in a few hours.

Dammit, that was going to cost another three hundred. She didn't have it. But she couldn't just give up. Her whole future depended on this.

"Putting yourself in *yet another* compromising position." He angled his head. "Tell me. What happens when you do that, Ms. Tamson?"

"Look, I'm real sorry I blew your cover and all. I don't want any trouble. So I'll just leave—"

"Sparks? Fireworks?"

"I don't believe in that magic shit." She held out

her hand. "My license, please?"

"What license?" he countered.

She stared.

"You really shouldn't be driving without one by the way. Do you need a ride somewhere?" he asked.

Shauna edged away from him and toward the tin can, compact car she'd stowed across the street. "I'll walk, thanks." His boss would be getting a call in the morning. By the time she finished with him, he'd be downgraded to dogcatcher.

He stepped in front of her. His gaze pinned on the large button of her trench coat that fastened just below her breasts. "A little troublemaker like you shouldn't be out wandering the streets. Let me take you home."

"Again, thanks but no thanks."

"Are you…resisting?" he asked.

She arched a sardonic brow. "Are you…using cheesy, porn-cop talk on me?"

His grin widened. "Maybe."

"Eww." She wrinkled her brow in disgust.

His frown said that wasn't the reaction he'd hoped for. "Hey, you're the one who started this, with your high heels and your little trench coat. I know what you're after. I know your game." He leaned in until his chilidog breath wafted over her face. "Nor do I like being teased." A rancid gleam of intent lit his eyes.

Forget the stone in her pocket. Between fight and flight, her nerves were charged with enough panic that Shauna could shimmy up the lamppost faster than a shiny vampire. "Look. You really seem to have the wrong impression."

"Do I?"

She edged to one side. "I'm flattered and all. But

honestly, I have a boyfriend."

"Even if you do, he's not here. Is he?"

She retreated another step. "He's here. He's," she lifted her voice, "Samuel?"

The agent made a skeptical snort and angled toward the crook of her neck. His arms curled around her torso.

"Sam. Sammy…*shit*!" She pushed at the agent's chest and twisted for the steps. "Oh gross. Get away." Her voice dripped disgust.

His squeezing pressure around her midsection increased. The tiny hairs on the back of her neck tingled. The rapid-fire sensation chased down her arms as the surface of her skin crackled and heated.

Not again.

A cold lump of dread dropped into her stomach. The warmth inside her body rushed to the surface. The porcelain skin on her hands took on a lobster hue. Anger and determination blasted through her body, stoking her external temperature.

She would not be a victim again.

She may not be able to control it, but she'd use it, by God. If she had to, she'd kill him. Her palms slicked with moisture. "Let go!" she screeched.

It was coming.

If he didn't release her, she wouldn't be able to stop it. A girl can only afford so many death-by-inferno cards. Even with self-defense paying the bill, it was still expensive on the conscience.

The energy in her muscles drained and grew cold. Her arms weakened. Her elbows ready to snap at the hinges as the heat turned up and her body turned helpless.

She shrunk down in her coat-turned-pressure-cooker and twisted to escape from the agent's grasp.

Somehow, his grip slipped. He rushed to regain his hold.

She jerked out of reach.

The moment her head managed to follow the direction her legs were taking her, she stumbled down the steps and yelped in surprise. Shauna smacked into a cool, bony chest. A puff of freesia-scented steam escaped her coat on impact. Her nose crushed against his sharp collarbone. She tried using her momentum to pinball away, but thin arms clamped down on her.

"Hey, baby," a familiar voice purred. Strands of limp, copper-colored hair brushed her cheek. "Did I scare you?"

"Samuel!" she gasped. The pungent aroma of his body odor, cardboard, and axle grease coated her senses, and like a hot poker plunged into water, her skin cooled. She turned in his arms to face the squid and tried to act more relieved than repulsed.

"I said the east door, *east*, not south. And you're late." A slight edge hardened Samuel's tone. One that didn't seem to fit the whole freckle-faced, schoolboy thing he had going on. "But we'll spank you for that later…" He paused.

A look of surprise creased his ruddy brow at the faint hissing sound that came from under her coat. He eased his grip. "What you got cookin' in there?" he asked.

The agent swiped Shauna's card from the ground near his feet. "You know this girl?"

Samuel paused from peeling back the edge of Shauna's coat as if just noticing the agent. "Hey,

Squeelinski."

"It's Squid-linski," Shauna spat. She swatted at Samuel's curious hand.

"*Squa*-linski. Get it right," the agent snapped. His putout frown deepened. "How do you know my name?"

"Nah, she's right. I like squid better. And for the record, I know everybody." Samuel looked at Shauna and his lips turned pouty. He looped an arm around her shoulders and led her away. His voice took on a patronizing lilt. "Did that man-handling squidster touch you? Did he?"

Shauna hesitated. Her tone deflated. "No." The last thing she needed was for someone else to fight her battles. Hell, the opponent might even *survive* that way. Besides, if she caused more of a scene, she might as well kiss this meeting goodbye.

She hesitated. "But I think he molested my license."

"Damn," Samuel muttered with an emphatic sigh. He lowered his head in feigned annoyance then twisted around, snatching the card from Squidlinski's reluctant hand. Samuel moved forward again, and lifted his voice as if barking to the agent behind them. "Try harder next time. I need a better excuse than a piece of plastic if I'm gonna kick your ass." He jerked on a chain protruding from a single door on the east corner of the building.

Shauna glanced up. The light had already been dimmed here. Samuel had told her a dark light post would be her signal. He never said it would be darkened *for her*. She closed her eyes. Of all the stupid—

The door swung open, and Samuel yanked Shauna inside.

11

The agent moved to follow. He opened his mouth. The scowl marring his forehead indicated a disgruntled reply, but before any words escaped, Samuel slammed the door.

The crash of metal echoed though the storeroom. He wrapped the chain around the door's inside handle. The *rattle-clang, rattle-clang* beat through the room with each pass around the bar.

Samuel muttered between passes. "Do you have any idea…how hard it is…to get people in here? You've gotten caught not once, but twice. What the hell! And FBI…?" He shot her a glance as he retrieved a padlock from the end of the chain. "He rarely accepts anyone anymore, you know that?—by the way, you throw like a girl, and I told you to wear something dark. That's not dark."

It's dark pink. She wanted to argue, but doing so would only fuel his anger.

Shauna knew her choice of dress was a risk. Adrian Sands liked his customers low profile. But Shauna knew something about Adrian her contact didn't. This had been Adrian's favorite color. Maybe not his favorite color in the whole world, but he had specifically picked this color for her.

Chapter Two

Her memory spun back to Adrian Sands. To the man he used to be. She'd known him throughout her small-town childhood as the neighborhood hottie. But with a two-year age gap, they were incompatible back then.

Pifft…with the number of wars they fought, the term "incompatible" had been an understatement. It wasn't until college that they formed any shred of an awkward truce.

Even at the age of twenty-three, he wasn't a big talker. His broad posture and brilliant smile might have said "large and impressive," and who knew, maybe he was—even between the sheets. But that illusion never confirmed or denied itself, even to the most provocative of community college cheerleaders. The power of raging hormones was no match for Adrian's blockade of good manners. No wonder he'd made the best house dad in Sigma Phi Epsilon history.

Shauna has been busy pledging to her own sorority the night of the SigEp hosted party. Even in a surging crowd with music thumping loud enough to blur her vision, the laser sights of Alpha Chi Omega were still trained on her from every corner.

"You. On the stairs!"

Shauna turned to the blonde-haired boy near the kitchen. His lips stretched to a cheesy grin and pointed to the paper cup he held high above the masses. "Drink?"

"How about a Coke?"

His pale brows cinched in disbelief. "What?"

Shauna cupped her hands around her mouth and shouted, "A Coke!" as the music lulled. Her words bullhorned through the frat house, and several heads turned in her direction. Laughter bubbled through the crowd as the music picked up again.

"I think she wants a Coke," offered a spaghetti-strapped redhead who appeared to be holding her own at the beer pong table. The attention wandered away, until Shauna caught the weight of one pair of eyes that had locked and held. The warmth that had receded from her cheeks returned full force.

Lounging in a battered chair with one ankle propped on his knee, Adrian Sands regarded her with an arch of his raven brow. Not a seductive, fancy-meeting-you brow lift. A what-the-hell-are-you-doing-here, don't-you-think-you're-a-little-young brow lift.

Shauna should know. When Adrian played her neighborhood big brother, she'd seen it hundreds of times. His hottie-authoritative combo made the perfect formula for years of closet fantasies and self-pleasuring role-play.

One by one, those thoughts marched through Shauna's brain like an erotic circus on parade.

Pity. She'd grown old enough to sneak a peek inside his big tent, but he still wanted to play safety net.

Was it the Coke she'd ordered that gave him license to treat her like a child? How could that one look of disapproval turn her stomach into such a shaken snow globe of excitement? With every chair and dark corner occupied, Shauna slunk down on the stairs. Maybe she should have ordered something stronger.

"Here you go, pretty girl." A freckled hand lifted the drink through the stair railing.

Her reflection danced back at her in the darkened liquid. Did she look that out of place?

"Well, don't just sit there. Drink up." His limp tangle of blonde hair flapped up and down as string-cheese-boy shifted and trotted past other partygoers on his way up the stairs.

Adrian's gaze shifted to the boy, and his eyes seemed to narrow.

Maybe Shauna hadn't done anything after all; maybe Adrian was in one of those hate-everybody moods. That seemed more fitting. She'd never managed to score his attention before. Why start now?

The flat, lukewarm drink left a chalky film on Shana's tongue. Her bottom lip pulled into a frown. Her next, tentative sip sloshed over her lips as string boy bumped her shoulder.

"That'll be five dollars." He sighed as he lowered himself next to her. "Or you could just tell me your name."

Shauna took another sip and looked away. "Is this diet?" She offered the cup back. "For five bucks, I'd prefer the drink I ordered."

He nudged the cup back. "Come on, don't make me feel bad. It's all we had left."

She looked to Adrian again. A wide-shouldered man had stepped in front of him, blocking Shauna's view.

Something had changed in him. She craned her neck for a better glimpse, but she couldn't see his face.

Adrian's hands had clamped on the arms of his chair, and he leaned forward, his posture tensed as if ready to strike. If she had to guess, the wide-shouldered guy had just given him some very bad news. Adrian looked ready to pummel him.

Of all the crappy timing. Shauna rose to her feet and stared at the shoulder blockade. Just a little to the left and she'd get the full view again—a kibble toss of excitement to the yapping poodle that was her curiosity. What sort of news could possibly animate the immovable Adrian?

"You okay?"

Shauna's attention spun back to the blond boy who'd planted himself beside her. "What?"

"I said, are you pledging?"

"Yeah." She waved the questioner away.

"Well then, you'd better catch up," string-cheese-boy persisted, pushing the cup back into her hand.

From her vantage point over the rim of the cup, Shauna caught sight of Adrian again as he jumped to his feet. A piercing look of determination darkened his features, and his chin jerked in her direction. *Was that really meant for her?*

As if on command, the shoulder barricade turned, and the man started for the stairs. Adrian fell in step behind him, picking up speed. A growl of hurricane force rage seemed to pull from every corner of the room, as Adrian heaved a mighty breath.

Had she heard that right? Shauna's heart leaped to attention and pumped out an urgent distress signal at first sight of the menacing clench of his jaw.

But one step closer and the snow globe in her stomach seemed to shatter. *Act cool. Act cool.* The excitement overpowered everything and fought her lips into a hopeless, groupie smile.

She lowered the cup just as the liquid jumped into her face. It splashed down her shirt, rendering her white-silk, butterfly-sleeved top completely ruined. She gasped at the wide-shouldered man who lay face down a few steps away. Adrian had apparently shoved him forward, dominoing the mass of stoop monkeys right into her.

He never did offer her an explanation that night, just a box one hour later that contained a new shirt *as colorful as she was* and an invitation to Casa de Adrian for the night.

Which she refused.

Well, except for the shirt. That berry-pink, sewn-in-heaven, wonder of a blouse came from Saks Fifth Avenue. It had been the most expensive item she'd ever owned.

Perhaps he'd been trying to protect her from the date-rape drug that laced her drink that night or the destruction of her self-respect a few hours later. But it's easy to pin nobilities on a girl's first crush.

Shauna flung the memory away. He had still offered his room that night. He still wanted something from her, just like the rest of them. He wasn't as innocent as he'd led her to believe.

Any opportunity to appeal to that marred nobility from years ago could save her future. If she could stand out and sweet talk him, it might earn her the privilege of being treated for her unwanted singe-skills.

"You know, you're not very bright. Pretty, but not bright," Samuel assessed.

She grinned. Some of that might come naturally,

but for Adrian, she'd dress it up a little. Act dumb and flaunt the package. If Adrian had some sort of weakness for her, she'd find it. She had to.

Her thoughts brick-walled as Samuel shoved a paper bag over her head. "Hey!" She moved to tear the bag free.

Samuel caught her hands.

She twisted.

Samuel's voice elevated over the crinkling sound of the attack paper bag. "Stop…*Stop*! It's the rules. He doesn't see you. You don't see him. It's how these things stay secret. Deal with it or leave."

Shauna jerked her shoulders away. "Okay, fine."

Shit.

Samuel hooked her wrist and tugged her forward. "Let's just get this over with."

She kept her head down and dodged the boxes, shelves, and advertising signs that littered the narrow view at her feet.

"You're lucky he's still here. He's usually gone by now. Moved to the next drop zone."

Shauna swallowed. Right. Him. The man she'd come to see. No longer the frat house overseer or the model neighbor boy but the elusive miracle worker, Adrian Sands. Shauna caught word of him not long after she dropped out of college for cosmetology.

The tiniest of patients at Primary Children's Burn Unit had been making recoveries beyond medical explanation. The staff was sworn to secrecy, but it's apparently inhuman for people to *actually* keep a secret. Word got out and the entire nation turned their microscope on Utah and Adrian, the local researcher, who had flipped the medical community upside-down.

Of course, the pimple-ridden debutants and wrinkle-fearing celebrities were the first to swarm. But the moment Adrian Sands' name came out, he disappeared.

If he could reverse the effects of charred skin and cooked muscle, maybe he could help with her own high-temperature affliction. Before time ran out.

Her mind whirred to a different memory from the SigEp party. Those few hours later seemed a lifetime away from flat drinks and staircase brawls. Where pained screams and ambulance sirens drowned out the thumping music and the smell of burnt bodies would forever brand her soul.

Shauna shook the memory from her head. She couldn't think about that. She had been a survivor, not a victim, and she hadn't meant to hurt anyone. With a little luck from Adrian, it would never happen again. She could fall apart later, but for now—focus.

Classic rock swarmed Shauna's paper bag as she entered some sort of concrete clearing and the toasted smell of spice and frankincense invaded her nose. A *clink* of glasses came from somewhere on her right, followed by a muttered curse and shifting steps. Her stomach twisted. Only one person in the room, as far as she could tell, and Shauna had a pretty good idea of whom.

"What is it, Sam?" His mellow baritone held that same gruff edge. Shauna's heart recognized it and chimed off an erratic response.

Oh, come on. She tried to quell the giddy tension in her chest. He might be a medical icon, and sexy as hell, but the guy was still a guy. A small-town guy—regardless of where he'd been the last ten years. He took off his pants the same as everyone else, one leg at a time.

A metal *click* would sound as he loosened his belt, followed by a snap of leather that cut through the room as he pulled it free. Then the quick and deliberate grate of his zipper. The image of tanned, muscle-corded thighs, and a prominent male appendage appeared as he shoved his jeans down, a motion that was all authority and purpose. Each deliberate step forward would cause his erect cock to nod an upward beat. The tempo, a lurid promise of the power it could deliver. One full, heavy thrust at a time.

The heat turned up inside her paper bag.

This time it had nothing to do with her unwanted defensive mechanism.

Shauna squeezed her eyes shut. Puts *on* his pants. That's how the saying went.

How fair was this? The mere sound of his voice sent her mind on a hasty jailbreak. It fled east of Beef Cake Street and promptly snapped its chain. Gone.

She could never evoke that kind of response from Adrian.

Not that it would hurt to try. If it took pulling out every dirty trick in her girly arsenal, she'd do it. With her fiancé, Richard, pushing the celibacy issue on an almost a daily basis, and her wedding night looming in just three months' time, she had to persuade him in any way possible to cure her problem.

She cleared her throat, the sound more timid than she wanted. She tried again, louder this time, guessing she still hadn't claimed his full attention.

Adrian always functioned with a singular focus. To divert him would be next to impossible. Even if a naked cancan dancer high-kicked through the room, he wouldn't look up. Not to mention, Shauna wasn't a dancer.

And she had a bag on her head.

"Adrian—" she started.

"You don't talk." Samuel whispered. His voice turned in Adrian's direction. "Hey, big guy."

"Hey yourself…and who's that?" Adrian asked his voice rather flat and unaffected.

"Sort of a special request." Samuel strained his words in a sly undertone. She could just imagine his arms splayed out like a swarthy magician. Or a *Price is Right* model.

The price was a little high to be truthful.

The noncommittal grunt that came from Adrian seemed less than fascinated with Samuel's mystical introduction.

"And I know how you enjoy a challenge," Samuel prodded.

Adrian's response came sporadically as the shift of boxes and shuffling feet continued. "I think you have me confused…with you."

Shauna's frustration percolated under the bag. He was shutting her down. She pushed out a huff of annoyance. "Can I take this off now?"

"No," the boys answered in unison.

Shauna paused. How about that. A reaction. Not exactly the one she'd hoped for, but a good start. "This isn't fair. How can you fully consider my case without putting a face to it?"

"You want a face?" Samuel asked.

Shauna heard a pop. "What—"

"Hold still." Samuel snared her chin and held her

there amid the panicked crinkle of brown paper.

She shoved at his hand and thrust her head back. "Stop it." The sound came out more annoyed than panicked. Like some unfortunate pet that fought the sweater and lost. She couldn't escape the assaulting smell of ink, in the form of two scribble marks for her eyes and the curvy line of what must have been her mouth.

"Here ya go...there," Samuel sounded a little too satisfied for his own good. He stepped back.

Adrian's voice held only passive dismissal. "I don't think she's smiling under there."

"Trust me, this is better... On second thought, her frown is kinda sexy." Samuel seemed to contemplate. "Maybe if I—"

Shauna put up her hands when Samuel neared again. "You touch me with that marker, and I'll scream."

Shauna could hear the grin in his voice. "Fine...be ornery then. But just so you know, you're smiling on the outside."

The paper bag crinkled as Shauna planted her fist on her hip. "Okay, that's it. Are you going to hear my case or not?"

"No."

"No?" Her breath caught in a futile attempt for an explanation, a point to argue, something! He had to treat her. He just had to.

"Believe it or not, princess, you're going to hear that word a lot in your young life. Get used to it," Adrian said.

Princess? Shauna's anger sparked. "Just who the hell do you think I am?"

Adrian paused between the scrape of boxes. His voice returned even more distracted than before. "Ugh...Strawberry shortcake?"

Shauna's shoulders dropped in their sockets. Well, at least he noticed the outfit.

"But you don't even know what you're treating her for yet," Samuel complained.

The bag crinkled as Shauna turned in Samuel's direction. She paused. Since when had he been on her side?

"I'm busy enough as it is. If you want this serum finished by tomorrow..." Adrian countered.

"You finished it three hours ago. Now you're just farting around."

The reassuring weight of Samuel's hands rested on her shoulders.

"Dude, this one's special."

"Aren't they *all* special?" Adrian drawled. "Really, you might want to focus on getting rid of your old flames before you build new ones."

"What can I say? Love all, trust a few, do wrong to none—" Samuel seemed to stop short. "Okay. Sorry." He leaned toward Shauna and funneled quick words near her paper barrier. "Just a note, he doesn't like Shakespeare."

"I get lonely," Samuel tried again. "The serum will take care of flame number one. I'm just lining up my rebound. No harm in that."

"I'm not your rebound," Shauna muttered. "You wanna see flames? I'll show you freaking flames." Despite Samuel's...revolting yet honorable efforts, the value of Shauna's situation dripped away, one millisecond at a time. Any moment Adrian would boot her out.

She lifted her voice. "No one else can help me, and I am not leaving. Take one look at me, Adrian Sands, and tell me you're not treating me. Say it to my face."

"I'm not treating you. Though it's kinda hard to be serious with that look on your um…bag."

Shauna fisted the paper and the tearing sound silenced the room. "Not good enough. Try again." When Shauna tossed the bag aside, she found a tight-jawed look of anger altering Adrian's initial surprise.

Her shoulders set back with victory, just before Samuel stepped in front as if to shield Adrian from some crazed groupie.

Shauna smoothed a hand over her hair and leaned deep to one side to see around Samuel. "You're not the easiest man to find, by the way."

Adrian's chest rippled as he folded his arms, partially obscuring the GNC logo on his chest. He offered a faint, congratulatory nod. "Yet here you are."

"You've been here, this close, the whole time?" Shauna demanded. "How?" The small town seemed to have an impenetrable orbit. No one ever left this place, but somehow she always expected Adrian to be immune to that sort of thing. Miles away on a yacht somewhere. With the public hunting him, how the hell did he manage to stay invisible?

Adrian didn't respond.

"So, you know each other?" Samuel demanded.

Shauna sent him a bitter grin. "Oh sure! He threw me in *a pond* once."

Samuel sat back. "Oh. How romantic."

"I heard about your work at the children's hospital," she tried again.

24

He tipped his head. "We're not at the hospital, and you're no child."

"No." She lifted a defiant brow. "Far from it, but thanks for finally noticing."

"You don't seem to have any burns," Adrian continued. His attention returned to the canister in front of him.

Samuel shifted to block her on the right. She jockeyed left. "Again, thanks for noticing. But you're right. My problem's different." She shoved at Samuel's shoulder when he blocked her again. "I'm the one that does the burning."

"Only not children. I would never do that to a child." She swallowed. "Just to men."

"I feel that," Samuel added. "She is pretty haaawt."

"I want to get rid of it."

"Why?" Adrian didn't look up from the table.

"Because—" Did it really need further explanation? Marriage, children, her *future*. It all depended on him.

"Sammy there doesn't seem the least bit uncomfortable," Adrian stated.

Shauna recognized the press of Samuel's palm, holding her at length. She managed to deflect it with an irritated shove of her hand. "That's because it's…it's a more intimate reaction."

The glass vial of amber-colored fluid looked so tiny between Adrian's fingertips as he nestled it into a container of powdered supplements. He twisted the lid with a few agitated flicks of his wrist and tossed it into a box. "Well, whatever it is, it's not life threatening. I'm sure you can work around it."

Samuel's voice grew with enthusiasm. "Yeah…we

can experiment a little."

A squeal rang out as Adrian swiped a packing tape dispenser across the box. "You're too busy for any more experiments." Adrian threw the box with a sharp flick of his wrist. The basketball-sized parcel shot end over end in a tight spiral until it collided with Samuel's torso.

Samuel jostled the box in his fingertips for a moment, then cradled it to chest. "Hey, careful."

"Stay out of my chocolates from now on." Adrian turned to leave. "Get her out of here." That last bit sounded almost like an afterthought.

Shauna's mouth hinged open with offense. He had forgotten about her before she'd even left.

Samuel gave her a once-over. He offered an apologetic shrug, and motioned a hand towards the exit. "Better luck next time I guess. Oh, and by the way, no refunds."

How could he do that? How could Adrian just dismiss her like that?

"I don't have time for this," she pleaded.

Adrian's snide tone echoed through the hall. "Late for a nail appointment?"

She glanced around the room for something to throw at the back of his perfectly groomed head. There, on the table, amid a scattering of dark business cards, she spied an apothecary jar full of brightly wrapped chocolates and rushed for it.

She attempted to lift the jar. The weight of it told her she'd never be able to throw far enough to make contact. What were these things made of? Solid lead? She lifted the lid, ready to fire a fist full of chocolate projectiles. The glass clinked.

The sound seemed to stop Adrian in mid-retreat down the hall. He returned.

Her gaze zeroed in on his chest. Center mass. Even better.

"Take two," Samuel whispered.

"They're not for her." An ember of warning seemed to glow in the depths his voice. It was little, but it was there, and something about that tone itched at Shauna's naughty side.

Adrian started toward her.

Samuel looked to Adrian and back to Shauna. His voice grew in urgency. "You'll probably need two. And one for me. Okay, so that's three."

Shauna's vision returned to its target and she scooped an entire handful. Loose candies tumbled to the floor on the way to her pocket and snapped near her feet.

Adrian planted both palms on the table that stood between them. He leveled her with a threatening look. "Put those back."

"Uh—no."

Adrian tipped his head in challenge.

She shot him a smarmy grin and batted her lashes. "Get used to that word, Poindexter, because I'm not taking it for an answer."

Chapter Three

That woman.

That adorably stupid, pain-in-the-ass woman.

Agitated steps carried him the length of the darkened GNC store before he met the wall and spun back the way he'd come. Where was he going? Hell, if he knew, but Adrian couldn't leave. He only had one way out after the gates closed, and *she* was out there. No doubt growling like a pissy kitty because he'd refused her.

But that kind of magic doesn't get undone. Especially because he didn't know how he'd done it in the first place. He's never intended for the flame powder to be deadly or even permanent. Teaching those hormone-driven frat boys a lesson hadn't even been in the equation, but they'd learned all right.

So had Adrian. Never step blind in the world of apothecary again.

From the moment Adrian's father first caught him playing with Shauna, the Barbie next door, he'd been warned. *Those feelings have power. You can't wield them without losing control.*

Barbie grew more powerful the older she became, and in the end, his father had been right. His own infatuation for Shauna had screwed him. Oh, he had kept his distance from the tender-yeared doll, just as his father had cautioned, while one relationship after another failed.

And why? Adrian massaged the tight cords of muscle between his shoulder blades. Good question. What was the point in staying away from Shauna if all the lower pedestals failed him anyway? Go big or go home, right?

Adrian snorted. He went big all right. The moment he decided to take control of the frat-party situation with that innocently powdered sweater, his power contorted into something far worse than he'd ever intended.

Now she wanted him to fix it.

He took a deep breath, trying to cleanse the faint smell of freesia and syrup from his lungs.

He couldn't. It permeated everything. He blew the air out again and sent the stack of receipts near the cash register fluttering. He'd detected it the moment she stepped in. The tiny grains of infatuation in her seemed to form a tidal wave that sloshed through the entire room.

With his heightened awareness for chemical reactions, Adrian didn't stand a chance. A scent like that could send an entire fleet of apothecaries to their knees. Good thing there weren't many of them. Maybe three or four in the state of Utah—less if they came anywhere near his girl. Then there'd be only one.

Adrian paused. Scowled. *His girl?* He shook his head.

The siren's song of wet heat between her thighs called out to him, and his body caved. Lucky his brain managed to hold on. His body's reaction had been purely instinctual. A little excessive, but his three-week sexual drought could explain that.

Or so he'd thought. Until she tore through that paper and his deep thinker went from semi-erect to near crashing through the table. She had changed over the years. Gone from adorable and adventurous to…to…preened for the groping hands of high society. Not that his cock cared much.

The entire time he argued with her, it swelled and pointed as if to say: *she's right there…right…Oh…for the love of…will you just hurdle the table and bury me already? I'm about to explode here!*

In that moment, he knew helping Shauna wouldn't be possible. Even after surpassing his hormonal peak, and screwing three dozen other women, his lust for her hadn't diminished. It only increased. The urge to spread her boot-clad legs wide…it felt beyond primal.

And that thing she did with her eyes. She'd learned a trick or two with men over the years. But had anyone seen them with the lust-filled glare he could coax out of her?

Adrian paced the length of the room again. He'd kicked her out. But could he really leave her alone after this? Shauna threw fate a major interception by showing up here. She disclosed her identity and blew his cover at the same time. According to Samuel, the FBI was already on her tail. How long had that been going on? It wouldn't be hard for the feds to connect the dots right to him.

Or worse, the O could be wooing her within the hour.

"Good hell." Adrian punched a nearby display tower. The powder-filled canisters and pill bottles exploded in every direction. Some hit the ground and busted open on impact, while others rolled a few feet away from the chaos. "Hellhellhell." His growl intensified to a roar. "Fuck!"

Samuel's voice lifted with intrigue as he entered. "Bringing out the big-boy words. I'm impressed, A. It's like duck-duck-goose…only more fun."

Adrian pierced him with a fierce scowl and pitched a stray canister at his head. "Shouldn't you be gone by now?"

Samuel's eyes grew wide. He dodged left. The canister exploded in a cloud of smoke and powder as it hit the wall. Samuel held up his hands in surrender. "Yeah, if some grizzled vagrant hadn't stopped me in the parking lot." Samuel shuffled cautious steps through the dust at his feet and held out a large envelope. "He wanted me to give you this."

Adrian swiped the envelope. His tone grew distant as he studied the paper. "Grizzled vagrant, now look who's pulling out the big words."

Samuel couldn't seem to contain the grin that split across his face. "Not my words, his. I asked the bum who he was. That's what he told me, A. Grizzled vagrant. Like that was his name or something."

Adrian mentally shook his head. The name didn't matter. The chicken scratches that formed the letter 'A' and the scent stain of crushed cloves told him exactly who the messenger was.

A eunuch. *The Eunuch,* to be precise; the one-and-only, hobbling, messenger boy of the Oracle. He had no real name and only one purpose. To deliver bad news.

He handed the paper back to Samuel. "You read it."

Samuel gave him a you're-being-a-baby kind of look, before retrieving the envelope and peeling it open.

All right, so maybe he was. But the Shauna bomb was enough bad news for one night. Maybe if Samuel opened the letter, it would dole all that rotten luck on him instead.

Samuel cleared his throat. "It says, your presence is requested by honor of the Oracle."

Adrian snarled. "I don't have time for this."

"It says make time." Samuel squinted at the paper. "P.S. Samuel, the candy jar is unguarded. Quick, run." Samuel looked up. "What do you think he means by that?"

Chapter Four

Show your face and get the hell out.

Adrian gritted his teeth as he approached the glass. Bold letters forming the name "Big O's Toy Box" were fogged with print smudges and grime from the countless clients who had passed through here.

His lungs tensed as Adrian suppressed his ability for chemical reconnaissance and grasped the handle. Sometimes it was better not to know where things had been.

He set his mental stopwatch for the twenty-one and a half minutes it usually took to get back out and yanked the door open with one hand. He covered half the distance to the Oracle's pulpit before the door sealed shut. The metallic, autumn air and rush of evening traffic died behind him, replaced with pulsing music and muggy warmth.

The owner leaned forward from the pedestaled checkout counter. His sand-colored hair took on a brash, pink glow from the halo of neon lights overhead. Even for Adrian's six-two, the counter seemed unusually high.

Deliberately so.

The shiny, plastic structure served two purposes: elevate the Oracle's ego and put his customers in their place, like scurrying rats, eager to pay and escape with their trinkets tucked under their arm.

Adrian should know. He'd been the rat often enough he'd actually lost his testosterone-driven taste for hardcore silicone and bone-seeping perfume.

At first glance, it seemed odd—why would an oracle run a sex-toy shop? But in truth, the wares weren't much different. Both forms of business served to provide immediate gratification that no one really needed.

Says the man who just became the next customer in line. Irritation itched in Arian's veins. He was hooked, and he knew it. Adrian didn't want to know how his life—or lack thereof—turned out. He wanted to beat the system and conquer his family's curse. Doing so meant slurping up whatever flavor of shit the Oracle had to offer and using it to his advantage.

The Oracle squinted through horn-rimmed glasses at his monitor. A grin of delight plied into the globes of fat most people called cheeks. He looked every bit the Buddha's white-trash cousin. Not the kind of guy who sought enlightenment. He tripped over it, often days, or if lucky, minutes ahead of time, and boasted of his find to any dumbass who would believe him.

And that made Adrian king of Dumbassdom, didn't it? He breathed an impatient sigh. Maybe more of that autumn pollution outside would cool his mood.

The Oracle's self-indulgent drone—which had been going on for some time—rose in greeting as Adrian approached. "—not in the number of breaths we take but from the moments that take our breath away…*like*." The Oracle emphasized the last word with a pointed click of his finger.

Adrian didn't bother suppressing his eye-roll. For an all-seeing deity, one would think the Oracle would be the first person to discover social networking. Not the last.

Well, let's be honest, he still thought he was the first.

"What's got you in such a poor mood, Adrian Sands…Sands….Adrian Sands?" he sang. The Oracle's thick shoulders dipped to one side then the other in time to the overhead music, like a pair of overweight merry-go-round ponies. That same stupid jingle greeted Adrian every time he came here. "Not that I don't just *adore* the brooding type."

Don't respond.

And what was it about always using his full name? Only his mother had that right, and she'd died the day she gave it to him. The spider-line threads that bound Adrian's heart pulled tighter. Yet another glimpse of the Apothecary curse in action. One of the many reasons Adrian hated prophecy in all its forms—and the main reason why the Oracle loved to pester him.

"Ohh and bitter." The Oracle clicked his thick tongue, but his attention held on the monitor.

Do. Not. Respond.

The Oracle's head swiveled atop the thick folds of his neck. His thin lips pursed to one side. "Boy, you need a vacation or a massage or something."

How does someone lisp with a tongue that big? Probably something he'd mastered over several centuries. Oracles had an unusual lifespan. Unlike Apothecaries—thank God. Death, at the ripe ole age of sixty or so, would be Adrian's one release from his loveless misery. But then again, in death he would probably be written in the night sky, a perpetual arm's-length from his one true love. That's the kind of fate the universe hands you when you go screwing with the world's most famous star-crossed lovers.

Or if your grandfather does it for you. Or even your great-great-great grandfather—

"Why, you pouty little drama queen. You're darkening my entire domicile." The Oracle lifted his head from the screen and snapped the laptop shut.

Adrian crossed his arms. "I haven't said a word." Until now. Damn it. Adrian closed his eyes and tossed out his mental stopwatch. No telling how long it would take now. "Just get to the point."

"How am I supposed to make a living here, selling joy toys to the masses, with you acting all—" The Oracle waved his arms in a conjuring motion. "—wilty-wallflower on me."

"The point. You do have one, right?"

"Your heart hasn't even been broken yet." The Oracle continued his rant unhindered.

Adrian plucked a travel-sized packet of lube from its clear, plastic candy bin and pretended to study the back label. He muttered under his breath. "Could have had a million other guides, and this is what I'm stuck with. An attention-deficient deity."

The Oracle's lips twisted in mock disgust. "Love sucks. You're a hermit beyond your years, boy." The Oracle turned. "Why did I bring you here, anyway?"

"Is that rhetorical?"

The Oracle's grotesque orange and yellow, candy-corn sweater jiggled as he let out a pelican's bark of laughter. "Of course it's a rhetorical. I already know why I brought you. I know *everything*."

"Then you shouldn't need *anything* from me."

"I don't."

Adrian paused. Most days, he could pacify his urge to strangle the deity and keep his opinions in check, but this time proved more difficult.

He'd forgotten just how powerful Shauna's pheromones had been and about their unpredictable half-life. The effect on him was wearing off, but as always, it came with the most annoying of adverse reactions.

Angst.

That love's lost, heart-sickened, why-don't-I-eat-a-bullet feeling that always overcame him. The entire basis for gauging just how dangerous Shauna could be for him. And vice versa.

A cold net of awareness collapsed over Adrian. Good hell. The Oracle's timing couldn't have been better, and judging by the Oracle's smarmy expression, he'd planned it like that. Adrian wasn't here for some sordid task. He had been summoned…for entertainment?

He narrowed his vision to the Oracle's slender nose. It didn't really fit his face. Pointy, not bloody enough. It could stand some rearranging. As far as mortality went, the common cockroach didn't have nothin' on these guys. To die, Oracles must suffer a violent death. And for that job, Adrian just might start polishing his resume.

He stepped forward, ready to hurdle the counter.

The Oracle raised both hands. "Okay, okay. I do want one thing."

"Get to it then," Adrian snapped.

The Oracle's thick tongue darted out, and then disappeared again. He glanced to the Eunuch whose thin frame skulked out from the cyan and fuchsia beaded curtain that guarded the back room.

The Eunuch moved forward with an outstretched hand, his smile strained and bright. Several dollars were clamped between his bony fingers.

Adrian frowned. "What's this?" But the guy didn't speak, not in front of the deity. A lesson Adrian still hadn't mastered. *Damn it.*

Adrian's attention rounded back to the Oracle as he drum-soloed along with the pulsing overhead music. His eyes squeezed shut in rapture, a pink, jelly dildo in one fist and a blue one in the other. They flopped back and forth, smacking the laptop's cover then the Oracle's wrist, and back again. *Sure hope those don't find their way into some lady's purse later.* Adrian swallowed back the gag that threatened to mar his hopefully impassive features.

"Maybe I should come back. When you're medicated."

"Already told you, Adrian Sands, I don't need medication to function." He wanded one dildo along the chair-puddled length of his body. "This is one-hundred percent pure awesomeness. Connecting to my enlightened state—"

"—is like bumper bowling with my grandma. Get on with it."

The Oracle sniffed. "You misunderstand my perception of things." His eyes half closed, and he settled his hands. "I take in information as I see fit. When a rare specimen such as you graces my presence, I have a natural curiosity. Distractions ensue…"

"Would you like me to knock your ass back on course?"

The Oracle's lips curved to a sly grin. "Oh, now

you're just teasing me." The Oracle's attention traveled Adrian's full length. Hopefully he hadn't missed the clenched fists, or the boot that was just begging to drop kick his face.

"If you tickle us, do we not laugh? If you prick us—"

"You *are* a prick," Adrian muttered. Oh, the games this guy played could make even the strongest of men vomit. With the Oracle's reputation as an imbiber of all things lurid, Adrian knew better than to threaten him. It only made the guy want to play harder. Secretly, the Oracle seemed to enjoy Adrian's sour moods more than his complacent ones.

The Oracle chuckled. His shoulders twitched in a sort of victorious wiggle. "Oh. Yes. I remember why I called you here." He set his rubbery drumsticks aside and motioned the Eunuch toward Adrian. The Oracle's messenger pushed the bills into Adrian's hand.

"You have a new toy," the Oracle declared.

Adrian nodded to the beaded curtain at the back of the store. "I think you own every toy in the metropolitan area."

"No—*your* toy. Your little doll. You've got one. In fact, I believe you've been hiding her for some time."

His heart thumped at the walls of his chest. In Adrian's early years of teenage promiscuity, he had mastered the shielding powder—and his ability to bring Shauna in contact with it on the thirteenth day of every month. It kept her well hidden from the Oracle. After college, he'd eradicated Shauna from his life. It wasn't long after that, he was using the powder to make *himself* disappear. The thought of hiding her hadn't even crossed his mind until she tore through that bag and by then, it was too late.

"What light through your window breaks, my boy?" the Oracle prompted again.

Adrian tried to sound impassive. "You've never been interested in any of my relationships before."

"But this one's special, isn't she?"

"Not to mention, you're gay."

The Oracle sat back. "It's true. I prefer the strength and stamina of a more virile crowd. But your toy isn't for me. Not really. You see, Nightingale's is getting a little stale these days. The same followers every night leave nothing to look forward to. So I'm calling in some rather unusual recruits. Stirring things up a little."

"No." Adrian leveled his glare. There would be no bargaining on this one. O'Nightingale's, the dirtiest underground nightclub in all of Utah, would burn to the ground the moment Shauna stepped inside—with her in it.

Didn't the Oracle know that?

"What are you afraid of?" the Oracle demanded.

Adrian didn't respond. The complete demolition of his future…or girlfriend flambé. It was a stupid question from either angle.

Wait. Now she's the girlfriend? Adrian grimaced and then blanked his features again before the Oracle detected it.

"You've passed the age of your ancestors. You've made it this far without provoking your curse."

"Because I was careful."

"'Cause I helped you."

Adrian folded his arms over his chest. "I could argue that one all day."

The Oracle arched a sandy brow in challenge.

"Would you like to hear what's ahead of you, Adrian? Would you like to hear the tragedy that befalls your one true love, should you fuck this up? How she dies? How lost you feel?

"How would you like to know every moment of every day how you will lose her and not be able to do a damn thing about it? To act against prophecy will seal her fate."

Adrian tossed the wrinkled bills at the counter. "She's not for sale."

The Oracle's voice lightened. His face changed to insidious delight. He stretched his chubby arms out wide. "Of course she's not. That money's not for her. It's for you. I already knew how *you'd* react."

"Go buy yourself something nice to wear tonight. And let me be the first to welcome you back to O'Nightingale's." The Oracle angled his head to Adrian's fist, where syrupy liquid oozed between his clenched fingers. "Oh, and uh, keep the lube. You're going to need it."

Chapter Five

Shauna swallowed the gasp of fear that seized her throat.

Jutting three feet from the treacherous threat of a clean-swept gutter, and well into the natural flow of traffic, sat Richard's Chinese-red Bentley convertible. Even under the scant light post it gleamed, the lower fender curved in a smile of privilege and self-assurance. As if to say, *"Go ahead. Try to outrun me."*

Shauna's gaze fled to the clutter-stacked bunker of her garage then to the remote clipped on her sun visor. What she wouldn't give for a working garage door about now. She'd lower it behind her before he could leave his car and take one step in her direction. Giving her a moment to think.

He always kept her on a stopwatch. With her shift having ended several hours ago, that left lots of explaining to do.

Richard's catapult of accusations came fully loaded and ever ready. The moment he spotted her—oh God, *and* the outfit—no doubt he'd open fire. And he wouldn't stop until he brought tears.

She needed an excuse—a plan—and something good this time. She came up with a dozen of them when she got dressed this evening, but all the good ideas fled her mind about as quickly as Adrian and his turbo-boosted better things to do.

Shauna careened into the driveway, as her cashmere sweater grew itchy and constrictive. The tiny, woven threads seemed to sprout serrated insect legs that chased up her spine. Caught. And she knew it.

She couldn't muster the guts to look at Richard and his ego-stroker-on-wheels. Not yet.

She steered straight into the garage. Eyes stuck on the dingy tennis ball that hung in wait to tap her windshield and declare her home free. Shauna pushed out a bitter huff. No freedom for her. Not anymore.

Come on, think.

A sick coworker could explain the late hour, maybe she had to cover their shift—in disguise, so her friend wouldn't get fired.

Or she could be flaunting the outfit just for Richard. Maybe she'd planned this. She'd been expecting him?

Yeah, like he'd believe that. She let her forehead *thunk* against the steering wheel. Why did encouraging her own fiancé's sexual intrigue feel like the very last thing she wanted?

Because then she'd have to spend the entire evening warding him off. That's why.

She clicked the remote button. It hadn't worked in months, but once. Please, just one more time. Shauna jammed the button down, harder this time. The tiny, green light on the remote flickered, but the door didn't budge from its propped state.

Come on!

She risked a quick glance to Richard's car.

Wait a sec. The car wasn't idling. The driver's seat looked vacant.

She craned her neck to the view behind her. Her

gaze flew to the dark carport, the prickly bushes that lined the drive, even the slender pole that caddied half-a-dozen birdfeeders—anywhere but inside. Please don't be inside.

She jammed on the emergency brake and shoved open the door. If her roommate, Kimmy, got a hold of him, no telling what kind of damage she'd do.

Shauna launched herself from the driver's seat and bypassed the attached door to the garage. She started for the front entrance. Rounded the four-foot, brick alcove that blocked her view of the front door. Her heels skittered on cement as she made an abrupt stop.

Richard, in his crisp, black tuxedo, stood hunched over the doorbell—too busy woodpeckering the button to notice her clipped approach.

The faint, honey-rasp of Kimmy's voice came from the other side. "That's it. I warned you—"

Richard leaned toward the door's crevice. "And I'm warning you, Kim. This is my house, not yours."

He paused for a moment as if waiting for Kimmy's retort. But nothing came. Odd. Not really her style. The roommate never backed down from a verbal assault. And if the fight happened to cross into her lair? Shauna would place her money on Kimmy any day.

Richard pounded the rough, wooden surface with his fist. "Open this door!"

Ah, the moment Shauna had been waiting for—or dreading, really. A year ago, their house had fallen into bankruptcy, and Richard offered to buy it. Not sure why he considered it his so-called perfect picture of domestic life, but finding a buyer had saved her bacon.

So she went with it.

He promised it wouldn't get creepy.

Maybe Richard hadn't noticed, but he'd just pole vaulted over the creep boundary like a champ. She'd picked a winner all right. Now to slip that gold metal over his head. And hang him with it.

Shauna folded her arms. "What are you doing?"

Richard pivoted slowly. His frown of determination intensified, and his lowered brows knitted with outrage.

The sudden sputter and hiss that came from behind Shauna overpowered Richard's sharp reply. She spun as the first round of sprinklers hissed to life, and erupted into a cheerful rotation of water spurts. Right into the open bay of Richard's car.

Richard's face paled. His hands rested in a ghost of a touch on her arms as he sidestepped her and raced to his car. "Damn it. I just had this washed." He jumped into the driver's seat and leaned to one side with his shoulders drawn up and his eyes squinted, as if to shield from the pelting water. The engine roared and Richard U-turned on spinning tires.

Shauna raced back for the garage, to where the sprinkler's time clock sat. She rounded the corner in time to catch Kimmy's self-righteous grin as she slapped the box shut and clomped for the attached door in her four-inch heels. "Sorry, Shauna. Had to be done."

There's the Kimmy she knew. "Thanks a lot." Shauna marched to the box and shut off the sprinkler assault.

She hoped Richard would continue down the road. But the screech of his brakes ended that in a hurry. She pulled in a deep breath. Maybe she should have left the sprinklers on.

From the other side of the street, Richard popped

back out of the car. He had one of those yellow, baby-buffer cloths and he wiped the glistening surface with quick, agitated strokes. He shot a brief glare in Shauna's direction. "You could at least lend a hand...Is this hard water?"

Shauna ambled toward the street. She lifted her hand, pretending to inspect her manicure. "Sounds like you're blaming me for this?"

He gestured to the house with the wadded cloth. "She's your roommate. I don't know how many times I've asked you to get rid of her." He returned his attention to the car. "There's another towel in the glove box."

"Good." It could stay there. Shauna pivoted. She hadn't checked the mail in over a week, but she couldn't think of a better time. If the mailbox just happened to suck her into another universe, the paper cuts would be worth it.

Richard's tone remained clipped. "Where's the costume I bought you?"

Shauna frowned. Wasn't this supposed to be about him? One balloon of a chance to take the attention off her and it already popped.

"In my closet, why?" The answer came to her just as the words slipped out of her mouth.

"Do you really think the one you're wearing is appropriate? It's a charity event. Just because it's a masquerade, doesn't mean people won't know who we are."

That's right. Halloween would hit in four days. There was the golden excuse. Not that she really cared for one at this point.

The mailbox lid opened with a metal *screech*

followed by a *clang* as it hit its supportive post. She reached for the mass of papers and envelopes crammed inside.

"I hope you'll consider changing before we go?"

That didn't sound like a question at all—or a polite request. She funneled the bundle of papers into her arms. "We're already late, and it's been a long day. I'm not sure I'm up to—"

"I just don't understand. If you already have a perfect costume, why would you come up with *that*?"

"Oh, I forgot about the party." The air of challenge that invaded her voice seemed to come out of nowhere. From someone else. Pretty sure, her name used to be Shauna.

Richard crossed the street with agitated steps. "How can you forget if you're dressed up?" His voice elevated. "Did you wear that to work?"

She flipped through the letters. "Yep…Work function. I didn't want to get the other one dirty, and this was more playful anyway." *Oh. Good job. Way to work that spine.*

Richard paused. "Just how *playful* were you planning to get—and what is this?" He snatched a small postcard from her bundle, studied it, and then tossed it back into her arms.

Shauna gave him a blank look.

His voice hardened. He shot her a curled-lip look of disgust, and nodded to the card again. "What is that?"

Her gaze followed the glossy, black postcard as it landed. "It's mail." She raised her brows. "My. Mail."

"Honestly, sometimes I don't even know you." He looked pointedly to the double knot tied in her coat, as if he expected her to not have a stich of clothes underneath.

She had a sweater. An *itchy* sweater—one he bought, by the way—and it seemed to get uglier and itchier by the second.

"I don't even know what you're supposed to be." He stepped closer as if to shield her from view. His voice lowered. "I don't think you should be wearing that outside the house. In fact, you know what? Leave the mail. You can get it tomorrow."

She motioned to her armload of papers. "But I'm already here."

"Exactly. Where all the neighbors can see you."

She gave him an incredulous look.

He snagged her elbow and tugged her toward the door. "Don't get me wrong, I love seeing you like this—"

Was that supposed to sound genuine?

"I just don't want to share it with the whole world."

She yanked her elbow free. "My thoughts exactly. So why don't you go on without me?"

"That's not an option." He put his arms around her shoulder this time and urged her toward the door. "But if you really want to stay in tonight, I'd be perfectly happy to keep you company." He nodded. "With the wedding looming, I think we may need to practice for those momentous traditions. The kiss, the garter, maybe even the wedding night?"

A cold ladle dipped into the pit of her stomach. Why did this escort suddenly feel like a serial killer ushering her into his basement?

Oh, I remember.

At the beginning of their relationship, Richard had

the patience of a saint. A phenomenal snuggle buddy. He didn't cause the reaction most men did.

Oh, she warmed a bit, but nothing noticeable. The reaction seemed mild enough that she even entertained thoughts of a normal life. A *perfect life*, as Richard would say. One picket fence, two beautiful children, and a dog with a jewel-encrusted collar.

So it wasn't exactly love. More of an unspoken, mutual agreement for obtaining the American dream. He would have every excuse to bail out on high-society obligations, and she could finally live in her own dollhouse.

But the closer to the wedding—or wedding night—they got, the more intense her reaction had grown. And the more possessive Richard had become.

His plans weren't moving fast enough, and apparently, he didn't want that pretty little collar to get cold, so he'd fastened it on Shauna.

And the leash? Suffocatingly short.

She pulled away and gestured to the front window where the flicker of the television light shifted from blue to white and the curtain swung from its sudden release.

"Kimmy's here. I doubt she'd feel comfortable—"

He gestured to the house with an impatient hand. "She's always here. She's a damn shut-in. And the reason why you have a bedroom door. We both agreed waiting for the wedding night was a cliché. How do I know our relationship is ready for a new level, if we don't test our compatibility?"

Shauna paused. Sound reasoning. Now to find a way around it.

"You already know I'm going to marry you," he

continued. "I agreed to that. You have your ring. What have you got to lose?"

Shauna curled her fingers under the pile of mail.

He pulled her in close and rested his forehead on hers. "Putting me off means putting off your family. Your future." His tone flattened. "You do realize this is how real babies are made, right?"

Low blow. Shauna clenched her jaw shut.

Hyper ovulation-induced menopause, they called it. Her eggs were on the slip-n-slide to certain demise. He knew children were always a concern, especially because she couldn't afford to store or inseminate her own eggs. Lending her the money seemed preposterous in his eyes, which to some degree, she accepted. They were to be married soon, after all.

Shauna zeroed in on the narrow points of his upper lip, hoping they wouldn't come closer and prayed that she wouldn't have to push him away again.

"Are you worried about your experience level?" he asked.

"No." She looked away. "Well, maybe." How could she pass up an excuse like that? Way better than being afraid of turning your fiancé into a French fry. The experience level, she could handle. She wasn't a virgin. Not that he needed to know.

She'd had plenty of time to conjure up what having sex again would feel like. She might be a little out of practice, but she wasn't immune to Google, or Youtube, or Redtube for that matter. But lately, her refined fantasy of writhing muscle and heat had nothing to do with Richard. It's a good thing the warmth in her cheeks couldn't spell out whose name those thoughts really belonged to.

"Because it doesn't matter. I'll show you. I'll tell you what I want." He hooked one finger in the lining of her coat.

"Thanks, but I think I'll pass." She offered what she hoped was an apologetic grimace and slid closer to the door.

Richard moved to cut her off her path. "Maybe if you'd spend some time with me, you can come to terms with what's expected of you before the big night."

Her vision narrowed to menacing slits. "What's *expected* of me? Did you really just say that?" Shauna turned on her heel and marched towards the door.

"Well, obviously when it comes to sex, you don't want any part of it, but I'm not the kind that goes without. So how else would you like me to word it?"

"I think you've worded it *perfectly*." Throwing his favorite word back at him didn't feel like enough. She reached for the door handle. Maybe she could fling it open hard enough to ram him in the nuts. Or plan B, a door-slamming penis guillotine.

Richard's voice hardened. "I don't mean to come off as an asshole or anything, but for God sakes, Shauna, I'm putting my foot down. A man has needs."

"And a woman doesn't?"

He splayed his arms out wide, and his brows lifted in innocence. "I'm right here. If you need something, let me give it to you." Richard shot a quick glance around as if afraid the shrubs were taking notes. He lowered his voice again. "Unless it's not me you want."

"No. It's not that." *Oh, yes. Yes, it was.* Shauna jammed her key in the door and turned the knob.

Richard expelled a frustrated sigh behind her. "Look, I'm getting tired of waiting. You're going to

51

have to prove to me that I'm not committing to a life of celibacy. Because I'm not up for that."

"I wouldn't expect you to do that."

"Well then, you know what's expected of you. There. We've come full circle." He gestured inside. "Now that we understand each other, what do ya say we go in? Kiss and make up."

"Why don't you stay out and kiss my ass instead." She solidified her statement by slamming the door in his face.

"Not appropriate, Shauna," he called from the other side. His voice muffled through the thick wood. "You're not yourself tonight." He paused. "I'm going to give you some time to cool off and get dressed. I'll be back in an hour. "

"You know what? Don't bother!"

He paused. "So…so it's over then?" More of a challenge than a question.

Shauna opened her mouth to speak, but no words would form. Could all of this end so easily? A relationship of this length should take at least a few more sturdy shoves before it completely toppled over. Shouldn't it?

His agitated steps quieted away.

Shauna pulled in a tight breath when she heard his car door open, then snap shut.

What had she done?

His engine started.

Her pulse hammered. What if she'd just made a terrible mistake? He had been the only man who wanted her. He stayed with her all this time. Now she'd refused him. Richard was right; she wasn't herself. Something had gotten into her. Or someone…

She pressed her forehead to the door, but refused the strength to lift her hand to the knob. She listened to the roar of Richard's engine until it grew soft and faded into nothing.

Shauna trudged for the closet with her head down, hating every matted-shag step. She could fix this. A little holy water and a priest would be great about now. So she could exorcise the spoiled brat who had taken over her body. No, she couldn't have what she wanted. She couldn't have Adrian. So get over it. Settle for the logical option and be happy with it. Reality. The safe decision.

"What you got there?"

Kimmy unloaded the mail from her arms and tore through it faster than a zombie after Einstein. "Junk. Bill. More bills."

Funny, such a ravenous appetite for the outside world, but all she had to do was take a few steps beyond the front door. Then again, at least Kimmy had control over her world. Complete control.

"How'd your date go?" Shauna asked.

The discarded mail slapped on the table. Kimmy's mouth turned down in a noncommittal frown. "Meh."

Shauna shrugged out of the coat and offered it back to its rightful owner. "What do you mean? I thought this one was totally sexy."

Her painted eyes widened. "He is. He's a hot body builder with muscles to spare, but when it comes to the bedroom—his wrinkled pinky isn't much of a Kimmy-pleaser."

"Really? On your first date?"

Kimmy expelled a teenage-worthy sigh of frustration and gestured airline-attendant style to the far end of the house. "It's hard not to take things to the next level when the bedroom is right there."

Shauna widened her eyes in disbelief and shook her head. "Lock your door ahead of time."

Kimmy's knees gave. She crumpled halfway to the floor in a dramatic wave before catching herself. "I can't. I have no willpower."

Okay, control over everything except the spreading of her thighs.

Kimmy's gaze lowered to the coat. "Did you steam clean this?" She seemed to weigh it with a floating motion of her hand, and then dug through the pocket. She gave Shauna a flat look and revealed palm-sized rock. She snorted. "You know, you really need a Taser if you want to keep Richard away. Throwing a stone requires space. He's too suffocating for that."

Shauna closed her eyes. "How did you know?"

"I know all, remember."

Shauna looked skyward. Self-proclaimed psychic. How could she forget?

She reached their shared closet space and pulled out the sleek, black dress. The hem looked short. Too short. The neckline formed a deep V that showcased an ample amount of both breasts. She slipped the dress over her head. Her jaw hinged open. Ample. What an understatement. Danger: explosive side-boob, would be more accurate.

Kimmy's voice muffled with the sound of crinkling plastic. "You're missing the under-thingy." Kimmy sauntered into the shared space with one of Adrian's chocolates caught between her teeth. She set the hangers to clattering as she pulled out a long-sleeved, black-lace undershirt. She tossed it onto the bed and then plucked the dress from around Shauna's neck. "Oh, sorry, and that's mine." She pushed a consolation chocolate into Shauna's hand. "Richard bought you…" She turned back for the closet and the rattle of hangers ensued. "This one." Kimmy returned with a triumphant smile and a God-awful, neck to ankle, polyester nightmare. "Going for the nunnery-chic look, I see."

Shauna's shoulders dropped in their sockets. "No wonder I didn't recognize it. Richard would never buy something that dramatic."

"You mean sexy?" Kimmy shrugged. "So your boyfriend has a taste for funeral wear. I guess that could be kinky in some really hard-to-get-my-head-around way." She blinked heavenward. "Maybe if it weren't Richard, it'd be more plausible."

Shauna's tone deflated. "Wanna trade?"

Kimmy grinned with pent excitement. "You'd seriously wear my dress? Take a leap to the other side?"

"Not with Richard. I'm not going." She still wanted Adrian. And tonight. If only for one night, she would wallow in that—and a slut-sexy, black dress.

And hell, maybe some vodka too.

And chocolate.

She twisted both sides of the plastic wrap until the chocolate dropped into her mouth. From the weight, she expected jawbreaker consistency, but the moment the nutty warmth rolled across her tongue, it melted. Tiny granules of sugar slid down her throat to warm her stomach.

Shauna squeezed her legs together and clenched her muscles against the yearning ache that tugged at her core. The heat of her arousal had been pulsing a steady beat since the moment Adrian had given her *that look*.

History proved she wouldn't be much use to the world until she got at least one good, hard orgasm under her belt. She looked away. "I'm going to need some serious *me* time."

"Oh, no, no, no. If you wear it, you're not staying here. This dress is meant to be seen. I know just the place." Kimmy tossed the dark card that she'd unearthed from the mail pile. A coy smile curved her lips.

"Ugh—I'm not in the mood to go *anywhere*," Shauna groaned.

"Hey, when you're happy—and I mean *really* happy—I'm happy, so let's make that happen, hummm?"

The card frizbee'd across the room to land on Shauna's nose. She lifted the stiff paper until the words focused. The same card that had Richard acting all defensive.

But not just that; she'd seen it before somewhere. In her past, or…

Oh boy. On Adrian's desk next to the chocolates. She remembered seeing a bunch of them, but they all looked so personal. Each one individually addressed. Why would she get one?

Elegant scrollwork of neon purple and green framed the handwritten card with a single message.

"O'Nightingale calls."

Chapter Six

Shauna trudged along the sidewalks pocked with disks of petrified gum and rain puddles as she made her way to O'Nightingale's. Her legs weighted heavily by the lateness of the hour and the emotional landfill that had become her night. Not to mention the snug fit of Kimmy's patent leather boots. She pulled another candy from her pocket and twisted the wrapper. The metallic foil squealed in protest.

Richard was probably off somewhere, still shaking his head.

From blushing bride to bitchzilla in a matter of seconds.

Shauna grimaced and flung the thought from her head. She didn't need guilt. She needed…more chocolate. She dug the candy from its protective foil, earning yet another squeal before crumpling the wrapper in her fist.

Richard deserved what he got tonight; the frustrations had been building up over *some time*. Sure, a little essence O'Adrian might have loosened her cynical corset, but that would have come undone eventually. Better now than after the wedding. Better to know what they were both getting into—or getting out of. Because at this hour, a mad dash for the border sounded a lot better than the altar.

She popped the globe of chocolate in her mouth

and chomped down. No, not even Mexico sounded far or fast enough.

She took a cleansing breath between chews. Her lungs infused with the scent of damp cement and chocolate. This time, Shauna welcomed the warmth that splashed into her stomach and the fuzz that danced with her thoughts. If she didn't know Adrian, she'd say these things were laced with something stronger than cocoa. Good, but it wasn't enough. She needed an escape of mammoth proportions. Another world entirely.

Something just scary enough to reset her perspective.

According to Kimmy, O'Nightingale's would be her quickest and dirtiest fix possible.

"A wish alone will not change your fate, but a decision will change everything. Better to move than be cursed forever," Kimmy had declared with an uplifted hand.

Quick fixes were okay.

Dirty ones? Shauna tilted her head. On a night like this, she could agree to a little dirty.

But what's with the mighty wallop of glittery, mystical stupidity? Why had she agreed to that? Kimmy's higher-being psychobabble couldn't be trusted. Under most circumstances, it was a good indication for an about-turn and sprint in the other direction. Shauna didn't mess with fate.

But when Kimmy threw the word *curse* into the ring…

Ding. Ding. Ding! The fight was over.

Shauna had already been cursed a-plenty. No other word could move her into trouble's path more quickly.

Except maybe "Adrian." That word caused all

kinds of trouble. Like the warmth of excitement funneling to her core. And the tight ache in her chest that had nothing to do with the push-up effect of her outfit. She knew the source of it and the more pervasive reason that she'd shed her usual reluctance for anything her promiscuous roommate suggested. Shauna needed a fix on multiple levels.

Kimmy's ideas weren't always this brilliant, but she couldn't pass this one up.

It's not as if underground nightclubs were infesting the state of Utah. The odds of a man as single and secluded as Adrian going anywhere else to blow off steam were zero to not happening.

Kimmy had mentioned that the cards were a one-time use. No turning back. Given the number of invitations strewn across Adrian's desk, the man came often enough to build a skyscraper house of cards.

Adrian had revealed something else tonight. He'd *noticed* her. Not only noticed, he'd *recognized* her. The same who-let-you-out-of-the-house-in-that look from years past had changed a bit. It stung less. More like a sharp slap on the ass now, and to Shauna's surprise, she kinda liked pissing him off.

He had unleashed the bratty demon within her; now he could deal with it. If he did show, and he happened to see her again…She glanced at the black trench coat wrapped tight around Kimmy's thigh-high dress and the scant light gleaming off her boots. She grinned. She'd bet every ball-bearing treat in that damn jar that he couldn't look away this time.

A little extra dig to settle the score would for sure make her night. After all, Shauna had been invited. Someone else wanted her here. And it wasn't Adrian.

How chocolate-coated awesome would that be to rub in his face?

Some foreign grain of protectiveness—or was it territorial—who knew, but something deep inside Adrian loomed to the surface every time Shauna stirred up trouble in his presence. Like with the chocolate, it really got to him. In an instant of recognition, the docile gorilla stood ready to assert his dominance and straighten out this troublesome neighbor-monkey.

She lifted her chin a notch higher and quickened her pace as she crossed the vacant street into the historic district. If that's what worked, she'd take it.

She had to.

All other options for a cure dead-ended with Adrian Sands. If he wouldn't help her out of kindness, her next option had to be the one thing she knew. Putting herself in danger got his attention—bratty and selfish as it was. She'd hate herself for it in the morning, but for now, she could manage a little wardrobe-tantrum at his expense.

Her attention turned to a slender, Victorian-style building on the corner. The darkness under the scalloped awning seemed to tunnel into nowhere. She tried to focus in, but still couldn't detect even a single body.

The three-block distance from the nearest parking lot must have been deliberate. Not to mention the odd destination time. It made sense. Better to stagger the crowd and move them in quick than to cause a scene in the open.

The streetlight had been dimmed. Nothing like Shauna's handy work—not broken, but diminished somehow to a scant ember of light. Just functional enough to avoid repairs but pretty darn useless. The interior lights of the building shed the same glow. To the common passer-by, it looked tucked away for the night. She squinted to the card, then to the sign fixed to the weathered hobby shop.

Grigori Bird Watching.

The nightingale silhouette on the sign matched, but the place seemed more welcoming to cane-toting retirees than the fetish-hungry elite Kimmy had mentioned. What about this place had caught Adrian's eye? Why did he keep coming back here night after night?

Only two stores down on the close-packed street was the same ice cream shop she and her grandpop visited every summer. The windows were dark, but the place probably doled out the same double scoop of strawberry ice cream as always.

In the daylight, anyway.

"Going somewhere?"

Shauna lurched forward and spun around to find Squalinski looming close behind, from the dark shadow of a building overhang.

"You scared the shit out of me!"

His lips twitched with a smug grin. "Well, if it isn't our little streetwalker, out for a stroll."

"Funny." Her gaze narrowed. "But I didn't think your pudgy little legs would make it this far."

Squalinski rocked back on his heels. "Yeah, thought you lost me after you went home, but you didn't...did you?" He turned his attention to the bird shop across the street. "Word has it, this place makes all kinds of calls after dark."

"Is that so?"

"Never been there myself. Your first time, too? How fortunate."

She smirked. "Closed party. You're not invited. Look, I'm not doing anything illegal. So *you* can't bother me."

"Public intoxication is illegal." Squalinski's pen light snapped on and he waved the bright beacon in her face. "How much you had to drink tonight?"

"None!"

"Really. Because your eyes are telling me something different." He angled his head. "Follow this light please."

"Nice try." Shauna marched forward. "You know, this game is getting old. And you still haven't figured out how it's played. You don't have anything on me. *You* can't touch me." She looked both ways, ready to cross the street. "Rumors of an abduction *here* would be bad for business. And something tells me, the guys in there? They don't like cops hanging around their establishment anyway. So maybe you better step aside before you blow your own cover."

She took two marching steps into the crosswalk. Then three. Four. Her nerve endings tingled with high alert for the moment the agent would charge from behind and grab her.

But nothing came.

Nothing!

Had she been right? The bluff paid off?

A hurried clip of spiked heels carried her forward as she chanced a quick look behind.

Gone? Not exactly, still skulking in the shadows, but the slime ball didn't venture a step into the open. From what she said? Or because of her destination?

A sporadic shift near the hobby shop snared Shauna's attention. Panic vised her heart. Several dark figures in the entryway ballooned to one side, then the other before settling into some sort of queue. She paused. Five? Twenty? She couldn't determine how many were there, but one thing was certain, this had to be the place.

Shauna started forward again with tentative steps. She eyed the shapeless ripple as it parted again and the shop's door swung open. She half-expected the pleasant jingle of entry bells above the door, the kind that plagued every Maw-and-Paw shop on this street.

But no. Not a sound.

A violet-blue light from within, arched into the entry, and then snuffed-out by a surge of eager bodies.

Her mind whirred to catch every detail as the darkness filled in. One, two…six. Pretty sure there were at least six heads. She expected some music, maybe a collective moan of disappointment from those who didn't get in. Anything but this intimidating silence.

As she neared the crowd, the closer outliers appeared to turn in her direction. Even the air around them seemed to pause in watchful curiosity. The hammering in her chest battled to overpower the steady pace of her clipping heels. She tried to quiet her approach with tiptoe steps. More of a courtesy really, it's not as though the entire place hadn't already seen her coming.

Perfume and the sharp tang of leather wafted from the building. Shauna clutched the phone in her pocket. Could she reach someone in time if she got in trouble here? With a following this tight? The image of scurrying shadows and grabbing hands flashed through her mind. They'd have her surrounded and silenced before she ever hit send.

A sudden spasm of fear shot through her. Inside the trench coat pocket, warm vibrations danced against her hand. It took a moment to register the phone's sensation. She wasn't used to putting the thing on silent. But again, Kimmy insisted.

Shauna kept marching as she pressed the phone to her ear, and used her other hand to shield its offensive glow.

"Hello?" she whispered.

Kimmy's voice projected through the phone. "You there already? 'Cause if you get caught with your phone, they'll take it."

Shauna turned from the crowd and cupped the lower end of the phone, hoping to dampen the sound. "You couldn't have told me sooner?"

Shauna could just picture the careless brush of Kimmy's hand. "It's no biggie. Once you're in, I'll have you on webcam. If you feel a vibe in your pocket, get out. If anyone asks, you're from the Seattle group. Oh, and one more thing. I think the safe word is still 'button nose' so if you get into trouble, work that into the conversation and you'll be left alone."

Shauna's attention flew to the eaves of the building and the corners of the upper floor window. "Safe word? You're kidding, right? And you're watching this whole thing?"

"Well…Yeah." Her tone smoothed with haughty assurance. "It's more fun watching you. As a member of Nightingale's soaring high club, it's old hat for me."

"*Soaring high club?*"

"Well," Kimmy scoffed. "Of course that was years

ago."

"Gee, glad I could be of service. Since when did I become your cheap entertainment?"

"Since…always. Now get in there and give me video feed. I need to feed!"

On any normal day, Shauna would tell her to go fly a kite but at present…hell, why not? Let Kimmy take in the show. She didn't care. Shauna didn't have a care in the world. Something about tonight blanketed her in a perfect concoction of blissful indifference. "If you want to feed that bad, maybe you should soar your lazy butt down here yourself? What happened to you anyway? Why is it that I'm *here*, and you're *there*?"

A pause of unsettling silence stretched through the phone.

Apparently, that blissful indifference came with a splash of saucy-bitch and a mouth that couldn't quit. This is what the world got when a sex-deprived Shauna went on parade.

"I know you're stressed—" Kimmy began.

"Stressed?" Was she supposed to be stressed?

"Maybe a little nervous," Kimmy corrected.

Shauna looked skyward in contemplation. Nope. Not that either. Not anymore. But she could have sworn that only a moment ago…

Kimmy's words picked up speed. "There's nothing to worry about. Promise. You're going to have fun. What's the worst that can happen?"

The worst? The entire building going up in flames—with her in it. Not to mention how many others she'd take down with her. Why didn't that bother her all of the sudden? Tonight, it felt more like a great chance to roast marshmallows. Or s'mores. Shauna slid her tongue over the roof of her mouth to savor the tinge of chocolate that remained. She twisted to her pocket in search of another candy.

A scamper of heels over wood erupted at the building's entrance. A disconcerted mumble of irritation came as the ripple of bodies shifted in all directions.

One woman's voice carried over the rest. "If you think, after I come *all* this way—" Her words lost their clarity, smothered to muffled grunts of outrage as a large man shoved through the commotion. He hoisted the woman against his chest with one hand clamped tight over her mouth.

The buxom woman kicked and reared. Her occluded cries became longer and more urgent the closer they came to the street. The bouncer bobbed his head to the left once, then again, to avoid her flailing arms.

The glittery, head-to-toe spandex the woman wore looked ready to explode—what was left of it anyway. The strategic holes cut from the fabric stretched and thinned like melting Swiss as the woman continued her spasms. Her doughy flesh bulged through a large hole at her thigh. One patent-leather heel clattered to the cement. The bouncer took lumbering steps toward the curb, and a faint grunt sounded as one of the woman's arms connected with his temple.

The bouncer stopped. He dropped the woman on her feet, and snatched her up again. One large arm banded her limbs down while the other clamped her mouth again, the woman's movements reduced to little more than a writhing caterpillar in her hole-eaten chrysalis.

A white limousine loomed into focus beneath the streetlight, like a shark through murky water. The engine purred at a leisurely few miles per hour until it reached the struggling pair. The passenger door opened by unseen hands, and the bouncer tossed the woman inside.

The woman managed a few curses of indignation before the door snapped shut, and the vehicle puttered away again at the same pace.

Creepy.

Shauna readjusted the phone to her ear as Kimmy's warning cut through. "Anonymity is everything here. Anyone seen dressing for attention outside won't get past the gate. Keep your goods covered till you're in. But for God's sake, get in soon. You're running out of time."

"Right, then it's all out and exposed. Got it. Anything else, puppet master?"

Shauna watched the bouncer stoop to retrieve the abandoned shoe and turn toward the building. Eyes forward and mechanical, he didn't even glance her way. Probably paid not to.

Shauna's phone buzzed against her ear.

"Don't answer that," Kimmy barked.

The urgency in Kimmy's voice grew distant as Shauna held the phone away. "Don't need to shout." She frowned at the unlisted number bannered on the phone's screen. "And the puppet thing was a joke. You can stop telling me what to do now."

"It's 11:02. Get moving." A digital beep sounded, and Kimmy was gone.

Only the incessant vibrations of the incoming call remained.

She looked to the entrance as the door opened. It arched wider this time and more bodies filed in. The skulking shadows under the canopy diminished and her view of the bouncer's vantage point became clear. Shauna had a feeling if she stayed on the street much longer, jabbering on her phone, she'd end up the next contender on The Quiet Ride Game.

She looked to the phone just as it went dark. The unlisted number vanished.

Just as well.

Chapter Seven

She slid the phone back into her coat pocket, but after just a few steps, the phone buzzed to life again.

Shauna pushed out a sigh of frustration. She couldn't get past the bouncer like this. Couldn't kill the phone either, it served as her only tether to the outside world. But with it dancing away in her pocket...she retrieved the phone once more and jabbed at the call with her index finger. "Go away. I'm busy."

"Where are you?"

Her lungs seized. The odds told her it would be Richard. What were the chances she'd hear the potent depth of Adrian Sands instead?

Pretty darn good, apparently. Looked like Shauna won the lottery.

"Are you in trouble?" he demanded.

She could hear the manual shift of his car as Adrian accelerated. Probably racing off to another chemistry convention.

"Trouble? Why Adrian, you sound concerned. You really must have the wrong number."

Wow. That saucy-bitch sauce has quite a kick.

"How did you get my number anyway?" Who was stalking whom here?

Shauna caught her breath the moment she recognized its hollow sound playing back through the phone.

Why wasn't he talking? Could he be *evaluating* her again? Shauna could picture that unnerving glare of his. The tiny creases that played near his eyes as he performed his microscopic calibration.

His tone remained even. Low, but even. "Your voice is slurred."

"Uh-huh."

"Clearly you're outside."

Yep, evaluating. She offered a congratulatory nod. "Excellent work, Sherlock."

"So, where are you?"

Perfect opportunity to add a little "dummy" to the sauce. "Umm, I'm standing upright. Is that bad? Should I be on my back?" The giddy warmth of excitement had returned again. Oh, this was too much fun. Shauna could play this game all night. "Because I wouldn't mind finding myself in that position right now."

She'd had her doubts when she first arrived. Would her spine be strong enough to go through with it, or would she melt into a quivering puddle of cowardly muck?

Now she had her answer. She'd march in with a cast-iron spine and Adrian's frown of disapproval fueling her pace.

Adrian's words paused amid distraction. As if the numbers in his head, if only for a moment, didn't compute. "Look. Sorry I couldn't help you before. But you need to tell me where you are."

"If you hadn't kicked me out, I'd be with you. Maybe even...on my back." Shauna waited for a response. "Legs spread...wet and achy....you know the drill."

Nothing.

"Or maybe even wrapped around your waist? I guess it would have been your business *then*," she continued. "But it's not now."

The accelerating roar of Adrian's motor served as his only reply. Could it be? Did Shauna's words actually have an impact on him? She didn't bother to hold back the grin as she marched for the entrance. The mouth that wouldn't quit was about to take a joy ride. She neared the entrance, and the bouncer motioned her to the front.

Shauna smiled in greeting to the pair of long-coated women. One frizzy head shook in disapproval, and then her attention fixed to Shauna's phone.

Shauna's mouth moved to silently frame the words "*I know*." Her eye's widened and rolled heavenward and she made a talking gesture with her other hand. "*He won't shut up!*" It was a furtive ploy for sympathy.

Based on the synchronous scowl from the women, it didn't work. They turned to each other with lips pursed in annoyance.

Shauna seized the momentary diversion and slipped ahead. She shrugged to a lanky man in a flannel shirt and windbreaker vest as she passed him too. Not an ounce of skin showing on anyone.

When Shauna approached, the bouncer frowned and held out one hand.

Shauna looked to the card in one hand, the phone in the other. No question. She handed him the card. He swiped it away and his hand jutted out again. "The phone too," he growled.

Shauna held up one finger. A nice one, thank God. At this rate, she didn't know who had control of this woman. Not Kimmy, Certainly not Adrian, and she had

71

serious doubts about herself either.

The bouncer's jaw tightened in irritation before turning away with her card.

Shauna returned her attention to the phone. "Besides, Adrian, you've already helped me out even more than you know."

"Why's that?"

"Because I'm eating the *chocolate* I stole from you. It tastes really good." Shauna moaned the last two words.

"You can't have that here, ya know," crowed one of long-coats. Which one, Shauna wasn't sure. They still wore identical looks of disdain.

The frizzy-haired one turned to the bouncer. "What makes her so special?"

"Not a darn thing," Shauna replied. She returned to the phone. "Look, I've got to go."

The screech of tires tore through the fabric of silence on the street.

"What on earth?" The ornery women turned; their eyes wide with shock and Shauna long forgotten.

A sleek, cobalt-blue Camaro drifted sideways around the corner. It straightened with a jerk and raced straight for the front entrance.

Was that Adrian? Did those tires echo through the phone?

"It's gonna ram us," one woman squawked. She grabbed her friend, but neither of them moved apart from a few jittery hops of suspense.

The distant sound of Adrian's voice came through the phone. "You're teasing me with a little harmless chocolate?"

Shauna's jaw fell slack. As the Camaro raced into

focus, her mind whirred to measure every discernible detail behind the Camaro's tinted windshield. It couldn't be. The Adrian she knew probably drove a Volvo, a sedan of some sort. Not. That.

The silhouette of broad shoulders and close-cropped hair made her stomach leap for safety.

She cleared her throat to force the shakiness away. "It...It's an aphrodisiac, you know." Shauna had to keep him talking, just long enough to know for sure.

A sharp screech of brakes seemed to come right at her feet, and her blanket of fearlessness billowed around her. The crazed jitter-squirrel that hid beneath threatened to seize the opportunity and dive under the velvet rope, shove through the door, and lose him in the crowd.

The bouncer stood facing the nearby wall, his large hands still cradling her card. He nursed it back and forth, under a wall-mounted black light. A sloth could out-pace the guy. The attempted assault by vehicle didn't seem to faze the bouncer, as if he'd seen it a million times. Shauna craned her neck to catch a glimpse of a faint inscription that glowed to life along the bottom edge of the paper, and inched closer to the door. Speed-reading. Not one of his strong points.

Shauna stole another glance behind.

Adrian's left shoulder dipped, as he shoved open the car door.

"*Shit*," Shauna peeped. The phone slipped from her hand as she made a panicked effort to end the call. She juggled the glossy plastic on its way to the ground. She managed to swipe it mere inches from crashing to the floor.

Shauna up-righted from her crouched stance inch-for-inch as Adrian unfolded himself from the car and straightened, only Adrian had several inches to spare—each one power and determination. His intense gaze of forewarning pierced through the handful of irritated patrons and hit her dead center.

He started forward.

Milliseconds ticking, Shauna spun back to the bouncer.

"Your phone?" It wasn't a question.

"Billy," Adrian called. A sharp jingle of metal sounded as Adrian tossed his keys to the bouncer.

Billy reached, and Shauna ducked under his arm. She finished-lined the velvet rope and the metal posts on either side crashed to the floor.

"Hey!" the frizzy one cried.

The bouncer rushed to quiet the toppling metal as Shauna stumbled over the clutter and body-slammed through the swinging door.

She blinked to take in her new surroundings and started moving.

No time to hesitate, but which way?

There's no clear direction, no exit.

The store corralled her in each direction with countless card racks, shelves, and aged display cases. A landmine for broken hips in the daylight, for sure.

Her only greeter perched four feet above, in a haze of swirling dust and smoke. With wild, round eyes, the plastic owl looked about as startled as Shauna. But something much bigger hunted her.

Her focus darted from one wall to another as she picked her way deeper into the store. The stale warmth closed in as she wound from one aisle to the next. Each row stood about four and a half feet high. It wouldn't take long for him to find her. Shauna's ears tensed on the commotion behind, waiting for the firm plod of footsteps to cross the threshold and begin their pursuit.

Nothing looked odd, out of place, or even a slight sketchy. Where the hell was her portal to this so-called sexual underworld?

Her gaze caught on a mosaic of bird feeders, swings, and perches displayed on the far wall. She frowned. One seemed brighter than the others. Not in presentation or size, but something—yes, a nightingale. The same spread-winged profile from outside and her card had been stamped on the wall in glowing paint.

Shauna slipped her hand behind the dangling collection of wooden blocks and twine, and traced its outline looking for any hint of imperfection. There must be a secret button or switch. She pushed on the glowing stamp.

Smooth and cold as painted concrete.

The door she had come through flew open, accompanied by a chilled gust of autumn air. The entrance erupted. Splintering glass and clanging metal skittered across the floor as a nearby display of wind chimes toppled.

Shauna flinched and shrunk down to avoid being seen.

Billy muttered, "...damn son of a..." more growling than an audible words. Adrian's deep reply interspersed the growling. "I'll handle this."

Something told Shauna he wasn't talking about the mess either. He sounded unrushed and at complete ease. He would. This was his playground.

Adrian's voice lowered beyond Shauna's grasp. The reluctant *scrape, scrape* of the bouncer's clean-up attempt didn't help. She could only imagine what *else* Adrian was saying to calm that raging bull.

I'll handle it?

Oh no, not this time he wouldn't. Adrian had his chance to handle it.

The handles were coming off.

She slapped her palm against the wall. The display trembled and clinked. She hit harder, and her palm stung.

Still nothing.

Her cheeks heated with frustration. Stupid kindergarten knickknacks were getting the better of her. She lifted the offensive swing from its hook and her view of the stamp became clear. As well as the sharp arrow below that pointed to the east-side wall.

Seriously? She let the swing slip from her fingertips. It hit the floor with a *clunk*.

Shauna's attention whirred east, and then she craned her neck forward and looked again. An illusion. The wall wasn't complete. From any other position in the store, she would have overlooked it. The thin slice of false wall obstructed a dark hallway, just wide enough to shoulder through. Beyond that, the faint luster of a brass doorknob and the outline of another door.

"Shauna—"

She stole a look in his direction.

"You're not going in there." Two aisles over, Adrian squared himself to full attention. The logoed cotton T-shirt that met her earlier still clung to his chiseled pecs.

She swallowed. Someone should really turn the heat down on his drier. Or confiscate it.

As if on cue, those proud pecs twitched as Adrian folded his arms. Massive shoulders lifted in a what-gives sort of shrug.

A new form of heat flared in her cheeks. She'd seen Adrian's recipe for challenge before. The higher her gaze traveled, the more potent it got.

The thick cords of muscle at his neck channeled upward to an iron-set jaw. She couldn't look past the dusting of stubble. She couldn't meet his eyes. Adrian already held enough of an edge to stay her.

On a normal day.

But Shauna moved again for the door.

What could he do? Nothing. He played here all the time. If he could do it, so could she.

In her tender, teenage years, his anger and disapproval would have thrown a proverbial bucket of ice over her spirit. But it was about time she outgrew him. No more spirit shushies for her.

She shot him what she hoped was her most impish grin and rushed for the hall. "Sorry, but I just can't help myself."

"Damn you," he muttered. Determined steps marched through the store, and echoed between the narrowed walls.

Adrian was gaining but not fast enough. Bubbles of delight chased around in her stomach when she reached the door. She didn't fight the urge to giggle as the knob turned with minimal effort, and Shauna rushed inside.

Chapter Eight

The door slammed and the steel cage surrounding her shuddered in response. There went the tiny, bat-like cry of what used to be her victory, as it flapped away in an irregular path.

She spun around; the clang of her heels echoed through the structure.

Please let it be an elevator, not a...whatever the heck else it might be. This wasn't familiar territory, but not even Shauna could imagine this much security just for a broom closet.

Urgent sirens in her head blared, *Doorknob. Doorknob.*

Any second, it would turn. She'd be face-to-face with that party-pooping Poindexter.

Within arm's reach on the right, a small, black box with two buttons stood out from the wall. She jabbed the lower button with her index finger. A buzzer sounded. Shauna's attention caught a slight movement through the door, as a metallic *click* sounded, and a bolt slid into place.

The cage bounced, then shook as it descended, but Shauna kept her gaze on that knob.

With the look on Adrian's face, would a simple bolt prevent him from crashing through the door?

Of course it would. This was Adrian. Content, everything in moderation Adrian. Not the neighborhood idol from her youth.

The handle jerked, rattled. Then it stopped.

The even prattle of the elevator's motor became the only sound.

She swallowed. Good…this is good. It would give her plenty of time to lose herself before the elevator returned for him.

And hope to God he doesn't find the stairs.

The cage sprang, and another rattle ensued as the elevator lowered itself in front of another door. Shauna took a tight breath and turned the knob. She pushed the door a fraction. Relief.

No Adrian standing in the margin of space. She opened it wide.

Another hallway, this time ornate stone tile replaced cracked linoleum. Still, no Adrian.

She stepped out and looked to the buttery-yellow recessed lights. No sound, no sign of her self-appointed babysitter. She looked to the steel cage. It wasn't returning for him.

Her steps slowed. What was this annoying ache in her chest? Not regret. Not disappointment. Couldn't be.

What the heck was wrong with her? She reduced her pace to a careless amble.

Twin entry tables guarded both sides of the hall; each bolstered enormous iron lamps. Their shades, a dense skirt of blue and purple feathers that swayed to life in a tepid breeze.

Who knew it would be this painful to play the dumb female card? She'd used it to her advantage at work a few times, maybe to get out of a speeding ticket, but never to this extent. And hormones, for the love of God, get a hold of yourselves. This wasn't about Adrian chasing her. It was about convincing him to give her what she wanted.

Sex.

No! She shook her head. A cure.

Right.

The purpose—the real purpose, distilled down to one word. Naughty. And how much of it could she aimlessly wander into before Adrian's good-neighbor morals came out, and he finally agreed to help her.

She couldn't use him as her safety net. Not this far into the game.

That wouldn't get her anywhere.

It might get her more chocolate, though. Shauna darted her tongue out to catch any remains of the stolen nuggets. She reached for her stash. Only one hard ball remained nestled in the pocket of empty wrappers.

Forget marriage and the picket fence. Sitting back and playing it safe all these years...and for what?

She squeezed the candy wrapper until the chocolate dropped into her open mouth.

Forget the normal sexual lifestyle too. Normal for Shauna had been nonexistent! And what's normal about that? Maybe here, maybe this place could give her what she'd been missing.

The hint of trickling water seemed real from the glass fountains framed on either wall, but the cricket sound, and what she could only assume was a nightingale singing, must have been piped in.

Shauna stopped chewing.

Lurid, low-slung voices filtered through the background as she neared the end of the hall and turned a sharp corner.

"Good times with that one," one gruff, female

voice noted.

A male responded after a brief pause, as though taking a drag from a cigarette. "I'll bet."

"You should try her." The female prodded. "Like a warm apricot—swear to God."

"Really. Is that right?" Another pause. "Who could pass that up?" the man asked.

Shauna tried not to make eye contact with the booth nearest her as she descended the iron-grate steps, but her curiosity couldn't let go. How quick could Shauna blend in a place this unfamiliar? What were these people like?

She knew what Adrian would do. He'd own this place. Her best bet would be to own it too.

The eggplant-purple walls grew further apart with each step, and the bottom of the staircase brought her completely into the open.

The sound of rubbing leather caught Shauna's attention near her left. This time her attention caught and held. The silhouette of a slender man—probably the owner of the male voice, slid to the edge of a rounded booth, and stood.

Shauna blinked to adjust her vision from warm halos to shadows and glowing neon.

The man escorted a curvy woman to her feet then angled his head for an older woman to join them.

The trio paraded through a room dappled with white leather furniture and oversized ottomans. Their proud gazes seemed to scour the darkened perimeter as if asking for an unseen crowd to gather in.

Alcoves along the far wall were fitted with king-sized mattresses and mirrored headboards. Tight fitted sheets glowed pink and blue against neon lights.

And a bar—thank God! The shell-shaped counter seemed pretty purposeful. Not familiar but at least recognizable. As for the rest of the place…call it a vacation spa of sorts. That sounded safe. Shauna offered a reasonable nod. A *sleazy* spa, but still, she could own a spa, no problem.

She took a deep breath and stretched her arms out to the new walls and shelves that boasted rolled towels and colorful knick-knacks.

Her thoughts played in soothing, singsong. *What a great place for releasing tension and inhibitions and promoting nothing but good feelings.*

She wound a path through the collection of booths as her gaze bounced from one surprise to the next.

The lit dance floor seemed strangely unoccupied for the number of people filing into this place. She expected a crowded room where she could blend in somehow. Not happening. The place seemed ten times the size of the store overhead.

She would have preferred the pulsing beat of a normal dance club like the ones she'd seen on TV. Shauna'd stayed away from parties altogether since the frat disaster. But at least that one had music. Here, the urban heave-and-thump from the speaker system had been subdued. It drowned under the authoritarian clip of her heeled boots.

She spied plenty of intimate hidey-holes, but they were all occupied. Patrons clung to the corners and walls. Milky-blue flashes of light sprang to her attention like fireflies in summer.

Her confidence screeched to a halt.

Spa feeling gone.

That wasn't light, more of a reflection, really. Pale

skin, hidden from the harsh rays of sun and society, had now been fully exposed. It glanced off mirrors and loomed under the neon glow. And plethora didn't begin to describe the amount of it.

Shauna's throat stretched around a painful lump as she swallowed the chocolate whole.

Those are just massages. The special, happily ever after, maybe a bit vigorous, and kinda-invasive...

She turned to the nearest pillar in a weak attempt to avert her eyes, and the flush that threatened to turn her cheeks into bright red homing beacons.

The distraction worked, until she studied closer. Those "knickknacks" of sculpted glass and chrome weren't just art, they were functional. Toys, tools, and devices...of the freaky kind. Everything had a price tag, and a big one. Some objects, like the nine-inch shafts, were pretty obvious. While others— Shauna tipped her head, trying to puzzle their use.

A well-dressed man slid into view from the other side of the pillar. "See anything you like?"

"No, but thanks."

The man's voice flowed smooth and as spiced molasses. "No need to thank me. I haven't offered anything yet."

Shauna changed direction, evading the suit and heading straight for the bar. Remember what Kimmy said. *"These are normal acts of human curiosity and affection—"*

Now she understood the disclosure. *"—just give it a minute to sink in. This is a natural urge that everyone has. Some people are just more open to exploring. Some are more comfortable."*

This went far beyond normal exploration in

Shauna's book. The pole dancers, caged behind the bar, seemed more modest than the crowd they'd been hired to entertain.

Who was she kidding? This was no spa, no summer ice cream parlor. She looked at the occupants on her right. And that was *no ice cream cone*.

Her gaze fled for the trio she'd crossed paths with. They seemed to know their way around. Maybe they were leaving. There had to be an exit on this level somewhere. It was fire code, right?

Shauna's hope deflated. The trio hadn't gone far. Center stage in the room, the curvy woman had perched herself on the raised inner portion of a circular sofa. She arched backward, her shoulders supported by the older lady—the gruff one, who reached forward and tugged the curvy woman's shirt upward.

Probably to get a better look at the show below waist level.

Pretty sure there were laws against spreading legs that far apart while wearing a skirt. Surprisingly limber for someone her size.

The man knelt between her thighs and pushed them further apart with both hands. Shauna blinked.

Correction. No skirt.

Shauna whipped her attention away as the man dipped his head into the limber woman's lap.

Shauna's gaze hit the ground. *Oh. My. Good-hell-someone-get-me-outta-here*. She pivoted back in the direction she'd come. Her head swam, slower to catch up with the rest of her body.

"Hey, sweetsome."

That suit again.

Shauna managed one wobbling step in retreat

before her path was blocked.

"Where you from?"

Shauna's line of sight traveled from loafers to flashy-pink tie. She hoped the look of annoyance would connect, but gauging the man's Mona Lisa smile, he wasn't taking "buzz-off" for an answer. "From?" she demanded.

"Haven't seen you around before." The suited man gave her a favorable once-over as he rubbed his baby-smooth chin. "I'd remember you."

"Oh, yeah. I'm from—uh, the Seattle group."

"Seattle?" The man rocked back on his heels. "I've got some friends up there. The name's Onyx." He offered a soft handshake. "Sorry to disrupt your show. The Grand Master's frolicking in the dungeon tonight, so I'm playing host. Can I take your coat?"

Shauna's shoulders dropped in their sockets. This guy was a big deal? She shifted out of her coat and handed it over. The warmth of the coat's silky lining slid from her arms.

"There. That's better, isn't it?"

Not really, Shauna hadn't noticed the sewn in heaven feel of the coat until it left her. If she'd known, she never would have given it up. Probably would have spent the evening rolling around in the coat closet too.

He half turned his attention back to the trio. "Sorry I didn't catch you when you first walked in. Awfully rude of me."

She followed Onyx's lead, turning back to the center of attention. "No worries," she murmured.

Shauna stared straight ahead, willing herself to look through the people. The undulating movements of the man's mouth. The dramatic arch on the woman's back. The spasm of her thighs, and the way she rocked her hips at an urgent pace, as if to goad him on. And the noise—oh God, *the noise*. Shauna's mind worked to bail out the images as fast as her eyes took them in. *Spa, spa, spa.*

It wasn't working. The throbbing tempo that grew in force around Shauna's lower half seemed to overpower her logic. The moisture that pooled in the confines of her panties seemed to welcome anything—anyone—that might relieve her infernal itch. And somehow *that* woman was getting what *Shauna* needed.

Her tongue slid over her cheery gloss-slicked upper lip, and Shauna chanced an angled glimpse at the man's expert ministrations.

His tongue danced over the glistening folds of the woman's outer seam. Wide flays from the full length of his tongue increased their tempo, as he moved upward from the lowest point of her genitals. A deliberate splay of his index and middle finger revealed the reddened inner folds of her most sensitive area. The tip of his tongue flexed sharp and quick as he speared between the swollen folds. Then the man settled into the upper crest of the woman's clit.

The woman's moans quickened to a feverish pitch of delight. One that played harmony with the mischievous anticipation tightening in Shauna's chest. She shouldn't be seeing this. But she couldn't look away.

"That there's Amanda. She's pretty, isn't she?" Onyx commented.

Shauna blinked. "Yeah, she's something else."

"We all are, darling." He angled his head in thoughtful curiosity. "You top or bottom?"

She offered a careless flap her hand. "Oh, top. Definitely top."

"Really." He paused. "Just how long've you been a player?" His tone seemed disturbingly casual over the curvy woman's accelerating moans.

"Not long." She swallowed. "Not really very long at all."

Onyx's lips eased into that Mona Lisa smile again. Was he wearing lip-gloss too? "Come now, there's no need to be modest here."

"What do you mean, modest?" Was he talking about her clothes? He didn't expect her to hand over *more,* did he?

The man pointed a manicured finger to Shauna's boots. "You've been in the game long enough to earn those."

Shauna followed his gaze to the glossy, black leather and row of silver buckles that bound her legs from ankle to knee. Funny how those heels seemed to beam back at her with a power all their own. "Oh. Yeah."

That damn Kimmy.

She offered what she hoped was a modest shrug. "I'm a quick learner."

His rich, golden laughter bubbled through the room. "That's wonderful." He moved in close. The slight weight of his hand rested on her waist. Tingles rushed over her skin from the warmth of his palm and swarmed through her body.

Caught somewhere between that delicious feeling and the violation from her own body, Shauna's chest heaved with what she hoped was an undetected gasp.

It wasn't.

Onyx's tone fell serious. Almost sensual. "I love the eager beavers. Tell me, who brought such a delightful present to our doorstep tonight?" His attention raked to the deep V-shape that framed her cleavage. "Or better yet…" The man planted a soft kiss on his fingertip and turned it toward Shauna. His path headed straight for the deepest part of her neckline. "Who befell the great misfortune of leaving you alone?"

Shauna's voice sounded shaky and uncertain, even to her own ears. "I wouldn't say he left so much as fell behind—" Her words cut off when Onyx's fingertip made contact. Long, slender fingers—like Adrian's—that could slide into her so easily. They could bathe in her moisture and massage away the unbearable ache from deep within.

A surge of fear busted Shauna free from the shiver that wracked her body. "He'll be along shortly."

Onyx's arm fell to his side. His bottom lip lowered in a sympathetic pout. "Oh, I scared you. I'm sorry if it seems I'm grilling you. Forgive me. I'm just intrigued. Never have I met such a perfect treasure. The more answers I get, the more you delight me."

"Thanks for that—I guess."

Onyx shook his head. "There you go again, thanking me."

"But like I said," Shauna continued. "My—my little *button nose* should be along shortly." There. She'd said it. The safe word was out, and now she would be left alone.

The man paused. His brows lifted in surprise. "Button—" he laughed. "Eager on so many levels, aren't we?"

Shauna shifted from one foot to the other, not sure how to respond. Had she said that right? Had the word changed to something else? The questions dropped from her mind. Not that it mattered. Her mouth stopped functioning anyway. The moment Shauna glanced to the entrance, her entire body seized in a steel grip of *deep do-do*.

Adrian's silhouette framed the entrance. He hadn't moved yet. Watching or searching, she wasn't sure which, but he was there. And Shauna's can was about to be kicked.

The look of dread must have registered somewhere on her face because Onyx seemed to recognize it and followed her line of sight.

"Ahhhhh, playing a little cat and mouse, are we?" He craned his neck to scan the far corner of the room. Onyx paused. "Wait. Adrian? You top...with Adrian?" His chest bounced in a delicate snort. "Never took him for a bottom sort of guy."

"He's, uh..." *He's getting closer that's what he is.* "He's both, actually." Shauna blurted. She pivoted in front of Onyx, hoping to block Adrian's view.

"Ha—*Ha*." He shook an impish finger at Shauna. "Now I know why you like to watch so much." He gestured to the trio. "I'll bet that Adrian's quite the spectacle to take in."

Shauna tried to stammer a response, but Onyx was faster. "Come, let's get you a drink, little mouse. And that button you've asked for."

Shauna picked a stool on the far end that backed against a pillar. The polite conversation between the bartender and Onyx clouded from Shauna's ears. Too busy tracking Adrian's movements from the corner of her eye.

He'd spotted her, all right, passing one booth after another without a glance in either direction. One woman stood with her chest puffed up, bare breasts exposed, and her partner—ahem—*partners* long forgotten. She stood on her tippy-toes and wiggled her fingertips in an attempt to gain his attention. One man shouted from across the room, "Adriaaaan!"

He ignored them all.

"And the lady's name?" the bartender asked, tugging Shauna's attention back to the bar.

"I don't know. Big-boobed-ho-bag sounds pretty appropriate."

Shauna paused at the sudden halt in conversation. "Oh, me. Shauna." She shook her head. "It's Shauna."

He slid a stack of papers over the clean surface. The first few pages were folded over to allow clear view of the dotted line. "Sign here."

She scribbled a hasty line that vaguely resembled her initials, then tossed the pen and made a hurried, shooing motion.

"This is your consent," the bartender assured. "Wouldn't you like to read through it?"

"No." No time for that. Just hand over the damn button before Adrian sees it. She didn't want him to know that mere seconds after entering, she'd already chickened out.

"All right," the bartender sighed.

"You know how to use it?" He traded the paper for a large, clear button about the size of Shauna's palm.

He extended the button, then retracted it again, back and forth as he spoke. "This is an all-inclusive pass—"

"Yes."

He continued, unrushed. "That means no restrictions."

Shauna half-nodded. For some reason her brain couldn't keep up. Everything played in dreamy afterthought.

"Your partner for the evening will be chosen at random and frequency according to the Grand Master's discretion. Protection and safe words do apply, but must be worked out prior to engagement."

Wait. What?

Chapter Nine

The bartender set the button down with a *clink*. "Entry's back there. Enjoy." He angled his head deep to the left, to a giant birdcage of chrome and green, behind the pole dancers.

Shauna thought the cage had been nothing more than a stage prop. But from this angle, she could just detect a thin metal railing that corkscrewed into a lower level of some kind.

She held a staying finger out to the bartender. "On second thought, could I get a copy of that?"

"But first, a drink," Onyx offered.

She nodded. "Something strong." Preferably cement and a swizzle straw. She had time to kill.

The bartender slowed as he set a blank contract on the counter. "Sorry lady, we don't serve alcohol here."

She glanced from the bartender to Onyx who held the same curious expression.

"Oh, no. I just meant caffeine," she rushed to explain. "Like a monster. With extra teeth."

The bartender—if you could call him that—frowned. "Extra-caffeinated caffeine?"

Onyx shrugged. "She's from Seattle."

"No drinks," Adrian barked. His palm slammed onto the bar, covering the button before Shauna could swipe it away. It scraped along the surface in what sounded like broken shards, as Adrian retracted it. He tucked it into his pocket.

"Well, that was rude." Shauna pivoted on her bar stool, ready for battle. "And very out of character." The stormy blue depths of Adrian's glare stunned her. She didn't even manage a warning shot.

The party, the drink, that same look of furious intent from years ago all came rushing back with hurricane force.

"Do you really think I'm going to chase you through this room all night?" Adrian demanded. He straddled the bar stool next to her, blocking Onyx off, and her in.

She looked to Onyx, and then lifted her chin. "It's hard to chase me if I'm not running. Do you see me running?" She tucked the folded contract deep into her bra for safekeeping.

"You *are* breathing a little hard. And you look a little warm."

She gave him a smarmy grin and offered a look around with her uplifted palm. "What's your point of reference for that?" She leaned to one side. "Onyx, could you get me another button?"

"Sure thing."

"Why are you here?" Adrian asked.

"Pretty quick change of subject." In fact, Shauna could use one of those too. She hooked one of the many clear saucers of liquid that lined the bar and slid it between them. The blue, mint-scented substance rolled around the saucer in a sluggish, half-set Jell-O consistency. "Maybe you're the one who needs a drink."

"That's massage oil." He meant that coaxing tone to annoy her. She being the wayward puppy and him tugging the leash. She moved for another one.

"Lube," he replied.

She elevated the brown one and angled the warm saucer like a tiny pie on a catapult. "Okay, how about a mud mask then."

"That's wax." He set it aside. "And it's hot."

Shauna let him take it. She'd need about six feet of it to get rid of him anyway. She breathed a sigh of frustration.

"Haven't you figured it out yet? You're out of your element. I don't care how you got in or what you actually planned to accomplish here, but I'm taking you home."

"Taking me home, huh? Unless that means what I hope it means, I just got here. I'm staying." She twisted in her seat for a clear path to escape. "Stop trying to be such a gentleman. Let a girl have some fun."

Adrian pivoted as well. His foot stomped down on the bottom rung of her stool. Blocked again. "This isn't the place for you."

Wasn't her place? Where the hell did he get off? "Unless your name is Grigori, I didn't see it on the door." She waited for a response.

Stone-cold Adrian wasn't offering one.

The little disk meant something completely different than what her roommate let on. Whatever it was, Kimmy wanted her down there. Above all, Adrian didn't want her to have it. Do the math. That button meant power and a bundle of trouble. Shauna wanted it all.

Heat and excitement shot through her nerves when she covered his knee with her damp palm. "I have just as much right to this place—*and that button*—as you do."

Adrian had come here tonight to get some. No denying that. The very thought of Adrian turned-on turned her knees to jelly. His erect penis, dusky and swollen with feral need, would be sliding into *someone* tonight. The heat of their bodies would permeate the room, beads of sweat forming as their bodies worked together, both fighting for release.

"How many of those chocolates did you eat?"

"What?" She looked up from his button fly. She started again, fingers walking toward his thigh. Her own body reacted in a rush of heat between her legs. "The night's pretty young. I have endless possibilities. Besides, what's it to you?"

"Let's just say I know the crowd."

"You don't know me. Not anymore."

Adrian leaned in. The curve of his nose nearly brushed hers. "I beg to differ." The challenge came with a hot breath of power and possession.

"You want to prove it?" The words caught tight in her rib cage. "If you're not going to help me, or even bother to hear me out, I'm entitled to console myself over *your rejection* by whatever means I choose. You have no right to deprive me." She slipped off her barstool and leaned in close. Her hand slid to the crevice of his thigh. "Unless you've changed your mind."

Shauna silkened her tone. "Have you ever wondered what would have happened all those nights ago? If I had taken you up on your offer?"

Adrian snatched her wrist in an enough-child's-play grip and forced her palm to center mass, the hard ridge of his erection. A soundless gasp of awareness spilled from Shauna's parted lips.

White teeth flashed in a split-second grin before it was gone. With a firm, one-armed grip, Adrian pulled Shauna in tight until his moist breath fanned her upper lip. The movement of his mouth played against hers with every word. "I'll tell you what would've happened. You would have been safe." He rocked forward against her hand, pressing his erection into her palm. "And warm—" He rocked again and slid her hand down the full length of him. "—and sleeping on my couch."

Flames of anger licked up her veins. Lie. That was a lie. She pushed away from his chest, and this time, he permitted her escape.

"Your button, Ms. Mouse," Onyx called from her left. His voice lifted with giddy delight.

Shauna ignored him and swiped the new button from the counter. "I'm not taking 'the couch' for an answer either." She took a step back toward the pit, then another.

Adrian shook his head in warning. "You don't want to go down there."

Shauna lifted her arms. "It's your choice, really. You or the pit." She blinked. "Your *help*. Or the pit."

"Dungeon," Onyx corrected.

Shauna's tone lightened with feigned interest. "Oh, it's a dungeon? How fun is that?" She started walking. "This I gotta see."

Adrian's voice hardened. "Grow up, Shauna. You know that's not what you want. They'll have you on your back, all right. That might sound good now, but I'm warning you, they'll put you in positions you never thought imaginable."

"Sounds great. I love twister," she shouted over her shoulder. The forceful turn of her head caused her to side step before continuing on course. Hopefully he didn't see that.

"Run little mouse, run!" Onyx clapped his hands with glee.

Halfway to the pit, Shauna's heart kicked up as Adrian's voice rumbled behind her. Close. Too close and too quick, as though he hadn't moved but suddenly *appeared* there. His words fired around her like whizzing bullets as she marched ahead. "You're pissed because I turned you down. You want to get even. I'm sure your blatant lack of sexual adventure is pretty damn frustrating."

"Oh, shut up."

A firm grip caught her arm. "Look. If you want to get off, that's fine. That's reasonable, but do it in the comfort of your own bedroom. Not here. You're in no condition to manage what goes on down there. Above all, you have no clue what you're doing."

Really. She stopped. Out of shock or confusion she wasn't sure. The last several years of her sexual history hadn't crossed the threshold of her own bedroom door. Don't say he could detect that too.

"I'm going to let you in on a little secret." He continued. The scent of hot cinnamon and camphor radiated from somewhere behind her. "You ever heard of love potion number nine?"

"Doesn't really sound like your fragrance."

He lowered his voice, and released her arm. The firm press of his body consumed her from hip to shoulder. Her head grew heavy and tipped back on its own accord to rest on his shoulder. If her bones could reach a melting point, she'd be a puddle at his feet.

"Those chocolates?" he murmured. The stubble on his chin grated the soft shell of her ear. "The ones you took? That would be lust potion number two. Though, I'm thinking I should probably rename it cock-tease number one."

Shauna jerked her head upright. "You're serious. That's your excuse?"

"How else do you explain your current state of arousal?"

"I don't know what you're talking about. I was just messing around—"

His tone dropped. "You're wet, shortcake. Soaking."

Shauna's mouth unhinged in horror; she moved to escape him.

Thick arms closed around her, holding her in place. Not squeezing, just holding. "It's a perfectly normal hormonal reaction, but it's royally screwing with your logic right now. You make this decision, you'll regret it."

So that's what this was all about? He didn't want to be held responsible later? That was it?

"Isn't that what this place is for? Making bad decisions?" she countered.

His arms lifted. His touch, gone. "That's what you want?" His voice grew tender and something in its depths tinged with regret. "Your first time? This is really how you want it?"

The shell of her heart crusted over. *Shows what you know*. She hadn't been a virgin since high school. Any chance at normalcy had been stolen the moment she stepped into that frat house. The doctor classified it as an "attempted sexual assault" because although she had been bruised and swollen, her perpetrator hadn't managed to "seal the deal" before the flames took him.

But he had stolen her life. Her chance to be normal.

Shauna tried to mask the anger boiling at her surface. She'd fight to get *normal* back by any tactic necessary. She pulled in a tight breath and forced it down. *Look dumb, flaunt the package. It's not that hard.*

But in a blink, the anger won and overtook her mouth.

"I want more than that. I want you." She lifted the button between them. She stuck out her bottom lip in what she hoped was a porn-star worthy pout. "If you can't help me, I'm afraid I just won't be able to help myself."

Shauna marched for the railing. A heavy sigh of what must have been annoyance rushed from his lungs.

"You're not settling. I'm going with you."

Well, that's just great.

Shauna's pride-filled chest deflated a bit. Adrian knew the crowd enough to let her into his playground. Now he had the upper hand, the knowledge, and the new kid parading in front of him down the stairs. All of the fun seemed to be deflating from her naughtiness balloon. She clomped down the spiral staircase, feeling more gangly and awkward with every step.

Shauna's attention fell to the barrel-chested brunette woman who perched on a bench at the bottom of the stairs. The woman's critical gaze drew lines of age near her eyes and red-painted lips. And not just any gaze, this was the kind that snared and sunk its teeth in. Whether eyeing Shauna up for battle or breakfast she wasn't sure.

When Shauna handed over her button, the woman's attention finally broke and lunged for Adrian. The verge-of-liver-failure hue that bronzed her cheeks pinkened. Her lips pulled back to reveal a wry, smoker's smile. "Surprise, surprise. It's my ole pal, Adrian."

"Evening, Darla," Adrian muttered, a reply that seemed more chore than friendly salutation.

The bottom floor opened to a ten-by-ten stone room. For the number of people crowding in, it seemed pretty quiet.

Shauna expected to find a carnival of outrageous sexual activity by now. Whip-cracking, chain-rattling, swinging-from-the-chandelier type stuff. She paused, still gripping the railing. Apart from the man-eating button collector continuing to stare Adrian down, there wasn't any of that sideshow business.

She panned the crowd of nearly thirty people. How long had they all been waiting here? Shauna hadn't seen any of them upstairs. Some unspoken order to behave seemed to be wearing thin. A squirmy vibe of sensual tension seemed to filter through the room. It touched and bounced from person to person, as one woman crossed and uncrossed her shapely legs, a tee-and-denim man paced back and forth along the nine-foot iron bars, and Shauna took a retreating step backward.

Her nerves flipped to panic mode.

The muggy warmth of body heat and perspiration saturated this place. The tiny hairs on her arms stood on end, and the sickening churn of her stomach went cold.

The heat would come soon.

Shauna swallowed. She'd been lucky to get this far, but now she teetered on the edge of an invisible threshold. She searched the room for open space. There wasn't much, not enough to get away from the hormones thickening the air.

She took another step back.

The closest ventilation took the form of an enormous black gate, but that seemed to be what everyone waited on. Not the place for Shauna. In mere moments, she'd become a flaming doormat trampled by a lust-driven stampede.

Adrian pressed his lips to the back of her head. The moisture of his breath seeped into her hair. A cunning smile curled through his voice. "Problem?"

Shauna jumped forward, abandoning her subconscious disappearing act. Pretty lame, trying the squeeze herself into the crevice of his abs. "No. No problem," she rushed to assure.

"Uh huh."

She took an extra step away for good measure. Her gaze fell to where her arms squeezed protectively around her abdomen. She pushed out a slow breath, thankful no visible cloud of heat rolled from her lips. "So…what happens now?"

Adrian's stormy-blue gaze lifted, and he offered a faint nod at the large gate.

A man, six foot tall and about that wide, had appeared on the other side. His grin stretched between the bars and his fidgety gaze danced eagerly through the crowd. A ring of keys jingled near the gate's opening, but the man didn't look down. He seemed to fumble in greedy haste at gaining access to his new patrons.

The hinges squawked in rust-eaten protest when the man swung the gate wide. He stepped back, but no one moved.

Shauna caught herself staring, too. That's where they were headed?

Hydrangea and white moonflower blooms glowed amid the pillars of candle light. Waxy vines clung to the darkened hallways running in both directions. They draped over a massive iron gazebo that centered the largest indoor garden Shauna had ever seen.

She nodded to herself. Maybe this wouldn't be so bad after all.

"Come on, come on," urged the man. His grin widened, and he made a jumpy, coaxing motion as if drawing an entire herd of Hansels and Gretels into his kitchen.

Inside, the cement walls and cobblestone floor radiated with the sun-beaten warmth of July.

A little strange for October.

Tiny firefly lights pinpricked throughout the foliage, and mirrored the star-painted ceiling above. It seemed difficult to find any beginning or end.

Finding pain seemed no problem at all.

Shauna tried to ease her stomach's rollercoaster drop. This Garden of Eden had been tended by Jack the Ripper.

Manacles dangled empty from each of the gazebo's five arches. A chandelier of chains drooped from the center. Along one wall, a medieval fence of stainless, metal chairs were interspersed among the foliage. The chair backs made of what appeared to be sharpened pikes.

Adrian's voice rumbled low near her left ear. "Seen

enough?"

She shrugged away from him. "Are you kidding? This is incredible."

"Ladies and gentlemen, it is my fine privilege to welcome you to the garden."

Shauna turned to the voice behind them just as the gate slammed shut. The foreboding *clang* of metal-on-metal seemed to stop everyone in their tracks.

The large man chuckled, a soundless laughter that could only be detected in the faint giggle from under his multicolored sweater. "For those of you who do not know me, I am your host. Your Orchestrator. You may call me O."

He lifted his hand in offering to the new world around them. "I'm sure you've noticed this is no ordinary dungeon. We pride ourselves on secrecy, discretion, and trust." His belly jumped again in a silent snort. "On some level." He cleared his throat and sped his words as if racing back to the task at hand. "As you can see, our garden has many secret pleasures and toys.

"The tool shed." O pointed northeast, to where a primitive stone structure had been fitted with what looked like a steel refrigerator door. Inside, shelved racks of surgical trays were draped with blue paper cloths. A large assortment of gleaming knives, scissors, and gloves hung from the structure's inner walls.

"The koi pond." To the right, fattened, orange and yellow fish lapped at the water's surface. Their white, gossamer fins floated eerily through the ten-by-ten-foot blackened pond. Attached, a wrought iron bridge led to a cement island pad. In the middle, a coffin-sized, metal fire pit. The jumping flames, which seemed more blue than yellow, danced in a silent reflection from the mirror-like, metallic pokers, irons, and shovels that lined the wall.

Shauna bounced up and down in her best attempt at schoolgirl excitement. "Oh, oh. Fireplay. I can do that one!" She nudged him with her elbow. "Or the pond. We *like ponds*, don't we?"

Adrian rounded on her with a scowl that would send most grown men scurrying.

"What?" she asked, biting back her grin of impending triumph. He'd give in. Any second now she'd cross one line too many and end up over his shoulder and out the door.

Or over his knee.

Maybe his bed?

She closed her eyes. Umm…. Or with a *cure?*

"Many titillating opportunities for you to try. To enjoy," O continued. His tone hardened to reclaim the crowd's wandering attention and titters of delight. "But make no mistake. Just because you've gained passage this far, doesn't mean you've earned the privilege to play in my garden."

He lifted his arms akimbo, pointing in opposite directions, airline attendant style. The dark, rounded alcoves that lined the halls were fitted with black metal bars. "To either side of the garden you will find a chance to earn that privilege." O's tone lightened. He closed his eyes and swayed a bit, as though entranced in a song all his own. "So make friends, my little love birds. Play nice. Sing pretty enough to please me, and you shall earn your key."

Shauna hesitated. "We have to sing?"

"Cry, moan, scream. It varies. But you won't leave until you give him what he wants. He'll know if you're faking." Adrian tipped his head. "Are we through now?"

Shauna ignored the question. The irritated edge in Adrian's voice seemed sharper—and more in her favor—by the second. As much as she wanted to, she couldn't leave. She might be on to a golden opportunity. A cure. "How do I know what he wants—"

"*You* don't." An unyielding command flashed in his eyes. "Don't even try. I'm coming for you, and you're staying put."

She snorted. "Like hell."

O paused. He issued Shauna a warning look. Seemingly satisfied with her apologetic smile, he continued. "Once you earn your key, you will be released into the garden."

The cogs in Shauna's brain picked up speed as she scanned her surroundings. If the hard-core stuff stayed in the garden, and Adrian wanted her out, guess who had the upper hand now? To sit in her cage and simply wait for jailbreak, where would that get her at the end of the night?

If she were lucky? A couch.

Not happening.

"But of course, this is a game of chance." O looked knowingly at Adrian. "We have many ways to make you sing."

Adrian's posture stiffened. A tiny muscle near his jaw jumped to attention.

Shauna stared. The look of defiance and mistrust that played on Adrian's face was like nothing she'd ever seen in him. Did he know about this?

Then she heard it. A soldier's march trailing down the stairs. Four men and four women proceeded down the staircase from where Shauna had come. Their gladiator physiques completely exposed, except for the wingspan of a large bird tattooed across their chests, and a black, mesh bag with a silver drawstring tightly synched around their heads.

A wave of alcohol and menace followed their purposeful stride until they fell into rank behind O. They turned their full attention to the crowd.

One woman made a slight pivot, back and forth, as if consoling the ten-inch, pink dildo that she held in both hands. Another looked transfixed on the crowd with her fists planted on her hips, and a leather riding crop dangling from her wrist. The final man, who seemed somehow paler than the others, stroked the hard length of his greased-up penis in a slow, foreboding rhythm.

"These, my love birds, will be your hawks for the evening." O ambled down the line of behemoths with his chest puffed in imminent victory. "Before you ask, there is no limit to their mobility and your cage will not save you."

Great. The cages weren't safe either? Shauna glanced at the hawks and then at Adrian, but her self-appointed babysitter didn't move. His eyes were still fixed on O.

She knew that look. Adrian was calculating again. This game of chance must have introduced a new element even Adrian hadn't anticipated.

"If you catch a hawk, he or she is yours for the evening. But if a hawk catches you, you become their prey. Their hoods remain in place at all times for the ultimate in anonymity. Our predators are the cleanest and safest of specimens, but you are by no means safe from their wrath."

The courage inside Shauna went from apple to sauce. What the hell had she gotten herself into? They'd be separated. Calling Adrian's bluff and acting exactly as he said—a spoiled brat—wouldn't get her anywhere now. They were trapped, both of them, and it was her fault.

O pointed to the ceiling and lifted his sandy brows in innocence. "You have all signed a consent. But if any of you wish to back out, speak."

Adrian turned to face her.

Swallow your pride. Choke on it if you have to.

Shauna opened her mouth and then closed it again, her tongue caught in a net of uncertainty. After tonight, and the mess she'd made, Adrian would disappear just as he had before. Then she would never find help.

What could she offer him beyond the threat to her safety? How could she become more than the troublesome neighbor kid he'd dolefully watched out for all those years ago.

She shrugged in defeat. "How else can I do to convince you?"

The stoked anger and frustration rushed to Adrian's surface. His cheeks turned red, and his lips twisted into a sneer. "Not putting yourself here. That's for damn sure."

"All right, birds," O called. "Choose your cages."

Chapter Ten

One gate slammed shut and then another as the remaining crowd galloped down the hall amid nervous laughter, and cat calls.

The first cell on the block hadn't been picked yet. With any luck, the others would pass over it in their haste. Shauna rushed ahead, not running away, strategizing. She nodded to herself. After all, who in their right mind would barrel headfirst down a path of certain destruction? She had a plan…somewhere.

Stepping inside, the heels of her boots plunged into the black, gymnasium-style pad that took up most of the floor.

She grasped the cell door to steady herself then jerked it to near-closed behind her. She turned, and with shaking hands, she nudged the door closer and closer to flush. Maybe no one would notice it wasn't shut completely.

Pushing Adrian out of his comfort level would be a lot easier if she knew *where* his comfort level was. You'd think Mr. Everything in Moderation Man would look a little out of place in this anything for ejaculation environment.

Nope, he looked right at home.

If he didn't give in, if he didn't rescue her, she'd get the hell out on her own.

But how?

Think. She pressed her back to the gritty wall and deep into the shadows. *Use your brain. Think.*

But her brain seemed too busy flinging insults for getting into this situation. Her heart, hammering for rescue, wasn't helping much either. Hell, even demon-brat who got her here wasn't finding *this* amusing.

The remaining herd clattered over the cobblestone floor with skips and spins. Amazing how delighted they seemed. Like imprisonment was next best to Disneyland.

That's where she was. Trapped. In an X-rated version of Pinocchio.

O's warning echoed through the hall from somewhere ahead of her cell. "Here come your hawks."

Now would be a great time to disappear.

Shauna shifted from one foot to the other. Hands up, she readied to thrust the door open. When the last person passed her, she'd make a run for it.

The cellblock fell quiet. Only the distant gurgle of the pond fountain met her anxious breaths. She edged forward.

She halted when a shadow eclipsed her cell.

Adrian's broad shoulders were steady set and unyielding as he passed her door.

The cold press of the metal bars knocked against either side of Shauna's temples as she reached for him. Her door hinged open a bit with a low groan. She pulled it back just as quick. She tried again. "*Psst. Hey.*"

Adrian strolled out of reach to a cell several doors down and across the hall, as if he had the world's best headphones and all the time in the world. As if the stupid cell had his name engraved on it. *Nanny-nerd of*

109

the month. All violators will be towed.

Adrian pivoted to face her as he reached for his door. The look of resentment never broke as he pulled the gate shut with an ominous click.

Stubborn. Shauna stepped back, and her arms fell to her sides. What did he have to go and do that for? With his cell locked, he couldn't reach her even if he wanted to.

Her heart tensed. Maybe he didn't want to reach her. From the scowl that pulled at the corners of his mouth and the shadow that darkened his eyes, he'd rather leave her for dead.

She scanned the dingy corners of her cell, fighting the hurt that threatened to consume her. So this was it. He'd never give in.

There had to be a way out, a loophole, something. She couldn't trust any of these people to form an alliance against Adrian. The ploy ended here. These people played for flesh.

She eyed the strange, dangling pendulum of Velcro and chains poised in the center of the room. Its metal links clinked together when the adjoining cell slammed shut. She wanted a chance to appeal to Adrian. He still didn't understand her dire need for his help. But she didn't want to show him this way. Not like this.

She expected to see a flock of plundering hawks swoop past her cage. It wasn't the case. They wandered by with measured steps. But they didn't choose anyone. They paced back and forth behind the portly ringmaster. They wandered a bit but they always returned to him, waiting for a final nod for deployment.

"Swing, baby bird," called the female hawk to the cell nearest Shauna's. Soft, yet somewhat orchestrated moans filtered into the hall. The hawk sneered. "Spread your legs and fly."

Shauna turned to the apparatus in the center of her cage. Some sort of sex swing?

She tucked back her chin. This wasn't Cirque Du Soleil. That key better be worth more than freedom and frolicking in a garden if they wanted Shauna anywhere near that thing. No telling where it's been.

The Orchestrator paused. Shook his head as if not convinced, and motioned the female hawk towards the moaning cell.

"Aww, but I wanted that one," cried a man from across the hall.

The female hawk turned from adjusting the strap-on dildo on her hips, giving the complainer her full, ten-inch profile.

The man put both hands up in an I-surrender pose. "Never mind."

The ringmaster—or whatever he called himself—ignored the hawk's delicate snort and the muffled snicker from the adjoining cells. Instead, he bubbled with animation as he neared Adrian's cell. The Oracle paused from his hippity-hop routine just a few feet from Adrian's cell. Was there anything more repulsive than a leprechaun jig of that size?

"So do you like the new curtains?" O's words ran together with pent-up excitement. He ignored Adrian's look of irritation, as usual, and his eyes widened with feigned surprise. "No? Didn't notice? Well, I guess that wouldn't be the first thing on your mind. We have made a few bigger changes," he allowed.

Adrian's teeth scraped against each other and sent shockwaves of pain up his jaw.

O offered a hand gesture to the row of hawks prowling the hall behind him. "Not quite the same potency as the legend of Adrian Sands, but we do our best to maintain a similar flavor."

Adrian's upper lip twitched on the verge of disgust before he clenched his mouth shut. Flavor? Hard to mask the rancid stench of blood and sewage that had seeped into the concrete floor over the years. To make it extra cozy, add the overproduction of vanilla bean incense and the cheap perfume and body odor that tainted every reachable surface.

Adrian's gag reflux twitched.

O's thick, sandy brows drew together in sympathy. He ticked along the row of bars with his index finger as he paced Adrian's cell. "Of course, not even my strongest hawk holds a candle to you."

Adrian's fist clenched at the chance to latch onto O's neck and slam him back and forth against the bars like a paddleball. He may have spent his youth poaching pretties here, but he never hurt people. Domination, pain, rape, the very thought dropped a cold stone in his gut.

His peripheral vision anchored to the cell Shauna had stepped into. His mind geared-up for the slightest of movement from her cowering silhouette. Too dark in there to see much. Wise choice.

The Oracle angled his body to the cell adjacent to Adrian. "Just look at them."

At the first hint of attention, the willowy man in the cell tossed back his mop of candy-cane highlights and flattened his chest against the cage. His voice strained with desperation. "Please. Let me out?" He snaked up and down the metal, blanching his colorless skin.

Might want to think twice before licking those bars, buddy.

The hawks paid no attention. They continued their dead-from-the-waist-up march up and down the hall. Their bare feet slapped the floor in steady rhythm.

"What's taking so long?" muttered a woman from somewhere down the row.

Judging from the crowd, the rape and pillage was running a bit behind schedule.

The candy-cane man's attention veered to a passing hawk. In a blink, his bony arms hooked between the narrow bars, his hands contorted into claws. He lunged for the steroid-swollen gym rat. Missed. "Come back," he insisted. His pale featured contorted in outrage, then eased again. "I'll do anything…"

O slowed his words as if musing to himself. "Look at how they react to the very thought of getting what you offered here." He turned. "They've missed you."

"They've missed the drugs," Adrian muttered.

"Not really." The Oracle pinched his thumb and forefinger together, as if holding the most precious grain of wisdom he'd ever found. His voice lowered to a serpent's hush. "You see, as far as they know, the drug never left. It just became a little *difficult* to obtain."

"You mean impossible."

"Yeah, pretty much." The O brightened. "Hey, business is business. They know the risk. None of these people are being held *or forced* against their will."

Adrian took a menacing step forward. "Or under false pretenses?"

"Sketchy pretenses at best."

His vision narrowed.

The O stepped back and held up his palms. "You can't go blaming me. You started this, honey. This was *your* game."

No denying that.

Finding pleasure in another person didn't come easy. Not unless it came five-three with honey-streaked curls. Legs limber and toned from jumping fences, and a dusting of freckles earned from days spent thieving through Jensen's summer garden.

A little hard to come by in an underground sex club.

So Adrian used his apothecarian gift to bend reality. A lot.

Only he saw the illusion through the air-light, undetectable powder. The women had no idea. It never lasted longer than a quickie, and it didn't work more than once on the same person. Perfect excuse to leave his relationships at the club the way they belonged. Short and meaningless.

But as with any of his novice concoctions, it came with a side effect. And this one fell right into the Oracle's food bowl. The residual powder that had dusted his one-night-stands left them with a rather gratifying taste. Or so he was told. The end result? A bunch of middle-aged, mental-Aphrodites offering themselves as the club buffet.

Night after night, no one could get enough. Passion turned to greed, then anger, violence. For the women, attention was attention.

Months later, when the effect finally wore off, the women went from seasoned steak to stale cardboard. By then, violence was the only thing left. O had been gnawing on the leftovers ever since.

The Oracle shrugged. "What did you expect? I can't *undo* what you've created here. When you left, this place became...watered down." He scrunched his nose.

"Not my problem." Adrian's peripheral vision yanked back to Shauna's cell as one of the smaller, male hawks paced by.

The hawk hesitated. He turned his full attention to Shauna's door.

Did he notice that she'd left it slightly ajar? Probably trying to hedge her bets?

No. The man didn't close it. He waited. He'd chosen Shauna as his first victim and was waiting for the order to strike.

Adrian worked to ignore the blast of anger powering through his veins. His gaze raced over the hawk's profile. He calipered the man's stance and the width of his shoulders. He sniffed. The sharp tang of gunpowder told him the guy packed heat on a regular basis. Not used to relying on muscle.

He could take him.

Blind him, that's possible. Distract him, maybe. But the urge to bust through the bars and smash a hole in the bastard's skull sounded best.

Forget the Oracle's demands or teaching that stubborn Barbie her lesson. Game's up. This ends now.

The Oracle moved to block his view. The edges of his smug grin plied into his fatty cheeks. "Not your problem? You sure? Because in case you hadn't noticed, your little toy is scared out of her itty-bitty mind over there."

"She's not for this world, O."

The Oracle snorted. "Well then, we wouldn't want

her to end up like the last one, would we?" O angled his head. "Probably never crossed your mind, did she? We kept her here." He grinned. "Fed her more and more of your precious chocolate to keep her willful, but in the end," he lifted a hand, "she didn't much appreciate our accommodations. Is that what you want for your little doll? It's not, is it?"

He erected his posture. "Because this one's special. If I didn't know better, I'd say this is the flavor you've been lusting after your entire life. Isn't that right?"

If Adrian told Shauna to run…No, she'd never make it up the stairs and out the building. The patrons at the bar would take her rape as an everyday scene. They wouldn't bat an eyelash.

Until their eyelashes singed off.

Shauna might be able to protect herself, but she shouldn't have to. Damn if he shouldn't have let her come down here in the first place. He should have been there to protect her the right way.

The first time.

If that guy touches her…

Adrian took deep breaths to clear the fog of rage clouding his mind. It must have registered on his face, because the Oracle's voice grew louder and more urgent, as if trying to rise above the drumbeat in Adrian's skull. "Give it to me, boy. I want the infusion, or that frat house memory of yours will be nothing! I'll send my entire flock over there for a gang bang you'll never scrape out of your mind."

The word grated through Adrian's clenched teeth. "All right."

Seeming satisfied, the oracle stepped back. He waved over a female hawk. "You'll start with a girl.

That will be easier for you, right?" He jabbed a finger across the room. "Followed by him, then him." He turned to face Adrian, his shoulders back. "Then me."

"No."

"No?" A look of profound hurt wrinkled his brow. "Where'd all those good manners of yours go, Mr. Sands…Sands…Adrian Sands?"

Adrian jerked his chin to the one facing Shauna's cell. "Him first."

"Oh." The oracle paused. "O-okay." He tittered with delight and waved the large hawk over with an urgent flap of his wrist. "And to think, after all these years. You rascal! I can't wait to see this tall drink of water turn into a pink lemonade."

O's pudgy fingers jabbed at the key pad attached to the cell door. "Or maybe it's to make your doll feel better about the whole thing." He waved the option away. "Oh, who cares?" He laughed. "You can do me next."

"It's a drug. Not a miracle," Adrian muttered.

"But you're *the miracle worker*." The Oracle's face fell serious. "You better pray this works."

The moment the lock clinked shut on Adrian's door, O bounded back, rear end first, to his vantage point. His bulb-shaped body jiggled as he trotted from one foot to another.

Shauna rose up on her toes. She pressed her cheek to the cold, stone wall, desperate to spy any hint of movement from her slivered view of Adrian's cage. A quick snap of O's fingers had turned away the beast about to enter her cell—but at what cost?

Maybe she didn't want to know.

A leering male voice echoed down the hall. "It's

playtime." Whether hawk or prey, she wasn't sure. Shauna's body tensed forward to pick up any sight or sound from Adrian's cage.

The building chaos around her clouded her efforts, frustration creeped along her nerve endings.

"Wait. What about me?" offered a female prisoner directly across the hall. The woman bounced up and down and made a scooping motion with her hand, as though begging for the last chance to pull attention her way.

It couldn't start like this. Not with him. Shauna's heart sunk into a murky thought.

Or had Adrian requested this. But why? To teach her the harsh reality that anything goes here? That he ran the show? Or was he trying to spare her?

The hawks paced, their force growing in every step. Taunts and pawing invitations from their soon-to-be victims grew more urgent as the entire dungeon charged with eager energy.

A few hawks reared their cloaked heads toward O and Adrian's cell, their expressions unreadable, before returning to the prisoners. Others faced the scene openly, as though waiting to act on the final outcome.

A scuffle ensued from somewhere within Adrian's darkened bars.

"Whoa-ho," shouted another prisoner. A grin edged in his tone.

"Get 'em, come on!" cheered another.

Shauna pushed out a huff of annoyance and glared at the overweight, dancing clown. *Move already*! She flinched at the deafening bang of metal that rattled through the corridor.

All sound cut off as the barred spectators

collectively flinched in surprise. O jumped back a step and the crowd roared with new enthusiasm.

Something must have hit the bars. Shauna angled her head, searching. A heavy shadow dragged back into the depths of the cell. Could that be Adrian? He didn't seem the grappling kind. He had the muscle for it, no doubt, but the guy who entered his cell looked like he could walk through a cinderblock wall.

The sound of shredding fabric met Shauna's ears. Then a loud smack.

Her attention raced over the distant row of bars. The hawk hadn't been wearing clothes. Whatever was happening in there wasn't consensual.

The chime of metal links seemed to spur on the prisoners nearby. Shauna's gaze flew to the dangling sex swing at the center of her cell, the same contraption that appeared behind every row of bars. She squeezed her eyes shut as her stomach took a sickening twist. This couldn't be happening.

The cheers rose up with guffaws and sharp whistles from the onlookers.

She blinked back the tears that flooded her vision. Not him. Not Adrian.

He had been the silent guardian over her childhood and at one point, the keeper of her heart. He couldn't be humiliated this way. Not for her.

The O's upper body leaned back in shock. As if remembering himself, O rushed for the keys to the cell. He fumbled. Looked, fumbled again. His mouth flapped open and closed as if panic had crushed his voice box.

His tone grew from rasp to panicked squeal. "Don't you dare…don't you hurt him. He's mine!"

"Adrian!" The name burst from Shauna's throat.

Chapter Eleven

She shoved her cage door open with such force it crashed into the stone wall adjoining it.

Her blur of action exploded into blinding pain the moment she smacked into the pale chest of another hawk. He snatched her torso bear-hug style, and pinned her arms to her sides then clamped down with a punishing squeeze.

Shauna clawed and tore at his arms like a wild animal. All the while, he fought her backward. Away from Adrian. Back to the cage.

"Nooo!" she roared. Shauna delivered a savage kick to the hawk's shin. The hawk staggered, and his grip crushed her arms against her body. She reared back and slammed her forehead into the mesh bag. The loud crack of bone against bone was quickly chased by numbness, then pain. A fine, white mist danced in front of her vision.

He dropped her, then delivered a brutal shove.

Shauna's feet flew from the ground. She scrambled midair to right herself.

Her back slammed into the mat. Like a ragdoll, her neck flopped backward, and her head quickly followed. A numb tingle swept up the back of her neck as she twisted to right herself.

"What's wrong? Not enough action in here for you?" The bitter malice in his whisper sent a shocking chill through her mind.

Shauna backed away on hands and feet like a tiny crab ripped of her armor. Her mind flew through his words, trying to decipher his meaning.

That voice. She squinted at the mesh head covering. Her attention coursed over the winged tattoo. The right side appeared blurry and smudged from their confrontation. It wasn't real like the others.

His tone hardened but remained low to not alert the others. "You really thought you could get away with this? With my connections? I know people. Haven't you figured that out yet?"

"Richard?" She shook her head. "What are you doing here?"

His head leaned forward as if searching for clarification. "What am *I* doing here?"

"You—you don't understand—"

"I don't care."

The riot of noise outside peaked to a thundering roar. Shauna scrambled to her feet and raced for the opening. They'd talk later.

Richard caught her shoulders and knocked her feet out from under her with a swift kick.

She slammed to the mat again.

"We're done. You got it?" He used the back of his hand to touch what Shauna assumed was his nose. He glanced at the faint smudge of blood that stained his hand.

"Fine!" No time for this. "Just lemme go!"

"No." His voice turned sly. "We're finished. But I'm not done with you yet." She couldn't see his face, but an entirely different person seemed to be confronting her from behind that mask. Not the doting fiancé she knew, but someone bitter, twisted with betrayal. "Know what? I'm glad you're here. I'm glad you finally came asking for it."

Shauna sent him a sharp look of disgust. "It's not like that—"

He came at her again until the mesh bag brushed her cheek. "I can't believe I didn't think of this sooner, actually."

The frothy scent of beer consumed her sinuses. She angled her head and backed away.

"It figures," he continued, ignoring her retreat. "Not the savviest pussy in the alley, are you?"

"Don't—" She parried his forward movement and scrambled to put the swing between them. "You're drunk."

"You're a whore." The flat of Richard's bare foot slammed into her chest.

She slapped against the foam pad again, and the air rushed from her lungs. Richard seemed to squeeze out what remained of her breath as he stepped his full weight on top of her rib cage.

Shauna pried her nails under his foot but it wouldn't give, she pushed at his ankle. He was too heavy. The burning pain in her ribs grew to the near snapping point. She made a hasty grab for the swing that shuddered above. Mere inches away.

With a callous brush of his hand, Richard held it out of reach. "In fact, I'd wager you're not anything that you say are. You're not a virgin at all, are you?" He thrust the heel of his foot against her sternum. The mesh bag flinched forward near his mouth as he shouted. "Are you!"

Her jaw hinged open in a mix of offense and pain.

Her mind struggled to register his words.

"So this is the problem, then. This is why you won't give it up." The weight on her chest eased a bit, sparing her precious gasps for air. "It's not holding out for marriage. One man's just not enough for you. How many do you need?" The weight returned full force. "Two? Three?"

Shauna scream forced itself from her lungs in a guttural yelp.

"Too bad for you, I don't like whores. But as a parting gift, let's make sure you get what you want." Richard's chest jumped as he blew out a sharp whistle, but the other hawk was already moving toward him. He released her with a final kick and moved for the exit.

One thought became clear. Even the dirtiest of money was cleaner than this kind of revenge. Richard didn't want to get his hands dirty.

His words were curt and expressionless as he passed the entering hawk. "Fuck her. Then bring your friends."

He pulled the cell door shut as he left and gave it a secure tug. He never looked back.

Shauna leaned away from the approaching assailant, but his military steps didn't falter. When he stepped within range, she kicked at the hardened length of his flesh-covered weapon.

He caught her foot before it connected. With a vicious tug, he yanked her forward. Her dress slid up, bare skin pulled and burned against the matt. She jerked her skirt back in place and twisted to crawl away.

Her assailant lassoed her throat with a tangle of Velcro and chains that hung from the ceiling. The animal scream that ripped from her throat cut off as he wrapped the swing around her neck and pulled tight. The man behind her shoved her lower half to the matt. Sharp pain branched from her overextended spine. The chains cut into her skin, and she scrambled up again, elbows propped on the matt to keep the pressure off her neck.

She sucked in air with tiny hitches.

The touch of skin against her inner thigh shot fear through her system. Her knees scraped the mat, routing for any chance of escape. Slick with moisture from her increasing body temperature, she couldn't gain traction against the weight that pinned her down. Her lungs burned.

Air.

Shauna squeezed her thighs together as he shoved her dress up.

Her vision clouded on the edges with dark spots. She blinked to fight them back, but the spots grew wider. They bled together, then fringed with a red haze.

An inferno of heat swirled through her core and raged to the surface. It ripped the strength from her muscles. Her arms trembled under the weight of her own body, then finally gave in.

Helpless to hold it back, the flames burst to life around her. They singed her tender eyelids, and the smell of smoldering cloth and vinyl consumed her.

Cries of agony blared through her head. Her own voice chimed with the pained screams of another person.

Oh God. She was hurting someone. A fresh dose of fear engulfed her system, and the flames jumped wider in a surge of blinding light. She couldn't stop it. She fought to lift her head, to escape, but her muscles wouldn't react.

Stop it. She rolled her head to one side, and pulled in a gasp of scalding air and soot. Her diaphragm clenched in spasms of protest. Each cough sent jolts of pain through her ribs and scraped up her throat. The vinyl straps had melted and loosened their grip, but the tangled swing still cradled her upper body in an arched position. Her lower half lay flaccid and useless on the smoldering mat.

Shauna strained to open her swollen lids. Through blurry, red slits the hawk appeared, several feet away, rolling and twisting on the ground in inescapable pain, beyond the reach of Shauna's flames, but locked inside the blistering shell of his own body. His waist and thighs were roasted to a lobster hue. Fragments of what could only be skin, hung like tattered rags.

The crackle of flames echoed amid scampering feet and the distant cry of fire from the other patrons. Pinpricks of water rained down from the cell's sprinkler system. It did nothing to quell the blaze. Piercing alarms rang through the hall and metal doors slammed. Ghostly plumes of human bodies raced past Shauna's cell.

Except one.

A large, dark figure marched toward her, through the swirling, back smoke. He bent over the lock near the cell door. Within seconds, the metal hinges screeched open. His attention never turned to the writhing man on the cell floor. He approached the ball of flames that fluttered and snapped around Shauna.

Too close. Stay back! She couldn't force the words through her swollen throat.

The flames answered for her as they expanded in a

threatening *whoosh*.

They consumed the man's silhouette until he stood in the center of the orbiting flames.

Illuminated by the fire's bright glow, no fear registered on Adrian's hardened jaw. His chest expanded with a mighty breath. He pressed a fist just under his nose. The air rushed from his body again, through the funnel of his fist.

A cloud of jade-colored smoke burst from his hand, expanding and curling through the room, pushing out the smoke and crawling along the ceiling of her cell. Tiny, cooling grains hailed down on her. They bounced off Shauna's skin like a hot frying pan. A faint, hissing sound grew until it overpowered everything else.

Shauna-flames bowed under the downpour. They weakened and flickered until they collapsed into nothing. The remainder of Shauna's energy disappeared right along with them. She fought the heavy sag of her eyelids. The watery rise and fall of her vision brought sporadic dark and light glimpses of Adrian as he knelt beside her.

One thick arm supported her upper body as he unwound her from the tangle of chains and charred vinyl, then lowered her to the mat. He reached for her then retreated, as though unsure the safest place to touch.

Her exhausted mind couldn't decipher the look on his face. Anger and concern tugged at his dark brows, and waged war in his eyes.

She wasn't burned. Couldn't he see that? She wanted to parrot the thought out loud, but the moment her mouth opened, she snapped it closed again.

Adrian rocked back on his heels and reached for

the hem of his tee. Bronze muscles rippled animating the winged silhouette tattooed on his chest when Adrian pulled his shirt over his head.

He leaned over her.

Shauna drew in a painful gasp. She sent him a wide-eyed look of caution. He'd extinguished her, fair enough, but not even *she* got to pick and choose who she burned. Why would he put himself in that kind of danger?

Adrian's face dropped all hint of emotion as he tugged his large tee shirt over her head. Shauna breath came easier as the dark cotton brushed her face. The warm smell of cinnamon and camphor soothed her charred sinuses. She wanted to burrow back inside the moment her head emerged, but Adrian wasn't wasting time.

Her sock-monkey limbs flopped to her sides, first one then the other when he pulled them through the arm holes.

He tugged her upper body forward to drape over his shoulder. His knuckles brushed the edge of her breasts and the inward curve of her waist as he worked the shirt back and forth over her torso.

A shiver raced through her body.

If she angled her head just right, her cheek would graze the cool strength of his bare shoulder. Her face could find refuge in the corded muscles of his neck, feel something real and unharmed in her presence, if only for a moment, before her curse found its strength again.

But no. Her body up and quit on her. The best she could do was drool on him.

Shauna pushed out her lower lip in a pouty frown. After all this time, not a damn thing had changed.

Chapter Twelve

"Does any of this make sense?" Shauna stared at Adrian. "No?"

Her gaze hunted for any indications of life. Was she speaking a different language? It probably sounded that way. Every other word came out slathered with wet hiccups. He hadn't asked for an explanation, But Shauna's tongue kept rattling anyway, like a runaway baby buggy. Her brain couldn't rise above infancy level. Her big girl britches had burned away.

First a brat, then a bawling brat. Could this night get any worse? She wiped her moist cheeks with the back of her hand.

The vehicle emitted a series of soft chimes. Adrian's attention flicked to Shauna, then straight ahead through the tinted windows. What was that? Her timer? Was Adrian waiting for her blathering monologue to continue? He hadn't said a word. His expression remained cool as polished granite.

What more did she expect? How should a man react to a wailing nutcase curled in his passenger seat? "You see? This is why I need you. My entire life has been ruined by this," she held up her palms, "this blazing chastity belt."

The vehicle chimed again.

Adrian's tone remained even, ignoring the alert. "I wouldn't say ruined. Inconvenienced maybe. You can still orgasm."

"It's not the same." She sent him a harsh frown. "Stop sounding so damn clinical."

The sharp-edged tattoo flexed its wings as Adrian gave an offhanded shrug. "Sex is overrated."

"It is not," she snapped. "Not when an entire empire can be built on it." Shauna thumbed a gesture behind them where O'Nightingale's had long since disappeared. "You of all people should know."

Adrian's attention leveled on the road. "I know what's of value and what's not."

"I'll be the judge of that, thank you."

A moment of silence stretched between them. The throaty hum of the engine continued, unaffected, like the stubborn jerk behind the wheel. Maybe if she blew her nose in his shirt she'd get a reaction.

"The entire relationship between a man and woman hinges on it," Shauna continued. "I-I'll never have children. I'll never be able to experience a moment so profound that it defies all reason and sends a person's mind into a million different places at once."

His gaze slid toward her and the corner of his mouth twitched with a wry smile. "You've been reading too many romance novels."

Shauna's eyes brimmed with fresh tears. Her dam of logic and resolve had crumbled. No way to hold it back now. She was melting. In a puddle of tears.

Oh, how attractive.

"Who spends an entire night in an underground sex club and still can't get any action." She jabbed an index finger towards her chest. "Me. That's who. *On my back*," she muttered in a smarmy tone. "What kind of lame ass come-on was that?"

"It served its purpose."

"Stop trying to be so damn cordial." The last word erupted in a pitiful cry. "What the hell is that?" Shauna asked as the vehicle chimed. Again.

"Your seatbelt."

"Oh." She stretched the belt across her torso. "Of course. Safety first." She attempted to shove the tab into its metal buckle. "Not that I couldn't use a good head injury about now." She jabbed at the buckle again and missed. Her voice grew in frustration. "What is wrong with me? I'm in the middle of a...a *fe-meltdown* here. That's not like me. I don't do this kind of thing."

The weight of his hand settled on hers, and the buckle clicked. "Hey. You're crashing. The chocolate's wearing off, that's all. You'll be fine in a few hours."

Shauna gestured to her half-naked state and blurted between chest-lurching sobs. "Even in a moment like this, the best I can get is a pity pat on the hand. Even then, you'll get burned."

She paused. Swallowed. "Why aren't you getting burned?"

"You're lacking a few things."

Lacking? Her brows furrowed. She lowered her glance to the perky mounds beneath the black cotton. When Kimmy's dress reduced to feather-light flakes of ash, it left her completely exposed. Maybe he didn't like what he saw.

He angled his head and sent her a lopsided grin. "Not the outside. You're body's flawless." He looked away. "It's a combination. Male hormonal rage plus your fear equals combustion. You're not afraid of me."

"Well, isn't that scholarly."

"You're not interested either. The chocolate's

elimination half-life drains sexual intrigue as it declines. You might crave more, but you aren't capable."

Shauna arched a sardonic brow. "Really. Well, mister smarty-pants, it just so happens that I'm *never* not in the mood. And I'm beyond *capable*. I'm a freakin' slip-n-slide."

Like a tumbling chain of clown scarves, she couldn't pull those words back fast enough. The embarrassment that warmed her face couldn't be hidden, no matter how deeply she pressed herself into the cool, leather backrest. "Just the whipped cream on my sundae, isn't it?"

Good hell. Could she stop with the euphemisms now?

Adrian didn't respond. His hand reached blindly for the pack of gum nestled in the center compartment near the gearshift, his gaze pinned on the road. The faint lines in his forehead deepened as though calculating her words.

"The only body that isn't aching for it is the one behind the wheel." Her sobs returned.

He folded a piece of gum into his mouth. His tone eased with a tender note of apology. "It's nothing personal. The female's tear composition contains a chemical component that—let's just say now's not the time."

Silence passed between them.

Shauna wrapped her arms around her legs and propped her chin in the crevice of her knees. She muttered aloud. "Who would want to make love to a leaky, red-nosed faucet anyway?"

A muscle twitched with every hypnotic churn of

Adrian's jaw as he worked the gum in his mouth.

"I-I thought I was getting better," she reasoned.

Adrian frowned. He opened his mouth to speak, but Shauna was faster.

"If I couldn't find someone to help me, at least I'd found a place where I'd be accepted. I mean, at least Onyx—"

"Was a woman."

"What?" Shauna shot him a deadpan look. "What." She demanded louder. "Oh—no—no, unzip those lips. I want an explanation. A *woman*?" she sputtered. She tried to shake the thought from her head. To clear the cobwebs that must have clouded her vision.

Her touch.

Her sense of smell, *and* her better judgment.

"Well, who else knew about this?" she stammered.

Adrian's chest bounced in a quiet snort. "Everyone. Didn't you notice you failed to react to him—"

"*Her*...No. I didn't notice. And I did react." She lowered her head. "Sort of."

Her nerve endings danced with delicious arousal every time Onyx touched her. The chocolate had swayed her body to react to everyone and everything. She got that. But what if all her male deprivation turned her awareness toward the safer alternative.

The safer sex.

It's not as if the thought hadn't crossed her mind a time or two. That would be the easier solution. But in the end, her puzzle piece didn't fit that way. Her heart couldn't fathom it.

What if her body had other plans?

The car slowed. "Shauna...It doesn't mean anything."

"You've turned me into a lesbian," she wailed. "And I don't even like girls!"

Adrian pushed out a sigh of frustration. The car rolled to a stop outside a mountain-style home with darkened, floor-to-ceiling windows and rough timber beams. The home looked new, but not the surroundings.

She'd seen this land before. Not from this specific angle, but the arched bridge over the pond—there weren't many of those around.

He turned off the ignition.

Shauna looked to the house, then back to Adrian. "Where are we? This is our old neighborhood."

"My place."

"The Wilson farm?" Her gaze spanned the overgrown, moonlit-field to the east side of the home. The quiet, rippling pond to the west. "But how?"

He jerked his head in the direction of the front door. "Come on."

Shauna crumpled with all the reluctance of a sulking toddler when Adrian opened her door. "You're killing me with this nobility crap. I don't want your couch. Just throw me back in your lake already."

He bent low and scooped an arm under her legs. "You take my bed. I'll use the couch."

"Isn't your bed big enough to share?"

"Nope." He grunted.

"I don't take up much space."

"I do."

"I only need a sliver."

"I need it all."

"Well, that's what I was offering you."

Adrian paused. He closed his eyes for a moment, then continued his steady pace.

133

"Adrian—" Her tone softened. "Please don't make me beg. I need this. No one else can give me what you can—the cure, I mean." Shauna tipped her head in consideration. "Don't get me wrong. I really need the other thing too, but they go hand in hand."

Adrian tipped her forward a bit as he turned the doorknob, then hitched her higher as he continued his march into the house.

"I'm sure you could get any girl in the city you wanted, but you did go to Nightingale's for a reason." She brushed along his stubbled jaw line with the pad of her fingertips. "I could be wrong, but I'm pretty sure you need a little something too."

"I really want to give it to you." Shauna's chest tightened with the giddy thrill of Adrian taking her up on her offer. The warmth of his arms against her bare legs caused a rush of moisture to pool between her legs.

His breathing grew weighted. Whether from carrying her through the house or warring with his better sense, she wasn't sure.

Better to tip the scale just in case. "You can turn off the lights if you want. Pretend I'm someone else—"

"Stop talking," he growled.

Was that a no?

When he lowered her into the bedside armchair, Shauna grasped his biceps. Her hands weren't large enough to circle them completely, but Adrian got the hint. He didn't move from his crouched position in front of her.

She searched his face. Would he really turn her away? "Please. Please I need this. You owe me this." She grazed his hand with the soft inner portion of her thigh.

Adrian's head lowered in defeat.

Somewhere inside Shauna, Marti Gras had unleashed. Complete with confetti, fireworks, and the urgent need to take off her top.

He paused. Pulled the gum from his mouth. His gaze considered it for several seconds before he offered it to her.

She frowned.

"Take it."

Her inward party faltered to an awkward silence. She plucked the wad from between his fingers and put it in her mouth. *ABC gum. This was his idea of intimacy?* She buried her curt remarks before they could form full sentences and chewed.

Her gaze followed Adrian warily as he stood and turned away from her. He lifted a wide-bottomed container from a collection of glass vessels on his nightstand and poured a cloudy substance into his hand.

His gaze raced over the pouring liquid as if taking stock of every atom. He hesitated with the bottle until a last, tiny drop let go of the container's lip and fell. He lowered the glass.

Shauna pressed her lips together. She craned her neck, leaning to one side then the other, catching sporadic glimpses of Adrian as he gathered secrets from all corners of the room and dove into his work.

This had been the closest she'd ever come to Adrian. It might not be sex.

Yet.

Her eyes squeezed shut. It might not be *a cure*, yet. But a step is a step. After all, how many people could he have chewed gum with?

He crossed the room to a sage-looking plant

affixed with dried, trumpet-shaped flower husks. Adrian curled his other hand around one of the out-branching limbs. With a quick yank, he stripped the husks from their stem.

Adrian clasped his large palms together and mixed his ingredients with an undulating motion of his hands.

Hello? Sex club? He'd been swapping spit underground with half the metropolitan area, and a little gum is supposed to make me happy?

Maybe it's like in *Pretty Woman*. No kissing on the mouth. Or in his case, sharing gum.

Her shoulders fell in their sockets. *Oh, who am I kidding? This is just weird.*

"How does it taste?" he asked.

Her response fell flat. "Like gum."

"More specific."

Her eyes rolled in their sockets, and she offered a reluctant head bob. "Like mint…strawberry mint."

He cast the mixture in his hand onto the bed of rumpled sheets. Fairy-sized globes of fluid scattered and jumped through the folds of cotton, but they didn't soak in.

Adrian grasped the bed linens. With a sharp flick of his wrist, the sheets billowed. The mixture arced through the air. It fizzled and popped like soda bubbles leaping over the edge of an ice-filled glass. Just as the nearly undetectable mixture began its descent, it slowed and hung midair. It danced and spun through the breeze, driven by the giant fan above the bed. The mixture's reach spread from ceiling to floor. It colored the air with a translucent purple glow, and flavored it with the scent of crisp, red apples.

Shauna opened her mouth to speak, but her words

dead-ended in wonder.

The weight of Adrian's stare brought her attention away from the glittery curtain of fumes. A sultry hunger grew to life from deep inside those stormy blues. A look that put her snow globe stomach from years past on spin cycle.

"It's not just a curse, it's a guardian too," he stated.

Her brows lifted with skepticism. "My flames? To guard against what?"

"Me." He crooked a finger toward her.

Chapter Thirteen

Shauna stood and skirted the bed in what she hoped was a slow, sensual routine, while her stomach opted to go freestyle, in more of a towel-in-the-wringer routine.

Adrian frowned.

"What?"

"You're nervous."

Shauna laughed. "Me? No…" She swatted away the accusation and continued toward him.

Adrian raised a dark, skeptical brow. "Prove it."

"Okay."

His attention slowed its appraisal. He angled his head. "Lick your lips for me."

Shauna's steps faltered. "Oh-kay." Was he serious?

Adrian folded his arms in front of his chest.

"That look…" The same look of unbendable stubbornness he had from years ago. She nodded to the window. "I remember that look, when I threatened to tattle on you for setting off homemade pyrotechnics over the pond." Yep. A challenge if there ever was one.

"Well, I'm not stopping you this time. You'll have to come get it…and you're stalling."

Shauna darted her tongue out to moisten the soft pad of her lower lip.

The corner of his mouth twitched in a knowing smile. "Try again."

She expelled a sigh. Okay, so maybe she was a tad

nervous, but who wouldn't be? How's a girl supposed to act when her tongue is summoned by a shirtless pillar of sexual intrigue?

Shauna had to prove she meant business. No more bluffing. Couldn't hardly blame the guy after what she put him through tonight. The man wanted a woman, not a lizard.

Perfect time for one last chocolate hurrah. If she had plucked the charred foil wrappers from the dungeon floor, she'd be licking them right now. Too bad that hadn't come to her mind sooner.

Shauna ducked her head and tugged in a deep breath. She could do this. She'd been practicing for years. All those evenings spent seducing her own reflection, hoping that one day Adrian would see her.

But to tempt her body with someone like him?

Not like him. It *was* him. The flesh-and-bone infatuation to end all others.

Giving herself over to a lust that strong could put them both in danger. She looked up through a fringe of moist lashes. But would she ever get a chance again?

Starting in the corner of her mouth, Shauna used the point of her tongue to follow along the sharp bow of her upper lip. She continued her painstaking circular path to trace her mouth's full outline.

Adrian's lips parted as his attention followed her. A feral, hungry sound seemed to drag behind his breath.

Shauna's gaze fled to the silent rise and fall of his winged tattoo. A persistent reminder of how far Adrian had traveled into the world of sex and a mysterious omen of where he was about to lead her. She stalled her approach and shifted her weight slowly from one foot to the other. What if she didn't know enough to please him?

"Closer." Adrian's word seeped in challenge.

Shauna's eyes squeezed shut, and she stole the remaining distance between them before her body roped him off with more excuses.

She cracked an eye open. Adrian hadn't moved. The most peculiar look of mirth formed in the sensual curve of his mouth. He dipped his head, mouth angling toward hers. The heat of his breath fanned her mouth just before he meshed his lips against hers.

A pulsing warmth funneled deep into Shauna's core as the pressure of his lips increased.

She jerked back. Had he flinched? Did she burn him? She stared, searching his tempestuous gaze and full, moist lips for any hint of pain. "I….uh." She pointed to her mouth. "The gum. I should get rid of it first."

He shook his head. "Can't."

"What? Why?"

"It serves as a compatibility test, which you passed. But in addition, its chemistry stimulates a biochemical impediment…"

Shauna frowned.

Adrian started again. "Because it lets me do this." He laced his fingers through her hair, and cupped the base of her skull. He steered her lips back to his. The firm press of his mouth disappeared before he angled his head and drove deeper.

The hot flick of Adrian's tongue coaxed against the seal of Shauna's lips. She parted on instinct to grant him access.

Adrian took his time, caressing the tip of his tongue against hers in a dive-and-retreat dance that grew more demanding with each stroke.

When Shauna urged him on with a throaty moan, Adrian tightened the grip on her hair. Tingles swept along the nerve endings of Shauna's scalp and she angled her head in compliance.

Oh yeah, she definitely needed more of that.

Heat pulsed at the swollen mound between her legs. She rocked her body against him in a desperate plea to gratify her throbbing core.

Adrian gripped the soft flesh of her bottom and met her stroke with the denim-clad bulge of his erection.

Shauna tensed.

Quick as anything, Adrian let go. The seal of his lips broke free.

Shauna couldn't contain her gasp of concern. "Did I burn you?"

"No."

"I did. Didn't I?" But where? His lips were moist and blushed with color, but no blisters. If not his mouth, it had to be his hands. Shauna stepped back and stroked a protective palm over the back of her hair. "I'm so sorry, I didn't mean it."

Adrian leveled his gaze in warning. "Don't—" The viper strike of his hand pulled back a fist full of her tee shirt. "Don't do this."

"I can't help it, I swear." Her vision brimmed with unshed tears.

"I know." Adrian tugged her back toward him. "Just...hang on—" He caught the shirt's hem and pulled the tent of black cotton over her head.

Adrian's gaze raked over her naked body.

Shauna clasped her hands behind her back, then in front. She folded her arms.

Adrian looked far more sure of the direction they were headed. He closed his eyes. His nostrils flared with a deep inhale as he flattened his palm on the center of her chest.

He nudged her backward several feet until she stood with the back of her knees hinged at the bed and a shower of purple vapor swirling between them.

The cool kiss of air billowed around her, and goose bumps rushed over her surface from head to toe. Tiny flecks of liquid bounced and jumped off her skin, leaving iridescent footprints behind. In mere seconds, her skin was soothed and lotioned. The apple scent turned syrupy. The long strands of her hair lay heavy down her back.

Adrian glanced up from slipping off his shoe and angled his chin toward the bed.

She put both hands on the mattress behind her and with shaking limbs, she pushed herself up to the chilled, damp sheets. She couldn't spare even the faintest diversion from the display about to take place in front of her. How many times had she imagined this moment?

Adrian leveled his gaze again, searching, no doubt, for any hint of hesitation as his hands moved to the button fly of his jeans.

Shauna swallowed to ease the desert that had become her mouth.

He worked the denim back and forth, over each button, popping them free with an expert flick of nimble fingers.

It wasn't anything like what her brain had conjured up. The vision of tanned, muscle-corded thighs never met appeared. Her gaze couldn't travel that far. It locked on the thick, swollen length of his erection the moment he released it, and even as he advanced into the swirling curtain that stood between them, she couldn't look away.

Erection? The word did no justice. The strong, upward curve of its posture and the prominent pout of its dusky tip hinted at so much more. Not a simple condition. That thing was an instrument of pleasure with a reputation all its own.

Only when the mattress dipped under his weight, did her attention snap free. She inch-wormed a backward retreat toward the headboard. Her gaze pinged from the double-paned balcony, to the collection of apothecary jars, to anywhere but him, as he advanced on hands and knees toward her.

She offered what she hoped was a sensual grin, but she could feel the edge of her mouth quiver with nervous energy.

Adrian stretched out on his side, his upper half propped on his elbow.

She glanced, and then glanced again, fighting the edgy giggle that tickled her lungs.

For a moment, he only stared at her. What could be so intriguing? The guy'd seen a hundred other women in his day. She opened her mouth to speak, but the words died at his first touch.

His fingertips traced her hairline then the curve of her cheek. They followed every feature with a feather-soft touch that left the tension melting from Shauna's apprehensive muscles. A thumb hooked the under curve of her jaw and urged her face toward his.

Adrian didn't utter a word.

His kiss spoke for him. It grew from patient taste

and exploration to a mounting demand for her attention. He caught her bottom lip between his teeth and nipped at the sensitive flesh.

His free hand continued its lazy drift over the alcove behind her ear and down the curve of her neck.

Shauna's hands mirrored his, taking cues and subtle encouragement through the growing weight of his breath and the low growl that vibrated through his chest. She splayed her hand across the solid pads of muscle that formed his pecs and roved further south, over a ripple of toned abs.

He closed a hand around her wrist before she could travel lower, and trapped both hands above her head.

He leaned over her. His teeth scored the delicate curve of her neck and then kissed to soothe her assaulted flesh. The process continued as Adrian's mouth moved downward. He brushed his thumb across the aching peak of her nipple, an unspoken warning that his mouth would soon travel there.

Shauna's breath came quick and anxious. She squeezed her eyes shut as he shifted toward the foot of the bed, gaining access to dangerous territory.

Yes, please. She'd say or do anything to have his attention there. An ache this strong couldn't be soothed on her own. Not now. Not after they'd come this far.

His hand wedged in the bend of her knee and he nudged her leg up.

Oh, God.

Adrian paused when Shauna tensed with uncertainty. His hand didn't move, but his mouth continued its roving torment until it closed over her breast. Shauna arched against the strikes of pleasure that shot through her nipple. She let out an achy moan.

"Yeah."

She couldn't bear more than a whisper, but he had to know. She might sound a bit demanding, but she couldn't let him stop. If she didn't tell him, he might leave her in agony. All the others had stopped long before now. She couldn't stand to be left alone on this crest. Not again.

With his hand still wedged behind her knee, Adrian angled her thighs apart.

Shauna's pulse sped as cool air kissed between her legs. She fought the urge to squirm and turned her head to the side. The sound she made ended with a plea of urgency.

Adrian spared her the distance between where his hand was and where she demanded it. He stroked over the wet juncture between her legs.

"Yeah," she whispered again. She bucked under his hand, her thighs tensed, and she bucked again. *Yes, please. I want. I want.*

Adrian seemed to understand her angst, and his touch became more deliberate, a circular massage that extended deeper than the outward folds.

His touch, slicked with moisture, tightened to circle the perimeter of her clit. Shauna's thighs lost all tension. She spread wide to welcome him. "Yeah...like that...oh, yes, please."

Many a time, she had touched herself in a similar way, but the sensation never came on this level. Shauna's nails dug into her palms and her thighs quivered as wave after wave of pleasure crashed over her. Desperation for release seemed to rack her entire body.

She had to feel him inside her.

"I need it," she cried. "Adrian, please. Give me...give me." It sounded spoiled. It sounded awful. To hear those words on any given afternoon would turn her stomach, but Adrian had to know what he was doing to her.

In Shauna's next ragged breath, Adrian's touch had left her. Her hands were freed.

She turned to face him, chest to chest on their sides.

Adrian wasted no time propping her leg onto his hip and nestling into the cradle of her thighs. He stroked forward slowly, along the slick outer lips of her vagina. This time, Shauna rolled her hips to meet him. Her plateau of sensation climbed higher with each stroke, until he paused and rolled his hips deeper, positioning himself at her opening.

Shauna was first to move, sinking down onto his shaft as it stretched and filled her. Perhaps all those evenings of self-gratification had trained her for this moment, but nothing compared to a living, breathing man. The mere size of him was both delicious and invasive as her walls conformed around him.

A bead of sweat slipped down Adrian's brow as he pulled back and then pushed forward again to fill her completely.

She wasn't sure what he expected, but the deep groan that chimed with hers must have meant they were both thinking the same thing.

More.

Shauna voiced her pleasure when Adrian delivered another thrust. "Yeah."

And another. And another.

"Yes. Like that. Like that. Oh, God. Don't stop."

Their movements increased in force until Shauna's throaty pleas became an unintelligible chant. They both raced for release.

Adrian gripped her hips and strained against her. He roared between clenched teeth and thrust himself deep.

Shauna tried to push back, anticipating another thrust, but Adrian wouldn't have it. He held her hip tight and pushed deeper still.

She paused. *No!* She was close. So close. It couldn't end now.

As if sensing her frustration he rolled to his back, taking her with him to straddle his thighs. "Take it," he gritted, guiding her hips to rock against him. "You know what you want."

She hesitated for a moment. Adrian rolled his hips and massaged her soaked genitals back and forth against his pelvic bone, his shaft still buried deep and unyielding.

Shauna understood, gradually building up speed and reclaiming the pressure she had lost. Her mind fled to somewhere else as tiny, sharp pangs of pleasure shot from her core. Her body took over. She plunged against the thick length of him again and again, increasing with haste and force until the friction exploded. Her muscles clenched tight in a final rush of brain-numbing shards. She cried out and managed to brace herself with one arm to keep from collapsing on top of him. Her body froze in place.

Good God all mighty, what kind of orgasm was that?

Chapter Fourteen

"Take the day off." Adrian's graveled, sleepy tone carried just over the hum of the idling car.

The thin lines at the corners of his mouth seemed deeper today. His eyes, heavier. She'd spent the entire night next to him, his body contoured to hers. The languid stroke of his fingertips came and went along the inner curve of her arm. At times when she'd shift to get comfortable, he'd tighten the large arm that draped around her waist, and nuzzle deeper into her hair. Not keeping her still, just close.

She smiled. "I think you're the one who needs a day off. Did you get any sleep?"

Adrian's gaze traveled over her body, lingering at her breasts. "Too busy thinking up ways to redeem myself." He tucked a stray lock of hair behind her ear. "I'll write you a doctor's note."

Shauna's stomach turned a gleeful somersault. "I want to, but I can't bail on such short notice. Besides, it's Friday. We'll have the whole weekend after this."

She looked at the low profile, brick home and the windows, where her villainous mastermind would no doubt be lurking with her coffee sidekick, and stroking her treasured, wireless mouse. "I'll just tie up some loose ends," *disarm one loose cannon* "and I'll give you a call around six?"

Adrian gave her a long look. He pressed a finger to

the tip of her nose and then pulled away. "I don't know. You look a little pink."

Shauna tossed him a quiet snort. "That's the color we girls normally come in."

Adrian's frown wouldn't be persuaded.

She sighed. "I'll get written up if I don't show."

"So."

"I could get fired."

He shrugged.

"Look, I know you live a private life."

He shook his head. "Not the point."

"Isn't it?"

He pushed out an exasperated sigh. "We'll talk about this later, okay? Do what you have to. I'll see you later."

"Promise?"

Adrian paused. The fine lines around his mouth deepened.

Shauna opened her mouth. An apology perched on her tongue, ready to take flight and erase the awkward silence.

She snapped her mouth shut when Adrian leveled his stormy blue gaze with hers. "As much as I'd love to make that promise. I can't."

Shauna lowered her head. Honesty. The most painful of his nobilities. He could do without that one.

"But I *will* do my best." He caught her chin as she began a reluctant nod of agreement. "Hey. That night at the pond?" His gaze turned solemn. "Those were fireworks."

Her lips spread into what could only be the dopiest grin she'd ever mustered. "Well, yeah, I knew you weren't setting off a bomb or anything—"

"They were for you."

Shauna paused. There had to be a punch line in there somewhere. But her stomach wouldn't wait for it. At first hint, it erupted in an erratic, hopeful flutter. "Your dad looked ready to kill you. Though I'm not sure what he was angrier about. The fireworks or drenching me."

The fine lines around Adrian's mouth smoothed to the epitome of serious. He angled toward her and brushed his lower lip against hers. "It was worth it."

The moment the car door snapped shut, Shauna raced through the tiny daggers of autumn frost that had formed on the lawn. Even though Adrian's oversized sweats hung heavy and damp around her ankles, her steps felt lighter.

Perhaps to everyone else, the sun had come up like usual. But for Shauna, it came up with no flames, the man of her dreams, and an entirely vulnerable world left unguarded. For once, she might enjoy exploring it.

Or...not.

The mangled door handle greeted her first, though it no longer served most of its purpose. Smashed and folded over itself, it had become impossible to turn.

Not that she needed it.

Fractured shards of wood buckled near the doorframe. She glanced to Adrian's car.

"Shauna, that you?" Kimmy called from somewhere beyond the gap in the door.

Shauna nudged the door wider. "It's me. What the hell happened to the door? Are you okay?"

"Fine. And your stupid fiancé, that's what."

"Geez...he's not my fiancé anymore." Shauna gave Adrian a final wave goodbye, and entered. She picked careful steps through the toppled lamp, scattered papers, and cast-off clothing as she made her way to the kitchen. "What happened?"

She rounded to the kitchen table, to where Kimmy sat with a rather smarmy grin and a cartoon-worthy black eye.

Shauna gasped. "Oh my hell!"

"Yeah, you're telling me." She pushed what appeared to be a crumpled eviction notice across the table. "He came back after you left."

"Let's get you some ice." Shauna jerked open the freezer door to find frosted bottles of liquid and cartons of sticky, half-eaten ice cream.

"I used it all. Though most of it fell into my glass." Kimmy snorted.

"Here." Shauna handed her a half-bag of frozen peas. "Did you call the cops? We should call the cops."

Kimmy set the peas aside. She used a tissue to dab the corner of her mouth, where it had cracked and bled. "No cops. I swear to God, the next time I see him, I'll beat him senseless. Then I'll be the one arrested. Did he find you, by the way?"

Shauna didn't answer. She glanced pointedly to the bedroom at the end of the hall. "How much did you see last night?"

Kimmy's gaze dropped to the table, and she shooed the question away. "Some of it. But your boyfriend busted in. He saw you on the video feed. Then all hell broke loose. I'm real sorry."

Shauna's shoulders drooped in defeat. She couldn't build enough calluses to lecture Kimmy. She'd already been beaten to a pulp. But she had to ask. "Sorry was a start, but why did you send me to the pit?"

"Rewind your face to twenty seconds ago and tell me, was it worth it? When you're happy, I'm—"

"Does either one of us look happy right now?" she demanded.

Shauna rolled her gaze heavenward when Kimmy bowed her head and tented her fingers under her chin. Here it comes. She knew that mystical, know-it-all gesture anywhere.

"*Some women are great; some have greatness thrust upon them*. That's Shakespeare, darling."

Shauna widened her gaze and her attention flicked around the room, searching for any leftover bits of sanity. "Are you kidding me? You're supposed to be my friend."

Kimmy nodded. Mimicking Shauna's crazy-eyed stare, only this one hit Shauna between the eyes. "Yeah. I am your friend. I sent you there to find something you desperately needed. You found it, didn't you?"

"Yeah."

"Well then." She turned away. "Hate me if you have to—most people do. But there's no other way I could have set it up."

"You didn't need to—"

"But I never would have sent you in there if I thought you would get hurt. I *knew* you wouldn't get hurt. I knew *he* would save you. This is what I do. My job. I align the situation and let the cards fall where they may. Sometimes the outcome is good. Sometimes not so good."

"Okay, enough with the transcending enlightenment crap. You work for an Internet service provider. That's your job—"

"You work at a damn make-up counter. Is that who

you are?" Kimmy flailed her hands through the air as if striving to grasp the right word. "A brainless...pampered...*powder puff?*"

Shauna grimaced. "Wow. You've really been holding this in."

Kimmy's rant elevated. She slapped the table. "I have a black eye and a date tonight." She pointed a cherry-lacquered finger toward her face. "How the hell am I going to cover this up? Granted. It's with a boxer. So maybe he'll understand. But still!"

Kimmy turned away, gesturing to the open window that once framed Adrian's car. "My point is, this is who we've become. Not who we are. You are just as impulsive as I am. I'm just as scared as you."

No arguing there. Shauna paused. She eased her tone. "So now what?"

Kimmy smiled. "Let your impulsivity take over your fear. You can't have both. Choose, you must."

Shauna closed her eyes. "What are you, Yoda now?"

Kimmy sat back in her chair. "I'm Yoda's wet dream, sweetie. Now go put that sexy little lab coat of yours on and toddle off to work."

"I gotta say. You're handling this pretty well, considering."

Kimmy held up a stopping hand. "That's because I'm medicated, and I have a plan. Now go. I'll take care of this mess and call a hit out on your ex."

Shauna backed away. Kimmy wasn't serious. She couldn't be. "We're talking when I get back," she clarified.

"Damn right we are. You've got some 'splainin' to do about the hot guy in that car."

****

"I'm not going to lie to you. The cost isn't cheap." The Oracle rubbed the dark grease paint between his thumb and forefinger. Betrayal and disgust seeped through his veins.

He looked to the man's lowered head. No response apart from the sporadic hitch that interjected the shallow rise and fall of his chest.

Had he passed out again?

"Wakie, wakie." The Oracle nudged the man's side as he circled him.

The man flinched to the left, indicating at least *slight* coherence.

Not many people could doze through a broken rib.

O gestured to the hall, to intermittent *drips* of water and a dense shadow of soot that marred the ceiling. "I don't know who let you in. I don't know *why*, but in a matter of minutes you've done irreparable damage here."

The Oracle fought to keep his voice pleasant despite the urge to strangle the boy with the trailing end of rope that bound him to the spiked chair. If O lost control, if he evoked violence, the visions might leave him.

For weeks, the chance with Adrian had consumed his fantasies. The skin that stretched over his swollen cock had become raw and inflamed from male prostitutes, rounds of sloppy blowjobs, and ultimately, the persistent stroke of his own fist. All vain attempts to quell an unsurpassable urge. Nothing could compare to the one. Adrian Sands.

O clutched the open cell door with both hands. His palms burned as he squeezed and twisted around the rough metal in an attempt to contain his boiling rage. How could he have missed this fraud? *How*?

How could he let this man suddenly appear at his side as a trusted servant and undo all he had worked for?

The moment O slipped from his observer role, and become the catalyst, his vision of the future went dark. He knew it would happen, but the urge to take possession of his tantalizing apothecary had been too much to ignore.

Adrian would have become the puppet, and he, the master. Complete submission. An undying loyalty. Pleasure beyond anything the Oracle had known.

He paced the boy with a candy-apple ball gag in his mouth. "You can. Not. Replace what you have stolen from me tonight."

The prisoner nodded to the contrary.

"Oh, don't worry. By God, you're going to try," the Oracle agreed. "Someone's going to pay. And right now, it's you!"

No...no.

O closed his eyes and took several deep breaths through his nose. He allowed his chest to expand full capacity, then released his breath. Slow.

Stay calm. Callllm. Taking anger out on this poor specimen wouldn't solve anything. Let's not forget our strength in this moment of unease.

Serenity and pleasure and his solution would come.

The weight of the boy's stare tugged at O's attention. He cracked an eye open.

The boy's pale lashes stretched high. His crystal-blue eyes widened with innocence.

O always was a sucker for blue eyes. "Oh, what is

it?" he snapped.

A low, unintelligible mumbling sound formed around the ball gag. His voice came deeper than expected. With the cherub curls and all, O expected more of a choirboy tone.

Against his better judgment, O loosened the gag, and slipped the warm, moist ball around the man's neck. This was safe. He could still strangle him this way.

If he wanted to.

"I can find Adrian Sands. I know where he is," the boy pleaded.

"So do I." The Oracle sniffed. "But knowing of his existence doesn't sway him. He wanted a toy. Now he has his toy. What do I have that he could possibly want now?"

The toy kept Adrian obedient, and she'd walked right into her own cage. This fool had set her free, shifted the gears, and set an entirely new future in play. A blind path. How could O head off a future so uncertain? How could he get back the control he'd lost and mold Adrian to his will again?

"The girl." The tip of the prisoner's tongue reached out to inspect the dried blood at the corner of his mouth. "I can get that too."

O's attention followed the tender exploration of his tongue until it disappeared. "My, but you're a willing one, aren't you? And what makes you so sure?"

"I have connections," the boy offered. His voice a low rumble, as though hesitant to admit his secret gift.

"Do you now?" O brushed a hand over the man's hair, careful to avoid the large goose egg at his temple. He savored the tickle of stiff, close-cropped curls that were gelled into perfect formation.

This one didn't flinch. Not an ounce of repulsion tugged at his full upper lip. Only hesitation and uncertainty stayed him. Then after a moment, he seemed to accept O's strokes. He leaned into it, just enough to encourage yet hopefully avoid detection.

Charming really. The boy possessed an untouched wonder about him.

The Oracle paused. Frowned.

Images came swift and dirty with this one. The rapid-fire vision of polished leather, and starched shirts slammed into the Oracle's mind. Almost…military. The authority that shadowed this boy evoked an awareness inside. Another image slammed over the first. The boy was turned away this time. Whether on hands and knees or simply bent over, O couldn't tell.

Knees sound better. He'd go with that.

The stout, rowing flexion of his shoulders had the tempo of a gold-metal sculling team and all the exertion of a man on the brink of orgasm. His head of golden curls arched back. Heady breaths belabored his mounting pleasure. Then a large male hand clamped down on the boy's shoulder. Not to stop him, but to encourage and leverage his movement.

The Oracle jerked back from the mental image. Could O's fantasy have interceded, ruining his concentration?

Never happened before…

It had to be—both the Oracle and the man shared this temptation. Some dark, unspoken knowledge forged a link between the two of them. The man knew O could give him what he needed.

This man with the angelic exterior, he didn't know

the Oracle could detect it. But the angel was prepared to make a most alluring request.

O swallowed the moisture that flooded his mouth.

The angel had privilege and power beyond anything O could hope to gain. A perfect confection of political influence and scandal. This guy enjoyed this domineering, military shadow. A little too much.

The urge to pursue the man's dark secret couldn't be ignored. Not in the form of this tender, polished angel all grown-up and eager to please. "But something more than eager," O murmured. "You can offer me something more, can't you? Lots more."

"I…I don't know what you mean."

The Oracle started again, willing to let the denial slide.

For now.

"You're military. Intelligence. Something like that. Something…rather unusual."

A frightful darkness passed over the man's crystal-blue eyes, as though caught in a lie and begging forgiveness.

And the charm runs deeper.

The Oracle narrowed his vision. "You're FBI."

The angel's gaze shifted to the door.

"What's your name?"

His attention jerked back. He shook his head.

O grinned. "But you must."

"If my family finds out I'm here, they'll—"

"Don't worry." O chided as he stroked the angel's head. "Don't you worry. This will be our little secret. Because it's ours now. You and I."

Again, *how* could he let this man suddenly appear at his side? Because it was meant to be. "What fates impose, that men must needs abide," O murmured. This man belonged here.

The man's brows furrowed with confusion.

O sighed. If Adrian were here, he'd understand. There weren't many things in life more delightful than watching Adrian get all broody over Shakespearian quotation.

The Curlicue Prince here made for a pretty mediocre substitute. A helpful distraction. For now. He'd settle for that, but he wasn't through with Adrian.

"Your name," O persisted.

"I'm not FBI."

Changing the subject. That's cute.

"They contacted me years ago," the man continued. "When I first met Shauna."

"Shauna. That's her name?" O let his arm fall to his side and he turned away. "How neighborly." The farm-fresh, school-girl type. She managed to snag Adrian's attention in only a few days' time. And form that kind of bond? Like an amateur porn plot. A little too convenient. Even for O.

"They started tracking her after college. She has this," the man searched for the word, "ability of some kind. It only comes out when she gets excited." His attention flashed to the Oracle and away again. "Turned on, you know? Only I…"

"You couldn't get her there."

The naughty angel didn't respond.

O sighed. It was a pathetic attempt to hide his own delight. "You couldn't get her there because you, my boy, don't swing that way." O pulled his brows together in a look that *bled* sympathy. Tetchy subject. A tender young thing, in his prime, afraid to admit to the world that he'd rather feel the rigid power and stamina of another man.

"You thought I didn't notice you stroking yourself earlier tonight." O leaned over the man's shoulder. He glanced pointedly to the impressive display of cylindrical flesh that lay between the man's thighs. "It's difficult. Keeping it up under such duress."

The man crossed his legs.

There goes that fearful look again. O fought to suppress the giggle that danced in his chest.

"I thought that if she went too far here, on her own, her secret would come out. If I didn't…wasn't here, I'd lose my cut."

"So what you're saying is you were hired as the fed's whore?"

The man raised both brows. "No, not at all."

Damn. O eclipsed his disappointment with what he hoped was a kind smile.

"They said to get a reaction by whatever means necessary. In a controlled environment. I wasn't planning to do it this way. I had the perfect plan—"

"Perfect?" The desperation in that word hit O at an odd angle.

"—but things changed. She left me no choice." The man looked to the floor. "We were set for marriage. I was doing it right, I swear. But the feds…" He shook his head. Crystal blues wide and pleading. "I hit my deadline. I had no choice. They promised if I made it happen, they'd take care of the rest. Shauna'd disappear—I don't mean killed—"

"'Course not."

"They'd fix her. Give her a perfect life somewhere else. Then I—" He swallowed.

"You could be a respectable widower." The Oracle rocked back and forth on his heels. "I see. An easy out." O wrinkled his nose. "All that pesky heterosexual peer pressure."

"I can get her back for you. I can bring both of them back," the man insisted.

"What assurance do I have?"

He shrugged. Gaze pinned back to the floor. "I'll offer you anything. Money, political influence…"

"We'll explore that." O nodded his assurance. "We will." The Oracle had time, plenty of it to seek the full extent of the angel's generosity, his willingness to comply and abide by the rules.

Because Adrian would be coming back.

This time, he'd never leave.

Chapter Fifteen

Toss the straw hat, the vacation from sanity is over.

Shauna steered her attention away from the mall's network of sleepy stores, where lights had flickered on and gates lifted half-open in preparation for a new day.

Heartley, the queen of coworkers, sashayed past the rainbow hues of pressed powders and lipstick tubes. "Team meeting time," she cooed.

"Right." Shauna squared her shoulders amid the deluge of heel clicks on the glossy tile floor. Time to drag herself, and her giant suitcase of dirty exploits, back to reality.

Too bad no amount of bleach would rid her eyes of what she'd seen last night.

Or how she'd behaved.

Better throw in some holy water and set her mental state for an extra rinse.

She rounded the makeup counter and fell in step with Heartley, and the other day-shifters.

"Late night?" Heartley called over her shoulder.

"Yep." Her gaze veered to the GNC store at the far end of the building. She could almost catch the faint smell of toasted spice.

Shauna yanked her attention back. She gritted her teeth. *Air Nutcase is now boarding aisle A. Get-the-freak onboard.*

She snatched a test vial of the monthly special and

spritzed it between her breasts. She ignored the raised brow look Heartley shot her and spritzed again for good measure.

If Adrian had kept his usual MO, he'd never approach that store again. Or her.

He wouldn't promise to see her again. He said he would do his best.

Sounded like the gentlest letdown in the history of ever.

Shauna stood in rank among the semi-circle of lab coats and mini-skirts. She shook her head despite the incessant tug on her heart. Fairies, unicorns, and Adrian Sands. They all belonged on the same irrational island. Time for Shauna's deportation. Whether she liked it or not.

She didn't. Not one little bit.

"Good morning, team." Her store manager's voice boomed over the jazzy tune trickling over the speaker system.

"Morning." The team droned.

"You sound tired," the boss baited with a lift of his palms.

Heartley lifted a limp strand of Shauna's hair. "We need more coffee…*Mike*," she replied absently.

"Is that all I'm good for?" he scoffed over the polite trail of laughter.

In Heartley's world? Yes.

The manager's speech continued, but the words couldn't penetrate Heartley's bubble of all-important girl talk. Her syrupy tone lowered "Not a haircut, but something's different about you."

Shauna glanced to her hopelessly frayed ends and smoothed them back into place. "I've—uh…given up heat styling."

"In favor of what?" Heartley leaned forward and whispered. Her lips pulled into a shrewd grin. "That freshly-fucked look?"

Shauna's eyes widened, and her mouth dropped open in offense despite Heartley's breathy giggle and the protective arm that wrapped around Shauna's shoulder. "Welcome to the club, hun. It looks great on you."

Heartley straightened her posture and her arm vanished when the boss paused and shot both girls a harsh frown.

The speech continued, and Heartley murmured quickly under her breath, "Seriously, you should bottle that stuff."

"Thanks." Shauna frowned. "But I'm afraid this one's not for sale."

She could never do that.

Adrian had fixed her. In a matter of seconds. Oddly disappointing that it took so little time. A fair amount trial and error could have been fun, but still.

To watch him manipulate the universe with so little effort... The hands that seemed too large for magic wielded it with a delicacy she'd never imagined. The calculation, the watchful gaze that seemed to measure every flick of emotion, it went beyond a simple gift. She couldn't deny the world his attention for her own selfish purpose.

Shauna tried to ignore the hollow ache in her gut.

She had gotten what she wanted, why the regret?

Adrian had gotten a little too. Win-win, right?

And about that more intimate *gift* her hulking intellect had offered—might as well drop the offered part. His prominent shaft, thickened with need had strained toward her, and she took it. Took it like a true cowgirl and raced to the finish. It left her muscles aching, her mind numb, and her body aching for more.

A pulsing warmth grew between her thighs. Even now, she craved a second helping.

Shauna sighed. That chocolate had turned her into a sex-raving idiot. She could have done so much better on her own terms, in her environment. She could have taken control of the situation before her body went on a hormone-induced rampage through Adrian's bedroom.

What if she had dragged it out a week, maybe two? They could have gotten to know each other. Before they crossed that final line and Adrian had to move on.

No. Adrian wouldn't have waited that long.

Neither would she.

He'd welcomed her to finish it last night, when he pulled her on top of him and urged her to take what she wanted. In that moment they were both ready to give everything and to accept their fate.

No longer the frat house gentleman. Adrian liked it once and done. After seeing his lifestyle and the kingdom he'd built at O'Nightingale's, she knew that's how he operated. Somewhere inside she had to have known.

Last night she didn't care. She needed a cure, and a cure she got. Why would spending one bonus night with him change him in the least?

Perhaps he had already forgotten her. Her heart squeezed. But how could *she* forget?

"Hey. Pinkie. Wake up."

She blinked at the manicured, snapping fingers in her face.

The downturned corners of her store manager's mouth matched the receding crop of hair atop his head. "Did. You. Have a positive experience with a customer yesterday?" He turned to the other members standing in rank and paced away with his hands behind his back and his chest puffed out *à la* Napoleon.

"Not that I recall…"

"No? Well, let's see if we can't make that happen *today*. Okay?" Mike clapped his hands. "Let's get to work."

Heels clicked in rapid fire over the glossy floor, as her coworkers moved to their stations.

Except for Shauna.

And the queen.

Heartley took a none-shall-pass stance. "Details!" Her voice tail-ended with a whine.

Shauna shrugged. "It's private."

Heartley frowned. "Well, something's brought the pink back in your cheeks, and I want some."

Shauna didn't respond. She edged to one side toward her counter.

"Don't you dare deny it." Heartley marched at her heels.

Shauna could feel the warmth in her cheeks growing. Her beacon of guilt glowing brighter.

She rounded the corner to where an overweight squid-in-a-suit had made an early-morning stake-out of her makeup chair. She stopped short.

Squid-dididly sent her a sideways grin, and all at once, the plug had been pulled on her beacon. Warmth vacated her face.

"Come on. Does he have a brother, a cousin, something? I'm desperate!" Heartley insisted. "Fork it over."

Shauna clenched her teeth. At this point, she'd do anything to get rid of her. "I'll give you a card, how's that?"

Heartley turned to one side. Her mascara-lined eyes narrowed, and she studied Shauna's face for a moment, then nodded. "Good enough."

Shauna swept by while she still had the room. "Be sure to ask for Onyx."

She pulled in a tight breath on her way to the counter and flung the squid a curt smile. "Something I can help you with?" She swept the scattered sponges and Q-tips he had clearly been playing with into the trash.

"I need to be done." He grinned.

She rolled her eyes. "You need your *makeup done*?"

"Make-*out*, maybe." His grin widened. He plucked a tube of After Party Pink from its rightful place on the display.

"Leave." Shauna planted her hands on her hips and flicked her attention to her approaching manager. "Before he makes you leave." The manager looked to be headed out of the accessories department, and into a very bad mood. He hated personal visits on the clock. Especially from family.

Perfect. Then Squidster was about to become her long-lost, freeloading Uncle Vic, who just finished five-and-three in the state pen. For shoplifting.

The clear, plastic chair squeaked in protest as the Squid leaned back. "What do you think I'll get? A slap on the wrist?"

Shauna skirted to the safe side of the counter and

knelt down, pretending to busy herself with the inventory markdowns. "I don't care. So long as you leave—"

"Hey, Mike. How's it going?"

Shauna heard the slapping sound. It wasn't slappy-on-the-wrist at all. More like a high-five.

"How long has it been?"

"'Bout—uh…ten years, probably?" Her manager's voice brightened.

She popped back up. The look on her face must have read like toddlerhood injustice. That's about the effect it had on the two men. None. What. So. Ever.

She interrupted their high school, glory-day discussion with the loudest *ahem* she could muster. "We have our own store security. We don't need you here."

Both men straightened with offense. "Actually, you do," the squid replied. "Because I'm a customer. No. I mean, really." He started again, looking to the manager for sympathy, then back to Shauna. "Can you make it look like I've been making out with the hottest girl here?" He tugged his collar off-kilter, and mussed his greasy hair for added effect. "It's for the guys back at the office. I can't really afford to lose this bet, ya' see?"

Shauna's arms slumped. How much more off the wall would this life get?

Her boss gave her that golden-moment brow lift, and finished it off with a you-dang-well-better-take-it jab of his finger. "Sure thing. Give him a hand, Shauna." He turned. "Nice seeing you." He laughed. "And no more bets."

Shauna stared helplessly for a moment, but the manager had already moved on.

She closed her eyes. "So would that be frosted pink or…"

"Whatever you're wearing."

"Of course," she said in defeat. She snatched the lipstick from his hand.

Shauna leaned in, forcing breaths in and out her mouth so as not to smell him. She did her best to make the make-up look as fabricated as possible. Like grease paint lined with stubble.

Pretty sure she'd never wear *that* shade again.

Fine way to ruin a perfectly good color scheme. Forever.

"Interesting thing happened last night in the historic district," he said. "You know, after our little conversation."

"Yeah?" Shauna's heart rate kicked up, but she kept her gaze lowered on the tube of lipstick.

"Fire broke out in the basement of a rather unassuming bird shop. So, I gotta ask…Since it sounds like your handiwork…"

She blotted the edge of his mouth with a cotton ball. "Smudged? Like this?"

"Did you enjoy yourself last night?"

"If you were a better tail, you'd know." Leaving in Adrian's car must have totally thrown him off. Shauna had become a pretty good shake when it came to the feds. With this guy on her trail, all the old tricks became new again. Suddenly it had become easier and easier. Which seemed odd. "Why is that exactly?"

"What?"

"Why aren't you better at your job?"

His voice hardened. "Doesn't matter. All you need to know now is that I'm your shadow from here on out." He took the mirror she dealt him and leaned in close. "You left behind a *live* one this time. Did you know that? The man you set on fire last night actually survived. Burns over half his body. He isn't talking yet, but *when he does*…I'll be right here to take you down."

He looked into the glass. "No. This is all wrong. It's more like…" He tossed the mirror. "Aww, what the hell—" He grabbed Shauna's shoulders and jerked her forward. He mashed his lips against hers.

He jerked back faster than she could push him.

"You ass!" She whipped the slime from her mouth with the back of her hand.

No satisfaction gleamed on his face. Only shock, then pain. "Oh. Ouch." He touched his lip. "What was that?" He looked to his fingers. "What *the hell* was that?" he demanded again. "Did you shock me?"

"You deserved that. You deserve more than that." She took a menacing step forward.

His brows drew together with disbelief and his voice lowered as though speaking more to himself than anyone. "You burned me."

Her next sentence got cut off by heavy, hurried steps. "Struck him? Did he just say *you struck him*?" her manager demanded.

"Uh, no." Shauna frowned. "*Shocked* him." *Good enough excuse for now, right?* "And it wasn't on purpose."

"We were going for the full effect," Squid added with a grin.

The manager's lips pursed with rage. "That's it. Mike, please leave my store. And you—" He turned on Shauna. "Interesting marketing scheme and all, but you're making a spectacle. No more male clients." He paused. "Except for Halloween, that's different." He spun on his heel to leave but paused again. "And until Halloween, that whole," he waved his palm in front of her face, "thing you've got going is against dress code. Wash it off and get back to work."

A silky voice appeared at her side. "He's right, you know." Heartley scrunched her nose. "It was subtle before; you should have stopped there. Now it looks like you're kinda mocking your job."

"What?" Her eyes might be still a little raccoony—a little swollen—whether from crying last night, or setting herself on fire. Or both.

But it couldn't be that bad…

Her friend widened her eyes and looked away as if trying to escape before the horror unfurled.

"What?" She snatched the mirror and stared back in horror. The lipstick smudge across her upper lip—that was least of it.

Her complexion was fine when she left for work.

She looked again. Her mouth framed the words in silent whisper. "Oh my God."

She hadn't even bothered with primer, foundation, or blush this morning. But now, her entire face looked like she'd powdered it with cotton candy.

And her arms! The mirror clattered onto the table as she looked from one to the next.

She tugged her shirt down several inches to reveal a pair of petal-pink breasts.

"This wasn't intentional." She blurted to no one in particular.

"Well, hun, next time, don't put your bronzer on in the dark." Heartley up-ended a bottle of make-up remover onto a cotton ball and handed it to Shauna.

Shauna lifted the hair from her forehead, and scrubbed her brow feverishly with the other. Up and down, side-to-side. The color only deepened. Her voice rose to a shrill note. "What if it doesn't come off?"

"Let's just hope it does…It usually does…maybe you should see a doctor."

****

Shauna's grip tightened on her phone. Its rhinestone-encrusted casing scored her palm and released a plastic *creak* of protest.

Words rattled off her tongue fast as her mind could form them. "Hey, it's Shauna. I know you said you'd do your best to be here, but I need you to do better than that. Something's come up—I think something went wrong—and I need your help. Call me."

She pulled a breath into her starving lungs and touched on the end button.

She dropped the phone into the center console. It clattered around in the shallow cup holder and nearly bounced free as Shauna veered a quick right around the corner on squealing tires.

She pulled in another sharp lungful of air as she entered the dim alley and forced her foot on the brake.

The car jerked to a stop.

Her gaze pinned to the cross-traffic in her rearview mirror.

One vehicle. Then another

No white SUV.

Frustration percolated along her nerve endings. She could just imagine the Squidster idling quietly on the other side of the alley. Humming to himself along with the radio's twangy tune. His index fingers tapping gleefully on the steering wheel. Just…waiting.

Erratic driving would only encourage him to follow more aggressively. This wasn't big city traffic. It was small town traffic. On a late Friday morning of all things.

The hidden drive next to the pasta shop hadn't worked.

Neither had the graveyard.

She never used the graveyard. Too many winding turns in the open. It made her an easy target, but to the average newcomer, the snaggle-toothed maze had no detectable exit.

Yet he navigated through that place like a funeral director on caffeine.

Suddenly, the worst detecti—agent in the business was excelling at his job. As though a flag somewhere had just lifted.

Or the flag holder.

Cold realization hit Shauna square in the face like a mop-bucket of dirty water. Richard said he had connections. He stalked her all the way to the nightclub and blended in like nobody's business. And now that he was gone…

Had he been influenced by the feds somehow?

Wedding night rehearsal…pifft. Richard didn't want her. She shook her head. Which explained her rather obvious reaction toward him.

Or lack thereof.

Her temperature hadn't soared nearly as high with him. The very reaction he wanted to witness the most.

She erected her spine. "Good…*jerk*."

She accelerated through the alley and veered right, cutting it close for a stray dog that had been bustling across the street at an awkward angle. She splashed through a waterlogged ditch.

Adrian better not have changed his number already. A pang of loss hit her chest.

How could she hide her condition now? With her face stained an unnatural shade of freak? And what's worse, she'd burned the agent. That's more than enough proof to haul her butt back to the observation room.

Anyone she associated with could be labeled a plausible connection.

Adrian had lived in secret for the better part of his adult life. Whether the squid knew Adrian's story or not, he would start taking notes the moment he caught them together.

Word might get out, and the nation would return to Adrian's doorstep. More than just clamoring for attention this time. Shauna remembered the anger and frustration of Adrian's potential clients who took to the nine-o'clock news shortly after he disappeared.

The lives he could save. The pain they endured. Their anger turned venomous. Their actions, deadly.

Shauna couldn't sacrifice him like that. She snatched up the phone again and scrolled through her list of contacts. Sammy. Maybe he could help.

Her attention flicked to the mirror again, as the hulking, white SUV turned the corner with all the ease of a Sunday afternoon drive.

Shauna clenched the wheel with her free hand.

When the phone connected, she heard Samuel's voice in the distance. It seemed to drown under the whirring sound of machinery.

Shauna looked up as red stoplight glared toward her. She gasped and pressed the phone closer as she jammed on the brake again.

"Samuel? Hello."

"Get another air mover over here. This one isn't cutting it." A crackle sounded over the phone. His voice drew closer. "Hello?"

"It's Shauna Tamson."

"Oh, the shortcake. Hi! Fancy hearing you again."

"Where's Adrian?"

"Not here." His lightened tone dampened a little. "I've been cleaning up his mess for over an hour now."

Her shoulders sunk under their own weight.

"You wanna reschedule or something?" he prompted.

"Kinda. We met up last night, but things didn't go as expected."

Shauna mentally prodded the vehicle in front of her as the light changed green. She eased forward. "Listen, how do I find him again?"

"You ate the chocolate. Without me," he accused.

She stomped on the brake when the car didn't move. Shauna hit the horn. Her attention shot to the vehicle's license plate.

The driver reacted midway through the prolonged *hooooonk.*

Red brake lights flickered off.

Shauna was moving again.

She glanced in the rearview mirror. Yep. Still there. Two cars back. "Sam?"

"Yeah."

"I really need to find him."

Samuel cleared his throat. His next words came with all the speed and agility of a monotone tax advisor. "Any late night escapades between client and provider are strictly consensual unless otherwise indicated. No animals were harmed in the making of your evening. Residual substances are for external use only and should not be bottled, processed, or otherwise reused. No threat of pregnancy or infectious disease is probable or possible as a result of your evening. Spoken expletives and sentiments during intercourse are not a guarantee of claims—"

She scowled at the phone, then pressed it back to her ear. "What. Are. You doing?"

"Giving you the run-down. You can't have his number. Your transaction's closed…sorry."

His last word. Sorry. *That* one sounded genuine.

And final.

Shauna paused. Searching for a loophole. "Well…what if I'm not happy with my service?"

"You mean sex? Or…"

"No, *my service.*"

"Again. You're talking sex, right?"

"This is not funny." She fought the shrill note that entered her tone. "I'm pink, Samuel. He turned me into a giant Easter egg."

She could picture the way Samuel must have rocked back on his heels and scratched his head. "Oooooh. That." He paused again. "That's never happened before. Interesting. The prophylactic mist has been used for years. I don't think I've ever seen that happen."

"Prophylactic?"

"Where are you?" His voice seemed a new mix of intrigue.

"Are you kidding me? You're telling me we were fu—frolicking around in a goddamn, airborne condom!"

Samuel lowered his tone. "You know, you really need to watch that mouth."

"I said frolicking!" Her voice came out thick with tears and desperation. "He didn't help me at all. He used me. How could he do that?" Caught on the verge of painful sob, Shauna refused to let any more words tumble free.

Silence stretched across the phone, and Shauna took several hard swallows, working her throat into obedience.

Samuel expelled a deep sigh. His words eased in. "Oh-kay. Where are you?"

"I'm..." Her heart dipped a little. "I'm going home." She dodged down a side street. "But don't let him go there," she rushed to clarify. "Have him call me."

"Aye-aye, shortcake."

Shauna couldn't respond. She didn't want words. Words gave her nothing. What she wanted was the protective warmth of Adrian's arms wrapped around her like last night.

But at this point, why see Adrian at all? He'd betrayed her. She swiped at the warm moisture that rolled down her face. She had been right. It *was* easy to pin nobilities on a girl's first crush. Too easy.

Adrian used it to get what he wanted, and now he was gone.

Her foot eased off the gas pedal. It wasn't entirely his fault. She'd pushed for it—pleaded. Even after he'd told her no. She'd brought this on herself.

She'd broken herself.

What good would a broken doll be to anyone?

Samuel's words seemed awash with helpless

concern. "Take care."

The connection severed.

Chapter Sixteen

The large, glass bulb tipped forward. Moss-colored liquid flooded into its long neck and pooled against the cork stopper as the glass bowed toward the floor. The glass tipped further, losing its perch on the narrow shelf fixed several inches over Adrian's head.

He sidestepped the footstool and brushed by a pile of dusty books, sending several volumes cartwheeling.

His attention cross-haired on the container as it plunged through the air. Corrosive? Explosive? It could be anything, and headed right for the wooden floor.

His fingers stretched wide, forming the largest net his hand could muster. The heavy weight plunked to the center of his palm.

He expelled a rush of air from his lungs. "Good hell." He cradled it to his chest with both hands as its contents sloshed and spun. Dark sediment billowed from the glass' bottom. Adrian sniffed. A heady licorice odor emanated from the bottle. Anise, if he had to guess. He glanced to the illegible cursive that stretched across the yellowed label, then to the petrified library of murky bottles towering overhead.

"Brewing some green fairy, Dad?"

"You know I don't indulge in all that boozing nonsense." His father muttered over his shoulder. The ground-shaking baritone had gone thin and raspy with age.

Adrian's reply came in the form of a quiet snort behind the old man's back. When did that change?

As if sensing Adrian's response, the old man's tone elevated. "My hand in the apothecarian trade has gone passive. Youthful stupidity has long since passed *me* by."

Adrian grinned. "What you getting at, dad?"

"Not a thing."

The dumpy cat that stalked along the shelf mewed in agreement. Her tail brushed the remaining bottles, and a chime of rattling glass echoed through the room.

"It's merely a collection of curiosities now." His dad used the blunt end of his cane to scratch behind the cat's ear. "I suppose it's grown a bit over the years."

The cat's attention followed his father's pot-bellied hobble until he moved out of reach. The cat then sprang from the shelf, dislodging yet another bottle.

Adrian snatched the second one more easily. "You still haven't managed to blow yourself up."

His father's tone lifted. "What's that?" He spun to one side; the handle of his cane crashed into a square decanter.

Adrian lunged again and caught it. The containers clinked together in his arms. He closed his eyes and pulled in a slow breath, then scowled at his father's back.

A growling chuckle paired with his father's shuffling steps.

"Very funny." Adrian placed the containers back.

"At one time, you found my collection pretty fascinating." His father continued to the couch, where scattered tissues and soiled plates marked his favorite corner. "I couldn't keep you out of here. No matter how many switches I broke over your backside."

True. The world of apothecary had strict rules. Secrecy was the biggest. Recipes weren't handed down, they were reinvented. In Adrian's teen years, he defied every one of those rules. Except for Shauna. Must have been waiting for that peak of stupidity to finally hit.

Adrian's father turned. "But enough of all this pantywaist nostalgia crap. To what do I owe the honor of this visit? Or better yet, to whom?"

"It's about the curse."

"So it *is* a girl then?" His father gripped the arm of the couch. He crouched slowly and then eased onto the couch's dark impression with a faint groan. "She pretty?"

"Yeah, she's pretty." Not that *pretty* even began to describe her. The hometown troublemaking that sculpted her slender frame and fed light into her smile—all that had infatuated him in youth.

But this whole new infusion of womanhood, the weight of her breasts that fit perfectly in his palm. Her nipples, like little bouquets of blush-pink baby's breath—with tiny petals unfurled and begging for his tongue. Her soft curves and even softer moans—and then, *then*, if she hadn't already pushed him to the brink, those moans formed words.

Simple enough words to come by in the daytime. She might even use them over Sunday dinner. But if she ever spoke like that again, he's sweep the cups and saucers to the floor and take her right there on the table. The woman knew what she wanted and how to ask for it.

The tight heat between her legs had welcomed him into a world his brain had conjured a million times over. His imagination, he could harness. But the real thing? The taste and the feel of her? For over ten years, he had waited for this. That's an eternity in cock years. When her fragrant nectar met his tongue, he dropped his brain at the door.

She had his blood pounding and his deep thinker begging for every treat her body tossed his way.

Of course, with the deep thinker in charge, holding back hadn't even entered his mind. Not until it was too late. But Adrian meant what he said. He'd redeem himself by whatever means necessary. Or spend an eternity trying.

Now if he could just arrange the eternity part.

"Well, isn't that nice." His father's tone hardened with its typical bitter edge. Then it changed, as his brows lifted in afterthought. "Got the implants?"

Adrian ignored the implant quip. "It's Shauna Tamson." He said the name slow, clear, and waited for the words to connect.

The man's gaze chased back and forth across the floor as if skimming distant memories until…

Yep. Bingo.

His father's pale lips clamped together, and a look of dismay etched into his forehead. "Well." He frowned. "This is good news then, isn't it?"

"Is it?" Adrian countered.

"Sure. Why not?" His gruff tone sounded a little too complacent.

"Are you going senile?" It had been years since Adrian visited the decaying cottage. Even longer since he stepped into the forbidden archive. What performance could his father have witnessed in that upholstered, front-row seat that would alter his outlook from caution-Nazi to Willy-fucking-Wonka?

The old man put his hands in his lap. "Look…that little sparkler of yours holds no match for the fates. But if it's a good time you want, you should have it. At least until it takes her." The bobble-head nod seemed to carry on longer than necessary. As though the old man had moved on, but his body forgot to follow. Or maybe he was still trying to convince himself. "It's your life now."

Adrian pushed a hand though his hair. "I don't want it to end like that. I need more information. Something else to go on."

The bobbing stopped. "You've come to an empty well." His father leaned forward a bit. The floor beneath him creaked in protest. "I told you that stuff was powerful. That it was dangerous. You have a gift, but as all gifts do, this one comes with consequences. You refused to ignore the calling, and despite my efforts, I could not keep you from it."

Adrian dropped into the chair facing his father and braced his elbows on his knees. "Okay…*When* does it happen?"

The old man searched his son's face for a moment, then shrugged. "It varies. For your mother and I, God rest her soul, it was two years after your birth."

"With no indication? No turn of events?"

The old man ignored his question and puttered on like an old, abandoned motorboat.

Round and round. No clear direction. No one at the helm.

"Your grandfather—he never admitted love—though he found her just the same. He sired the curse eventually, but he died a wealthy man." He looked away in puzzlement, and then returned with a pointing finger, directed at Adrian's chest. "A Hugh Heffner type fellow…if you know what I mean."

His father widened his eyes in clarification. "He got laid."

"I know."

"A lot."

Adrian let his head drop forward. "I know, dad."

"You did well to follow his footsteps." He stroked a hand down his grizzled beard. "You should have stayed a playboy and done the world a service. Maybe then the fates would have forgiven you. Look at all the lives you've touched."

His grip tightened on his cane. Desperation sparked in his grey eyes. "Maybe if you would've saved enough, you'd save *the right ones*." He paused again. His Adam's apple bobbed up and down just over the collar of his wool sweater. His eyes gleamed with moisture. "Not that you'll ever find them."

Adrian looked to the floor.

Several moments crawled passed in silence.

This wasn't getting him anywhere. He needed answers. Not the audible rendition of How to Screw Over Your Life: Volume One and Two. The scholar's edition.

"Romeo and Juliet," his father declared, with renewed gusto.

"Don't need to remind me."

Not that it mattered. When the man's mouth opened, his ears shut off. His father's voice grew with force, as though something had taken a hold of his soul and shaken it from its afternoon nap. "The first apothecary robbed the world of those star-crossed lovers, and the fates will never be satisfied. We have taken, and we must pay our debt—or you do, in this case."

His voice softened a bit. "Sorry, son, but I failed at this one." He looked to the side table. His shaky hand reached out to where his mother's picture once sat. Fifteen years ago, they had finally put it away, but they both knew its rightful place. "I wish they would have taken me too. But that isn't how it works. We're left to rot."

His father held up one finger. "Great Uncle Lance, now there was an idea. Tried to hang himself." His father scoffed. "Showed him, didn't they? Paralyzed him from the chest down.

"Your grandfather was a major ass too, parading all his gold-digging bimbos around him. The lap dances. And the—" The he made a conjuring motion with his hand. "Oh, what do you call it?" His hand froze mid-air. "Blow jobs—"

"Dad!" Geez. Maybe he liked the bulldog from his youth better. This old hound could do little more than lick old wounds and fart obscenities. At least in the growing years, there was a boundary of respect between them. Back then, they weren't stirring the same sexpot.

"What I'm saying is, you can't push that misery off onto someone else, and you can't delay it forever." His father breathed a heavy sigh. "I was wrong to keep her from you. The fact is I was only keeping you for myself." His father's pale fingertips traced a shapeless pattern through the layer of dust on the tabletop. "I see the light of your mother in your eyes. I'm afraid that's the only thing they haven't taken." He swallowed and looked away. "Yet."

"You met her so young, Adrian." He shook his head. "Until the paired hearts of young love cease to beat, your curse will follow you."

"Can we cut the poetics, here?"

His father's cane cracked against the wooden floor, and all the fury that Adrian remembered in youth came roaring to the surface. "I mean it, boy!" His gaze turned wild. The deep furrows in his brow became a battlefield of determination. "If you fail, and she produces an heir to the curse, they will take her."

Something cold and spiny seemed to dig its talons into Adrian's heart. He couldn't lose Shauna. Not after starving for her all this time.

The future had run backward until this point—for both of them. Shauna, God, look what he'd done to her. He's already put both of them through a lifetime of misery.

Could the fates really be so cruel as to force down another poisonous ending?

"There has to be a way."

His father nodded. "Then you find it. It's selfishness that fuels our demise. And for coming here, perhaps you've done yourself a service. Do what you are. An Apothecary. Do not let this curse run your life by running from it as I have, as they have. You find a way to work with it. Find a way to let her go, and who knows? Maybe the fates will find a way to bring her back to you."

"It's not worth it. It's not worth the risk."

His father tipped his head. His voice softened with wonder and inspiration. "Isn't she? Isn't she worth every risk?"

****

It took another hour of winding turns, one-way streets, and switchbacks until Shauna lost him. Stopping for gas must have really pissed him off. But that blind turn-off, the one just before the eternal stretch of desert road, was *such a shame* for him to miss.

She grinned. *Have fun in Nevada.*

Shauna's nagging paranoia tugged her gaze toward the rearview mirror one last time before rounding the corner into her neighborhood.

Or was it?

She slowed her vehicle to a crawl and looked to where the dented mailbox once stood. Had the neighbor kids down the street taken a baseball bat to it again? Maybe a cherry bomb?

She couldn't get too mad. She'd victimized plenty of boxes in her youth.

Adrian's twice, actually.

But she never took the post with it. The impish curl of Shauna's lips faded as she leaned over the steering wheel and peered closer. Only a gaping crater remained.

And the house. The faded shadow over the garage, where the house numbers had been, was that really necessary? Her gaze veered through the ant-scattering of construction workers and landscapers, then to the other flat-faced bungalow next door, and to the one across the street. Yep, Vanillaville, as always.

Quite the short-ordered facelift Richard must have organized. As though the place suddenly had to meet his caliber before he took another step inside. Guess the "perfect picture of domestic life" wasn't perfect enough after all.

She pulled to the curb and put it in park, beside a

pile of overstuffed bags and suitcases. Even if she *could* squeeze between the commercial trucks, the driveway just didn't seem fitting.

It wasn't hers any more.

A low buzz rattled in the cup dispenser of her center console. She picked up the phone.

Speak of the devil…

She stared at Richard's name through several rings, as the heat crept up her face and fueled her pulse into a pounding beat. What if she just ignored it?

What more could he possibly have to say?

She touched on the "accept" button. Her voice laced heavy with disdain. "How dare you call me?"

"Sorry. Are you home?"

Shauna's jaw unhinged with offense. Reverting to pleasantries. Just like that. And what was last night? A werewolfing, full moon? Alien abduction?

"Look, I don't know what happened last night…" he began.

So we're playing amnesia now are we? Oh, Shauna knew that game. "Who is this?" she demanded.

He paused. "It's Richard. I need to meet with you." His voice sounded cordial but urgent, as though he feared that with one false move, she might hang up. Or come through it and strangle him.

If only.

"Why should I waste even one millisecond of my time—" Shauna's words quivered.

"Hang on. Let me explain."

No. Something small and pained cried out from inside her. Not even the slickest of excuses could mask what he'd done. Any attempt at all would ooze off his face, like dog barf in the summer sun.

It'd smell the same too.

Shauna tossed the phone to the passenger seat and stared it down with her arms folded tight.

Richard started, and then restarted his defense. Or at least that's what Shauna assumed was happening. The word "sorry" wasn't in his vocabulary, and it took far less time than the blabbering, gnome-like rant that sounded from her phone. Only when he yelled her name, did the words take shape. "Are you even listening to me?" the tiny voice demanded.

"Nope," she called into the mouthpiece.

"That's it. I'm coming over," he said.

Shauna's stomach clenched. Wait. She was supposed to be at work. How'd he know her location? She gasped at the gray, lit screen. The unassuming keypad display. He probably bugged her phone.

Tracked her this whole time.

If that were true, what were the odds that she'd really lost the agent on that turn-off road?

She looked back to her rearview, expecting him to screech around the corner at any second.

Nothing.

She twisted in her seat to take in the full three hundred sixty degrees. Still not there.

All the more reason to believe Richard and the feds were connected somehow. The agent never showed up here. That was Richard's job.

Her attention whirred to the street, and she jabbed the down-window button with her index finger. She could go without a phone for a day. Get a new one. Transfer her contacts.

She snatched her phone, poised to throw, and the image of shattering plastic flashed in her mind.

But what about Adrian? Her lungs fought to expand under their own weight.

"If you want Kimmy to keep that home, meet with me," the distant voice said.

"Why?" Couldn't they settle this over the phone? She liked him better gnome size. The kind that can be pancaked with just one swift-moving vehicle. Hell, old Ms. Jonas, down the street would be ideal! Slow and painful. With a big-ass Cadillac.

"I just need a break-up, that's all."

"A break-up?" Was he serious? "Isn't it obvious by now?"

"You know my family. Relationships don't just dissolve without being accounted for. The public will want answers."

"I'll call the paper myself."

"They'll want a face. A conference," he countered.

Shauna breathed a sigh of impatience. She could feel her inner resolve crumbling in the long pause that stretched across the connection.

"I'll think about it." She pressed the end button. Then pressed again, extra hard, for good measure. The pad of her thumbs popped and skidded along the phone's surface as she applied more force. If only she could squish the damn thing like putty.

Kimmy would want her to agree to it. No question. She'd jump at the chance to stay locked inside. She panned the house again. Taking the deal would only offer her a well-manicured prison, and an abusive landlord.

Her attention veered back to the front when a flash of color appeared at the door.

Kimmy leaned out from the brick courtyard that

guarded the entrance and waved a staying hand. She turned away and made a few hurried, collecting motions, then crept from the alcove with cigarette and lighter in one hand, chunky, black stilettoes in the other. She glanced from one end of the yard to the other then back again.

Shauna stared at her. She figured she'd have to pry her little agoraphobe out of that house. How much medication had she taken?

Kimmy dropped into a crouch when a pair of construction men crossed her path. She cringed down behind the replacement door they were carrying until it passed and left her exposed. She looked and crept forward again. Her knuckles whitened as she gripped her shoes and held them to her chest, spikes pointed out.

Her red, silk robe billowed behind her, its ties flapped wildly on either side. Its golden embroidery glinted in the autumn afternoon and danced with the sequined, cocktail dress underneath. The morning's events seemed to have transformed her from woebegone victim to an ancient Chinese fighting champ. On the outside, anyway.

Shauna hoped her grin looked encouraging. "Now look who's being thrust into greatness."

She waited for Kimmy's smarmy comeback. Probably something high on the shock-and-awe scale, something about sex and the importance of great thrusting, but Kimmy ignored the comment. Her friend clamped the cigarette tight in the corner of her mouth. "How about this? He doesn't bother to lift a finger to fix the place up until we get kicked out." Her voice quivered with a mixture of anger and bitterness.

Shauna released a heavy sigh, and her last bubble of optimism went with it. No witty relief today. The undercurrent of Kimmy's anxiety was still there; it showed in the beads of perspiration on her upper lip and her painted-doll complexion. Makeup could do wonders, but it couldn't hide everything. "So what now?"

The flutter of Kimmy's lashes seemed delayed when she blinked at the huge orange and white moving pod. "Temporary storage for most of it. Moving guys will be here in a couple hours."

Shauna frowned. "But where until we find something permanent?" Sure, there must be some sort of grace period on the eviction notice, but if she could escape this place today, she'd do it. Before Kimmy's medication wore off.

Her friend didn't answer. Too busy nursing her cigarette to the lighter. She swayed and missed a few times before finally connecting. "I've packed all the necessities." She drew on the cig for a moment, then pulled it away. She nodded toward the street. Smoke wafted from her lips with each word. Her tone lightened. "We'll stay with him."

Chapter Seventeen

Shauna followed her gaze to the blue-ray Camaro that had just turned the corner.

Her heart stumbled through its next painful beat. "What? No." Not Adrian.

Kimmy watched his approaching vehicle. "Yes." Her grin turned sly, further staining her crimson-rimmed cigarette. "Oh, yes, sir, it's perfect timing. It's meant to be."

"But I haven't even talked to him." Uh. Actually, she had. Shauna mentally face-palmed herself. She'd left him an urgent message what seemed like a lifetime ago. Of all the rotten luck—and timing. Now he'd think that she called about the move.

"Wait. Hang on a sec," she pleaded, as she shoved her car door open. She dashed around the front of the car toward Kimmy. The open and shut of Adrian's own vehicle echoed through her mind, but she still couldn't face Mr. Prophylactic.

Hell, she didn't even want to talk to him. And moving in? *Pifft*, the crazy-cation ended hours ago, remember?

Shauna swallowed against the panic that pulsed in her throat; it squeezed tighter with every beat. She'd move back home with her parents. That's what. Kimmy could…do whatever Kimmy does.

But even as the plan struggled to materialize,

Shauna knew she could never pull the seams together. It had been a prideful move to stay away from her parent's home since she graduated high school. Even after the attack. Putting that aside, how would Kimmy survive on her own? She stared at Kimmy and the expectant fist she'd planted on her hip. That woman needed someone. Until Shauna could safely offload the burden, she *was* that someone.

"Here. Lemme help," Kimmy said. More a challenge than an offer as she reached for the luggage.

Shauna's whisper turned fierce with urgency. "I don't need your help, because this is not happening." She stuck out her thumb and gestured south. "There's plenty of decent hotel rooms by the freeway. Wi-Fi and everything."

Kimmy paused. She squinted at Shauna. "Wha-happen' to your face?"

Shauna touched her cheek, then glanced to her fingertips. Oh yeah. "It's a long story," she began then snapped her mouth shut.

Ah. Distraction. Kimmy's favorite. The conniving brat had already turned her back and moved for the real target. She'd snatched a hefty, powder-red tote and lumbered toward Adrian's car.

Shauna plopped onto the remaining stack of suitcases. She couldn't suppress the cringe; Adrian was still an opportunistic jerk, but the poor guy didn't know what he was in for.

Maybe Kimmy would deliver the tongue-lashing he deserved. Pointless to stop her, Shauna may as well see how this played out.

He'd tell her no. He told everyone no.

Her gaze flicked to Adrian, who had folded his

arms and leaned against the passenger door of his vehicle. Then to the barefoot-bullfighter staggering toward him.

"You remember me? Right?" Kimmy insisted, her voice a bit louder than necessary.

Adrian's jawline hardened.

Kimmy pulled the trembling cigarette from her mouth long enough to call over her shoulder. "He remembers."

The pounding hammers and saw blades swarming the house seemed to freeze, as though a giant puzzle piece had dropped from the sky, squashing Shauna's world under its weight. Her thoughts misfired with dysfunctional twitches. "You know each other?"

How could they possibly?

Wait. Her stomach churned with a sickening thought.

He, the mighty hawk of O'Nightingale's. She, a self-proclaimed frequent flyer.

But she'd seen Kimmy topless way more times than she'd care to admit, and she hadn't seen any tattoo. She couldn't be a fellow hawk. Which could only mean one thing. Kimmy had been on the receiving end. She'd already given him a whole *different kind* of tongue-lashing.

Kimmy touched her painted lashes as if to dam up threatening moisture. "Pop the trunk for me, will you, dear?"

Smooth as polished granite, no expression registered on Adrian's face. His arms remained folded, but his thick forearm twitched as he thumbed the button on his key chain. The trunk clicked.

Of course it did. Adrian was too damn polite not to

follow a ladies' request.

But that was no lady.

Every she-devil ounce of territorial rage hit Shauna. Her lungs kicked on, and heaved with anger. She could practically feel her glossy pink manicure flake away and her nails lengthen to razor-sharp claws. She speared her glare between Kimmy's shoulder blades. "What are you doing?"

Kimmy tossed her a scant glance. "Don't worry, he'll get over it." She dropped her load into the trunk. The car bounced under the weight.

"And speaking of baggage, you and I have something to discuss, young man. I might have lost my right to you, but it's only because I refused to go blabbing my big mouth." She neared Adrian with a pointed jab of her glossy, red finger. "You just *had to know* what was going to happen. Well, I hope you've learned something by now. You align yourself with O, and this is what happens."

Shauna's tone hardened. "Kim? You need to stop."

She rounded to Shauna with a wide-eyed look. "I might be a little pill happy, but I'm not stupid. In case you haven't noticed, we have no other place to go. It's not safe here for you. It's not safe for me. At the moment, our lives depend on this. We're moving on."

Shauna clenched and unclenched her teeth. Her jaw notched up. "Okay. You go. I'll find something else." No way in hell could she stand to watch her best friend cozy up in Adrian's home.

"Oh, no, you won't." Kimmy scoffed. "You're getting in the car."

"How do I say this?" Shauna shouted. Her face pinched with rage. "No—"

196

"You don't." Adrian moved toward her.

Her attention smacked pavement as his measured steps drew close. Damn him and that evenhanded authority of his. He didn't own her, couldn't tell her what to do, but that tone still put her in line. Even after all these years.

The warmth of his hand cupped under her chin and he steered her gaze back to him. "You never say that." Gentle warning brewed in his eyes and eased her rage from inferno to rolling boil.

The damn kindergarten teacher to her tantrum. She jerked her chin away, despite the delicious tingle that danced across her skin.

His arm lowered to his side as if he hadn't noticed. He gave Kimmy a long look when she folded herself into the front passenger seat.

A look that damn well better not be pleasure. Not one grain of it.

Shauna shook her head. Look at this, geared for a battle with no war to win.

So they had a history together. With as much as Adrian—and Kimmy—got around, in this tiny town, it was bound to happen somewhere.

Shauna had a history of her own. A few childhood years and one night that ended in a cotton-candy disaster.

Had she really put herself on the same playing field as *Kimmy*? New anger frothed in her veins. She jabbed an accusing finger toward the car. "She's self-destructive. Unmanageable. She's…she's constantly meddling—"

"She's an Oracle, Shauna. She always has been."

Shauna blinked. She gave him a quizzical look.

"Don't tell me you believe all that crap." Or better yet, did he expect *her* to believe…that he believed that?

Shauna frowned and mentally untangled her spaghetti thoughts one thread at a time. Adrian was all logic and order. He didn't believe in magic—or love. Or happily ever after. How else could he abandon so many? How could he use them?

Or her?

Adrian pushed a hand through his dark hair.

Shauna straightened. "That's the best excuse you could come up with?" A bitter-almond film of disgust tinged the back of Shauna's throat. She let the distaste register in her expression and pushed to her feet. "You two can have each other. I'm done."

"It's not like that," he warned.

"Bullshit." She pivoted to the luggage and began shoving the pile apart.

"I didn't sleep with her."

Aw, come on, how can that be? The guy sleeps with everyone. Suitcases toppled and bounced on the pavement with heavy thuds. Even the nagging neighbor girl—if she nags him enough. She scoured for any one container she could identify as her own.

"Shauna, be honest. What's the problem?"

"Problem?" She ripped one zipper open and began sifting through what appeared to be a tangle of sweaters and shoelaces. "Oh. I don't know." She sat back on her haunches. "Maybe that I'm still *burning people*." she splayed her hand over her cotton candy complexion. "Not to mention, the obvious." She moved to the next case. The zipper squealed open.

Jeans. Awesome.

"No, there's more than that," Adrian prompted.

She snorted in response and snagged one more bag that she knew belonged to her. Who cared what was in it. She'd make do. With arms loaded down, she lumbered towards the car.

"You need to stop running from me."

Shauna heart rate kicked at the sound of Adrian's footfalls close behind. "*I'm* the one who chased *you* down after all those years, remember?" She skirted for the trunk. "The nightclub? I figured you'd be there too."

"Then why avoid me? I don't like the chasing game."

"Neither do I." She dropped the bags near the back end of the car and dug the keys from her pocket.

"Then come at me, Shauna," he fired back, hands coaxing toward him and legs braced for battle. "What do you want?"

"I wanted you. The whole package." Jagged, metal keys dug into her palm. "I needed you." She clenched her teeth together, willing the tears to stay back. "I needed you to fix this."

He dropped his arms to his sides. "I tried. It didn't work."

She closed her eyes and took several painful swallows, fighting to keep her voice in check. "And was there—oh, I don't know—some time before *this very moment* that you could have told me?"

"Like maybe—" The first fissure in her voice cracked open wide. "—before you used me?" Waterworks. Great. Way to own those emotions.

"Used you?" His tone sounded lost in a flurry of shifting equations and scenarios. "Shauna, I haven't left. I'm standing right here."

His hand covered hers as she reached for the trunk. "When were you going to tell me about this move?"

Her glance fled to the remaining suitcases.

"What kind of game are you playing?" His tone sounded…surprisingly pained.

Her voice dropped to a bitter note. "We were evicted. Today."

"No notice?"

Shauna shook her head. "Doesn't matter. Kimmy's right. It isn't safe to stay." Not for either of them. No matter what deal Richard had planned.

He breathed a weighted sigh. "Come on. You're staying with me."

****

When Adrian glanced at the Technicolor goddess standing in his kitchen doorway, his grip tightened on the pan. He forced his attention back to the pale wedges of chicken that popped and sizzled in front of him.

Too late, though. He'd already caught it.

That robe drowned her. If the tie came loose, the whole thing could end up in a pile at her ankles, starting with the deep V shape that plunged between her breasts. Then all that rosy, heated flesh would be his for the taking.

He expelled a short sigh. "Forgot the luggage. Sorry." Probably could have made it sound *a bit* more genuine.

"I'm okay for now," she assured him. "Dessert?"

He paused. Her brows pulled together in skeptical look. Like he wouldn't take her up on that offer. He cleared his throat. "Dessert?" Wasn't she pissed at him for one reason or another? She had plenty to choose from.

The Shauna he knew didn't come off any grudge that easy. She probably still hated him for destroying that shirt of hers during the frat party years ago.

Some asshole had laced her drink with a cheap, mystery drug of some kind. He should have detected it before it got in her hand. He had tried to keep her from drinking it. What choice did he have but to knock it away?

The drink splashed down one side, and the damp, silky material had clung to her breast. Her bra didn't do much to save her either. It formed a proud triangle frame around the tiny, blush-pink bud of her nipple.

Of course, back then he didn't know how pink they were.

But last night things had changed. He closed his eyes. Why did all of his memories have to be wet ones?

She nodded to the clear, plastic container he'd picked up earlier that morning. "You're really planning that for dessert? I thought you were a health nut or something."

Adrian frowned.

"Well, you follow the whole vitamin franchise, and you're brilliant with chemistry, so…"

He tossed her a lopsided grin. "Those just happen to be the ultimate confectionary masterpiece." If he couldn't have her, they would have to suffice. For now.

"A donut?"

He shrugged. "Doubt if you will…" He looked back to the pan "But some things are worth the consequences."

"Okay, chef, if you say so."

He matched her patronizing tone. "Thank you, professor. Loved the lab coat by the way." And where did that go? He hoped she'd wear that instead—and only that.

Or he'd settle for a towel.

He'd overlooked the damn robe behind the door.

She ambled around the island countertop and peered into the pan. "And fried chicken? Wow, you really had me fooled."

He straightened. "Why is that a surprise? It's your favorite." Nothing wrong with being a good host. Taking care of her. Making her comfortable.

Not just trying to get her alone again. *Certainly not* getting her to talk as she had last night.

A smile tugged at the corners of her mouth. "How'd you know I liked chicken?"

Adrian prodded the thick slices of meat across the bottom of the pan. "When we were kids. You invited yourself over for dinner. My dad wasn't much of a cook. We had KFC."

"Yeah, and you weren't much of a host. You wouldn't let me play with your toys."

Adrian's abdominal muscles clenched in surprise when she poked his ribs with her index finger.

A warm giggle sounded at his right. "You blocked the door completely and refused to let me in your room."

He crowned the chicken with another sprinkle of fresh rosemary. Not that it needed more. But he had to keep his hands busy and his brain in neutral, otherwise he might suggest making up for lost time. He knew of one very eager, big-boy toy just begging to come out and play.

"Pretty flowers."

He glanced to the oversized bowl brimming with a

cloud of baby's breath.

"Are these for cooking?" she asked.

"They're mostly medicinal."

"Oh. What kind of medicinal?"

His gaze rolled heavenward. Shit. How to respond? He returned his attention to seasoning-crusted pan.

It's a spermicide. You know, in case you accidently blow your load. Like last night.

Or the real reason, because they reminded him of her nipples—among other things. He should've known. Shauna loved to accessorize. The glistening folds between her legs just happened to match in that same color.

He flipped the chicken over and an aggressive hiss filled the room.

Ignoring her. That's nice.

"I got them for you." There. That's safe.

"To go with the chocolates?" she quipped.

Adrian snorted. "Yeah, you'll never be getting those again."

Shauna's delicate fingers spanned the width of his bicep and charged his nerve endings with awareness. "Look…I'm really sorry about the way I acted last night. It was completely out of character."

He paused. "*You're* apologizing to *me*?"

What an ass. A load-blowin', luggage-slacking, lazy ass—and let's not even get started on the shielding potion. The one he still hadn't managed to lift. Or the fairly suggestive color of her *entire body*. How many more man points could he afford to lose in one day?

"How was your shower?" He should've apologized before she bathed—or during. Maybe washed her back for extra credit. He really needed to stop putting off all these golden opportunities.

"The shower was…wet." She brushed a hand down the length of her damp hair. "Do I need to be more specific about that too?"

"If you insist." This time Adrian permitted the penile nod of approval, and he didn't bother to hide his grin. His mind raced to the thought of what else might be a tad damp, and exactly where he could find it. How easy would it be to coax back the taste of honeyed freesia that he'd found there last night?

"I liked your shampoo," she offered.

Adrian nodded. Him too. The wild orange serum in that bottle must have lifted her mood. "Anything else?" he prompted.

Shauna's eyes narrowed to mischievous slits. "Nope."

Okay. False alarm. Time to get down to business anyway. "Sounds like it cooled you down enough. Ready to talk?"

Shauna's attention fled to the sizzling pan, then the sink. Hell, it bounced all over the room. "Is there anything I can help with first?"

He knew that look. Shauna was about to evade. "Here."

Her pert lips hinged open with surprise when he picked her up. The gasp she expelled came so softly, he ached to catch and swallow it whole.

"Front row seat. How's that?" He set her down on the counter. "You can supervise." It went better in his mind when she'd wrapped those silken legs around his waist. Maybe tugged herself closer to him with a deliberate flex of her thighs, and the feel of the damp heat between her legs pressed against him.

He planted both fists on the counter to either side of her. "The first thing you need to know is that I never meant to hurt you."

Shauna leaned back a bit. "Nice introduction. Sounds like something very bad is about to head my way."

Yep.

Her line of sight veered to the nearest cupboard, which of course, she opened. "Impressive spice rack," she murmured. "I can't even pronounce some of this stuff."

"Let's keep it that way." He moved to close the small door.

She opened it wider.

His gaze returned from its skyward roll of annoyance to catch Shauna with a smile of victory curving her lips.

She returned to the shelves. "Where's Kimmy? Is she in on this conversation too?" She collected several dark vials from the front row and placed them on the counter.

"She's resting." With the amount of sedative he sifted over her, she'd be doing that for a very long time.

"You remember my father," he started.

Shauna's attention remained on her stolen collection as she unscrewed a vial of lavender and took a sniff. "Sure. Your dad used to run the pharmacy by the hospital." She left the first bottle open and moved to the next, lifting to inspect the label. "I'd ride my bike down there in the summer whenever I got money. One of the few places that still had penny candy." She dabbed a bit of vanilla behind her ear. "He was nice to me."

The oil mixed with Shauna's own pheromone to form a come-hither scent that stretched toward Adrian and surrounded his brain in a heady fog. The muscles that enveloped his rib cage grew tense and a rush of heat swelled his cock with a pulsing chant.

Adrian cleared his throat. "He liked you. Thought you would make a perfect rival. Teach me about the better parts of this world. From a safe distance."

"I was a young girl. What did I know?" She moved back to the lavender.

"It's what you didn't know. The innocence of youth. Girl parts are the best kind this world has to offer, and at that age, they're off limits." He lifted a hand in consideration. "Safe distance."

He kept his palm open and urged her to hand over the oil with a crook of his fingertips. Instead, she ignored him and up-ended the tiny vial on her wrist.

"Don't do that," he groaned, closing his eyes.

"Contaminating your precious chemicals?"

"Something like that." He massaged his temple. Barely managing as it was, and then she had to go enhancing his temptation.

Chapter Eighteen

"You weren't an infatuation. Or so my father thought. How could a boy so young find the girl of his dreams on the first try? It's unheard of."

She frowned. "You're unheard of. You're nuts. The best you did was avoid me growing-up. Otherwise, you were deliberately spoiling my fun."

"I was trying to protect you."

"You weren't my babysitter."

He chuckled. "I remember those words. I pushed you away—"

She set the vial down with a *bang* and thrust a pointing finger toward the waterside view. "You *pushed me* into a muck-infested lake!"

"Because I had no choice. My father discovered my fascination with you. He forbade it. Said you were dangerous. I believed him."

Shauna twisted the lids back on at a feverish pace. "That's bullshit. How can you say that?" Accusations fired off as she slammed each vial back to its rightful place on the shelf. "You're a grown man. Look at all the women you've been with. Flings left and right. I had to beg for your attention last night. If you really wanted me that bad, then you would've..." She froze. "Wait. You knew." She rounded to face him slow as the knowledge hit. "You knew about my problem. Even before I did? Is that why he called me dangerous?"

He shook his head. "I created *that* problem."

She snapped her mouth shut.

"It's not something I'm proud of."

Pain threaded through the fine lines on her brow. It glistened in the copper pools of her gaze. "The burning…why?"

Adrian took a deep breath, fighting the ache in his chest. "I heard what those guys were planning, and I stopped it. It wasn't the best approach—I know. I didn't realize the effect would be so severe. Or that it would last—"

Shauna attention flew to the ceiling; she blinked, how does he know this? She swallowed. She seemed to nod to herself. Whether assuring her soul of the truth she'd always suspected or soothing it into a new and harsh reality, he wasn't sure.

Her voice cracked with emotion. "How?"

He shrugged. "My father ran the pharmacy because that's what he's good at. That's what I'm good at."

Her tone hardened with a bitter edge. "Kimmy mentioned something like that. Who you are versus what you do." Turbulent pools of pain and mistrust speared his heart. "Now you're telling me you're a pharmacist?"

"An apothecary."

She stared in disbelief. A slow blink sent two large tears racing down each cheek. "Like in Romeo and Juliet, get thee to an apothecary?"

Adrian frowned. "Exactly."

Her voice wedged up with sarcasm. "Oh, so you were helping me? How noble! What a fair night…" Shauna's expression dropped to a deadpan scowl. "Well, I'm no longer in distress, so you can just go joust yourself!"

"Shauna?" He closed his fist over the knot in her robe. For security purposes. She couldn't run that way. "Calm. Down."

She elevated to a shrill note. "Or better yet, fix it. Undo it, All Powerful Apothecary. Go on."

Adrian took a slow breath, willing himself to remain calm. "It's not an exact science."

"Yes, it is. It's chemistry."

He pushed a hand through his hair. "Don't you think that if I knew how, I would have done it already?"

"Good question. Why haven't you at least tried?"

"I didn't want to."

Surprise stunned her in her tracks. Shit. Must have said that one out loud. He'd worked it together on the way to his dad's place. Her cure had been locked away in his brain the whole time. Why he kept driving there, he didn't know. Until he got there.

He wanted Shauna for his own. Time couldn't change that. "I was young. Stupid. I was selfish," he admitted. "That night at the party, if I couldn't have you, neither could anyone else. I wanted you. By God, you consumed my every thought. I was sure you'd show up that night."

She looked away. "Well, your boys had other plans."

He could only imagine what must be playing back through her mind. Her gaze chased across the floor for a moment, back and forth in short bursts before she squeezed her eyes shut. Her delicate frown deepened with grief.

The sickening guilt that festered below the surface of Adrian's thoughts clawed its way to the surface.

"Did they hurt you that night? Did they—"

"You know what? I don't think I know you at all," she blurted out.

"I need to know. I can't make it right if I don't know how much damage I've done."

"No." She shook her head as if rejecting the thought. "I don't know." She shoved herself backward on the counter in a feeble attempt to escape. "It doesn't matter anymore, anyway."

Adrian cupped her backside with both hands and slowly drew her back to the edge of the counter. "It matters. It matters to me."

"I wasn't conscious. I don't know. The doctor said they didn't, but it felt like…" Her words skipped with what must have been a painful hitch. She looked away. Her chest hitched again, and this time, the sob slipped out before she could cover it.

"Okay," he whispered.

No more. He should torture himself through every detail. He deserved that much.

But she didn't.

He couldn't make her say anymore, and his heart couldn't stand to hear it. But the quiet landslide of Shauna's emotions couldn't be slowed with the simple word. He could do little more than hold her as the tears overtook her strength. The sobs jarred her body. He pulled her face to the crook of his neck and wrapped his arms around her. Warm tears dappled his shirt and slid down the crevice of his neck.

This is how it should have been from the very beginning. He should have protected her. He should have shielded her from the world and hacked off the parasitic curse on his life the moment they'd met.

Adrian pulled back after Shauna had quieted. He steeled himself from immediate loss of her warmth and brushed the pad of his thumbs across her cheeks. The remaining rivulets of moisture smeared, and a dusting of youthful freckles glowed to life from beneath. In a moment, the moisture dried. The fuchsia tint returned to her skin, but Adrian had his answer.

It was time.

He flipped on the stainless ceiling fan and collected the mortar and pestle he'd prepared earlier. A few quick grinding motions and the lemon-infused concoction hit the perfect, powder consistency. "Come here," he whispered, offering his hand.

She edged off the counter but seemed reluctant to follow as her hand slipped away. A few residual sniffs formed her only explanation. Her lashes clung together with moisture and lay low, refusing to lift and show what misery continued to wade through those copper ponds.

Adrian gestured to the open space under the fan. "Step one was the shower. You need the catalyst—the next ingredient."

Shauna moved to where he indicated, at the center circle of a large, braided rug. Her actions appeared numb and mechanical.

"It works better if you lose the robe—"

Before he could get the final word out, the heavy cloth dropped to the floor at her feet. Her toes curled under and her head lowered with what could only be described as shame. More potent and stirring than all the wasted sex slaves in Nightingale's trash heap.

Because this one was innocent.

Shauna hadn't asked for any of this. Adrian, her

would-be protector—turned asshole—had abandoned her. Not once, but multiple times. Adrian swallowed back the gut-clenching guilt. If he could wrap her in his arms again, he would. At this rate, he might never get her back.

He stepped close. "Breathe shallowly." When her chest rose with a faint intake of air, he tossed the powder high. The fan's narrow, metallic blades sliced through the air. The thin powder billowed and spun into a tight cyclone that enveloped Shauna. It brushed and lifted her damp strands of hair and a rash of goose bumps chased across her rosy flesh.

The powder didn't seem to bother Shauna much, but Adrian's knack for chemical reconnaissance made breathing a bit more difficult. He snatched a kitchen towel and covered his mouth and nose, not that it did much good. He squinted and blinked back the moisture that brimmed in his burning eyes. His sinuses filled with the sharp citrus tang. His lungs tensed. They spasmed with a protesting cough. He'd have a raging hangover in the morning, but he could fix that.

After several seconds, the cloudy air near the fan dissipated. Adrian hit the switch, shutting it off. He tossed the towel aside, and bent to retrieve Shauna's robe giving it a firm shake. Tingling particles danced away like fireflies on the wind, while others clung to his hand and seemed to crawl up his arm.

"The powder bonds to the oil found in human skin, so the robe shouldn't bother you for now." He draped it over her shoulders and waited. The golden powder that coated her skin seeped inside, and it took the fuchsia stain with it. Her skin returned to the sun-kissed hue that Adrian remembered.

Still, Shauna wasn't lifting her head.

He cupped her chin with his palm and gently urged her features to meet him. "Color's gone. You want to see?"

The negative shake of her head would have been undetectable had he not been touching her. He breathed a deep sigh. "I'm really sorry." He lifted one shoulder in a reluctant shrug. "I know it's not enough, but I'm not sure how else to say it. I'd give anything to make it up to you, but I think I'm in debt for life."

The dark, spiky fringe of her lashes stooped in quick succession. She'd opened her eyes, but she still wouldn't look at him. Maybe she needed time to think things over.

"I'll go get your stuff," he murmured. Adrian shifted his weight towards the garage, but paused again when Shauna closed her hands over his, her grip desperate.

Oh-kay. Maybe she wanted her stuff to stay in the trunk. Adrian opened his mouth to argue, then snapped it closed again.

He didn't want to hear her rejection. If he didn't plead his case to keep her, she wouldn't argue back. Though the suspense stirred his heart into an erratic rhythm, and his stomach soured with dread.

She leaned into him. Her damp head settled on his collarbone.

Adrian's arms closed around her again. Was this a hug goodbye? Did she need more time to fight through her emotions?

No hitching breaths erupted. The rise and fall of her chest remained even over several minutes. Adrian stroked up and down along the delicate ridge of her spine, soothing and waiting. Waiting and soothing. Why wouldn't she speak?

Both her palms, caught between them, flattened on his abdomen and began a slow upward stroke. Her breathing deepened.

A muggy warmth blossomed from the terrycloth cape wrapped around her. Not hot, she wasn't scared, just warm.

Then it hit him.

An undeniable scent of honeyed freesia carried on the air.

Now he got it. Shauna wanted an entirely different cleansing. Something that would take her away from the heartache, if only for a moment.

Only one problem.

The tears had done him in.

His deep thinker had amnesia. It had deflated with the first drop and wouldn't be found again for hours.

He stopped stroking her back. "I'm not sure this is a good idea." If she got any hint that he couldn't get it up, she might blame herself. Given his history with other women, what other excuse was there? "You remember what I said…about tears?"

Not even a pause. Shauna reached under the hem of his shirt. A rush of nerves jumped to awareness when her hands slid across his bare abs, and continued upward to his pecs.

Maybe he could keep her busy some other way. He had plenty of other resources. But if he took her to the brink and she started begging for something she couldn't have…again…

Her hands slid back down toward his waistband, and he caught them just in time. "We need to stop."

That sounded like genuine's fourth cousin, twenty times removed.

Her words reverberated against his chest. "You owe me." Not angry, resigned.

Adrian couldn't argue it.

Nor did he want to!

The shielding potion hadn't been lifted yet, but with Shauna doing all the work—which she apparently intended to do—there wasn't much threat of being burned.

He shot a frustrated glare to the lazy bulge somewhere below his belt. He couldn't see it with Shauna in the way, but maybe it was better not to look at the disaster about to unfold.

She fisted his shirt and shoved it up, baring the lower half of his chest.

His gaze flicked to the wall several feet away. The fan had dried at least some of her chemical cues, but not enough. He could speed the process if he could reach the damn switch.

When her mouth closed over his flesh, his thought process reduced to a useless buzz. She cupped a hand over the bulge in his pants and began an inviting, up-and-downward stroke.

The groan that escaped his lips caught somewhere between pleasure and frustration.

Shauna still hadn't looked up, but a sly grin curved her lips. She placed both hands on his hips and dropped to her knees.

Dear God in heaven...

His attention ripped to the spice cupboard. Honey, ginger, cinnamon...shit. If he could just get there and whip up a potent meal of aphrodisiacs...

The slow grate of his zipper seemed to echo through the room.

Underwear would have bought more time, but when he dressed this morning, he hadn't expected the afternoon to turn out like this. He'd planned for quick, easy access.

To be a willing participant, for Christ's sake.

With slender fingers, she coaxed out the limp appendage, its half-interested growth thickened mostly around the base. In all its wrinkled humility, the damn thing begged to be nursed back to health as it lounged along the entire length of her hands.

The pink edge of her tongue swiped across her lower lip.

No, not a gesture of nervousness. Her focus told him something else entirely. Her mouth dropped open, and her breaths came and went in a heady pant as she drew closer.

A simple hand job seemed appropriate for a first-timer. But Shauna clearly had other plans. Her mouth widened a bit, and she caressed the mushroomed ridge of his cock with her full lower lip.

She pulled away for a moment adjusting her stance, and Adrian swallowed the eager moisture that flooded his mouth. He embraced the growing tension in his chest and urged his body to beg for more. Her tongue flicked and swirled around his erection with growing enthusiasm. Then her motions softened and she pulled away again.

"Shauna—" His moan of torment came out louder than expected.

"I don't know what you call it." Her head tipped to one side. Her tone hushed with wonder. "I mean, I'm not *that* naive, but shaft…erection…None of those fit."

Call it whatever you want, just don't stop. He opened his mouth, but Shauna spoke faster.

A small smile curved her lips a moment before she returned. Her gentle kiss started at his hilt and trailed an agonizing path towards the tip. "All I know is I want it. All of it." Her mouth grew moist and fervent with every inch.

His cock grew heavy. A glistening bead of pre-cum greeted her by the time she reached the tip. When she took him into the heat of her sweet mouth, the growl of pleasure offered more than any word he could muster.

His hand brushed over her damp hair in encouragement as she took him in completely and delivered on the up-and-down ministrations her hand had promised moments earlier.

He slid his palm to the back of her head, and with gentle nudges, he coaxed her into his favorite rhythm. His head eased back with pleasure as Shauna continued, picking up speed and depth. The rush of arousal swelled his cock with a throbbing beat. One that fell in perfect rhythm every time he met the tight confines in the back of her throat. An all-too-familiar tingle swept through his body. He wouldn't last much longer. He gripped her hair, urging her to slow.

Shauna refused.

"I won't last—" His groan of half-hearted dismay was cut short by an uninvited female voice.

"Chicken's burning."

Adrian snapped to attention. "Damn it, Kimmy!"

Shauna gasped. She sat—or rather fell—to her backside and wrapped the robe tight around her. Embarrassment already blazed in her cheeks.

"You were supposed to be sleeping." Adrian let the anger show in his voice. Part for Shauna, part for the stone-hard rod being wedged back into his pants.

Kimmy snorted as she brushed behind him, heading for the sizzling pan. "Yeah, nice try. It's called chemical desensitization. But you wouldn't know anything about that." She moved the pan from the heat and prodded it with a suspicious frown. "Is this lemon?"

She looked over her shoulder when neither Adrian nor Shauna responded. "What?"

Chapter Nineteen

Pale cords of tension stood out between Richard's shoulder blades. "I don't know yet. But if you don't let me handle this, it won't work at all."

O propped himself up with one elbow and scowled at the phone Richard had cradled to his ear. That damn agent *again*?

Richard said he'd never been with a man before. Sounded plausible as far as his technique was concerned, but with as much time as those two spent together...

"I told you. I'll handle it," Richard insisted, his voice elevating.

Where had all this purpose and authority come from? O had been too sore to play the Dom, and it seemed a pleasant change to let someone else take control. But that was sex. And it was over.

Richard used his free hand to shift his perch on the edge of the bed. He leaned forward as if to stand. The motion cut short. He flinched in pain. Apparently, thinking better of the idea, he dragged a nest of satin sheets around his naked waist.

That's right. The man had enough determination to get off, even through the pain of his injuries. But without the drive of his arousal, and a little chocolate incentive, the fair-haired angel couldn't fly.

Richard ended his call with an exasperated sniff.

"He's not giving me any more time."

"Quite frankly, neither am I." O didn't bother suppressing his irritation. The man served as a common link to the loss of his empire and the loss of Adrian. It'd be better for Richard's health to remember where his motivation lay.

That old saying about keeping your enemies closer? Maybe the bedroom had been a bit too close. But this tender angel needed a little incentive to remain on his tether.

The act might temporarily blind O's ability to foretell, but it also forged an alliance the man couldn't break. Richard would probably give his left nut for the good graces of family and high society, but his first taste of the dirty underground wouldn't be his last. He'd get hooked. They all did. If he wanted to feed his addiction, he better hand over Adrian's toy.

"You need to get rid of that agent."

Richard didn't respond.

"You can't kill him," O prodded. "His buddies will start asking questions."

"I don't have the money to pay him off," Richard muttered.

"Pity. That would be the safer way." O lay back and laced his fingers together behind his head. Truth was, Richard *had* the money, but he didn't want to risk the funds being traced back to him.

When a moment of silence stretched through the room, Richard glanced over his shoulder again, his crystal-blue eyes imploring.

O grinned. "What? You want *me* to pay him off? Sorry, I'm not a charity. If you want the anonymity of Nightingale's for yourself…" And of course, he did.

"We could barter," Richard suggested.

O stifled a laugh and pretended to consult the neon-blue light waves that played across the ceiling. "What'd you have in mind?" With the number of law enforcement officers already tripping to do O's bidding, what good was Richard, a piddley, political-official-to-be?

"Favors," Richard murmured.

O arched a regal brow.

"I'm offering you my services. As often as you'd like." Richard sat straighter.

Oh, a sex slave, is it?

And who would win there? Not O. He expelled a deep sigh. Damn chocolate. Those Nympho Nibs were more trouble than they were worth.

"I've only bartered with one man. I'm afraid you're just not that good. You have a lot of learning to do in the art of pleasure." He traced a fingertip down the smooth notches of Richard's spine. "Not that I'm discarding you by any means."

Offering a freebie lesson from time to time might quell the looming boredom. His taste would remain pleasant for several months after the powder's administration. It might take that long for the headstrong apothecary to come around to O's way of thinking.

O's mouth flooded with moisture at the thought of the real thing, the real Adrian Sands, here, in his bed. No more fleeting illusions.

He'd kept the last of Adrian's vision powder for himself, but over time, the aftermath of one over-eager imposter after another only fueled his disappointment. O's attention veered to Richard. Case in point, just look at that sour expression. Adrian didn't look at him that way.

Okay, maybe he did.

But Richard should at least have the manners to *play* grateful after the gangly, noodle-fest O had been forced to endure.

"The only way to be rid of Agent Squalinski is to give him what he wants. Shauna."

O paused. "Watch that feisty tone, young man. That's not going to happen. You promised me both, and you'll bring me both."

An urgent fizz consumed O's stomach. He couldn't risk losing the girl. Ensuring his good fortune meant driving a wedge between Adrian and his toy—permanently. It wasn't easy driving a wedge between moving targets.

Richard lowered his head, his expression unreadable. If O didn't know any better, he'd say the angel was sulking. "The agent doesn't want Shauna, silly boy," O admonished. "He wants my apothecary like everyone else. Adrian's little toy was given some interesting powers, for sure. But the feds are hunting for the main source."

"So Squalinski isn't *just my* problem," Richard countered under his breath.

"Oh, don't get ahead of yourself. He's *definitely your* problem."

Richard may have earned a fair amount of trust, but he still needed to prove his loyalty. Making the agent disappear would be a telling chore. Would the fledgling recruit be frantic and messy, or methodical?

His bedroom manner pointed to both. Long awaited plans, then too quick to execute. No willpower.

Even less tact.

That delightful vision powder might make him *appear* as Adrian, but Richard's flaws bled through. O had to turn out the lights before he could even come. That never happened!

"Squalinski doesn't know about the apothecary yet," Richard said in warning.

O's gaze narrowed. "True. And he better never—"

"I won't tell him," Richard rushed to assure. "What I'm saying is, you keep Shauna until you get Adrian. Then, let's hand her over." He shrugged. "You won't need her anymore after you have the apothecary."

O masked his features. "With his toy gone, why will the apothecary do my bidding?"

Richard's pale brows lowered in confusion. "You can't keep him happy some other way?"

Happy? Embers of resentment burned deep in O's mind. Who said anything about happy?

"Every man has his drug of choice. For Adrian, it's her."

Sending that toy anywhere but an icy grave meant she could return some day. O couldn't allow that. He'd cage her, far away from Adrian, or he'd kill her.

Not that Richard needed to know that. The aptly named angel had *feelings* for her. On some minuscule level, he didn't want to see her hurt. Hence the reason O found him cowering and sobbing like a baby instead of sticking around to watch her flames of carnage.

Richard's pondering tone stirred O's attention. "But the powder." He nodded to the side table, where O's remaining stash lay tipped on its side. "We could use it on Adrian. We could bring any one of the whores from the club. Your apothecary'd never know the difference."

"Too risky." O frowned. "I don't like it." O paused. Lifted a finger. "But for the agent…" It just might work. Who cared if the agent's vision produced Shauna or Ms. December from *Porn Girl Monthly*? Squalinski would see what he wanted, and he'd take it. No questions asked.

"Find a replacement. A decoy. Someone who couldn't just get up and walk away."

Richard nodded. "Consider it done."

****

"First, you hot little love muffins." Kimmy pivoted from the stove. She moved with such force, tiny bits of chicken took to the air as if they were born again. She staggered to one side, and then righted herself with a you-didn't-see-that toss of her hair. Kimmy tipped a remaining forkful of chicken to Adrian, then Shauna, and back again. Her meat metronome kept time with her words. "We need to know how far the curse has played out."

Shauna gave her a flat look. "Curse?" You mean it gets better?

"Yeah, yeah, the star-crossed ass whoopin' thing." She looked to Adrian. Her shoulders slumped. "Tell me you've explained this to her."

"I was working on it," Adrian bit out.

"Looked like *she* was the one doing the work." Kimmy muttered an off-beat tune. "Work it, girl. Work it, work it, work it, girl."

Shauna frowned. The sudden morph of her lushly-slut-friend to a mystic know-it-all could have happened at any time. Why now? Why in the middle of her second best sexual encounter in the history of ever?

Even more important, why rub it in?

This wasn't Kimmy at all. The mystic thing had been a quirky, little seasoning that Kimmy sprinkled on from time to time, not the oozing, sassy snot that seemed to have consumed her. Like the blob or something.

Adrian seemed to reflect the same caution, as he looked from Kimmy to Shauna and back again. "Okay, something's not right," he murmured.

Shauna shook her head. "Okay…About the curse thing?"

"The men in Adrian's family are cursed to find love and tragically lose it." She waved the fork in circular, magic wand fashion. "Kinda like Romeo and Juliet. It's a curse on the ancient apothecary who enabled their death." With the last word, Kimmy emphatically flicked her fork-wand, and the wedge of chicken shot across the room. It disappeared with a wet thud, somewhere opposite the large island counter.

"Oops, sorry." She returned to the pan. "Anyways, you've already met. That's when it started." Kimmy sawed away at the meat; her shapely rear end jiggled back and forth from the effort.

Adrian's stormy-blue gaze rolled heavenward.

"Let her eat," Shauna murmured. "She'll talk less with her mouth full. Kimmy, why don't you take that to the other room?"

"Clearly, you've found love." Kimmy stuffed a forkful of meat into her mouth. Her next words came out muffled and thick. "So the next step is when Shauna bears an heir…mmm, this is good."

So much for the not talking. Or the leaving.

Adrian pushed out a heavy sigh of annoyance.

"Ugh…Kimmy, what's *wrong* with you?" Shauna demanded. "A little privacy here?"

Kimmy blinked. "But I have the munchies."

"She's in a trance," Adrian grumbled. "They require a lot of energy to prognosticate."

Shauna returned his statement with a wide-eyed look of why-the-hell-would-we-want-her-to-do-that?

"Which reminds me," Kimmy piped up. "You get delivery out here?" She retrieved the phone weighing down her oversized pocket.

"Hey, that's mine." Shauna frowned.

"I know." Kimmy blinked several times as she slid her thumb across the phone's surface. She murmured to herself. "No. No, that's not right—who are all these calls from?"

Was Shauna caught somewhere in a fifties sitcom? Did she really have to clutch her hand bag, dance back and forth on a stool, and cry for Adrian to *do something* before he took action? For the love! Drop the gentleman bullshit and kick the mangy goat out of the kitchen!

But Adrian's stony expression and belligerent arm folding wouldn't be moved. Probably not short of a raging cat fight to break up.

Fine. If he wanted a catfight, he'd get one. "Kimmy? Out!" She gestured to the door. "And leave my phone."

Kimmy looked up. Her expression turned serious. "I saw your face when you walked into the house this morning. I know that look. You were getting busy last night. Hell, you almost got busy right here amongst the cooking utensils. You love bunnies can't keep your hands off each other."

Shauna's defenses hardened. "So. As if that's any of your business…" Not like anything on heaven or earth would ruin *her* appetite.

"*So*, if you get pregnant—or what if you *are* pregnant…"

"Not possible," Adrian stated, his tone a little too calm for Shauna's liking.

She adjusted to face Kimmy. "No. It isn't possible," she snapped.

"You're sure," Kimmy challenged. "How are you sure?"

"Well," she gestured both hands toward Adrian, "the float-a-condom for starters."

"Doesn't count. Look what it did to your face. Obviously it's defective." Kimmy set the phone on the counter and angled her nose to a regal height. "Too much risk. I'm still not convinced."

Shauna tightened her grip on the fluttering ribbon of hope. Pregnant? The thought of white picket fences and backyard family barbeques had been farther from her mind than ever over the last twenty-four hours. But Kimmy's statement brought it bounding to the forefront of her mind, rattling and jumping around in its neatly wrapped package. "I don't need you to be convinced."

"It's. Not. Possible," Adrian insisted.

Kimmy snorted. "You'd be surprised—"

A warning rumbled low in Adrian's chest. "That's enough."

"You better tell her," Kimmy warned.

"Tell me what?" She fired back at Kimmy, Adrian, both of them.

Were they talking about the same thing? She hadn't *completely* gone barren. Not unless Adrian knew something she didn't. With his knack for detecting all things biological and beyond…her stomach squeezed in on itself. God, don't let him be the one to deliver *that* bad news. Anyone but him.

Adrian's rumble grew to a shout. "I know what you're doing. I said that's enough!"

"Tell me." Somebody damn well better say something useful, or that frying pan would go off like a church bell over the blob-she's head.

Chapter Twenty

"I had a vasectomy…okay?" Heated breaths of anger pushed out in quick succession from his flared nostrils. "Are we good now?"

The quick heave and flow of air became the only sound in the room.

"A what?"

"Vasectomy," Kimmy intruded. "You know." She opened and closed two fingers in a menacing motion toward the poor impaled chicken bits on her fork. "Snip, snip."

Oh, Shauna knew what it was. But why? How? If he could easily deploy the float-a-condom, wouldn't that have taken care of it? Why go to such extremes? A paralyzing grip of dismay latched onto her heart. He hadn't lied to her. Or betrayed her on any level. It wasn't her choice to make. It was his body. So why did it hurt so much?

Kimmy's sly tone continued to coax. To needle. "Doesn't have to be Adrian's blood heir, you know. He could adopt. Emotionally or legally. That means a child can be spawned by any means possible. Love, marriage, insemination, even the attack last night."

Shauna's gaze narrowed to menacing slits. "About that. How could you send me in there knowing—"

Kimmy issued a commanding look. "We'll address that in a minute. The attack, Shauna. This is important."

"No, now."

"Was it Richard?" Kimmy offered.

Adrian turned. "Who the fuck is Richard?"

Kimmy's tone lightened with smarmy mischief. "Her fiancé."

"Ex-fiancé." Shauna's nails bit into her palms. She rose to her feet. "I'm going to kill you." Her teeth gnashed together with crushing force. Her marching steps toward Kimmy were thwarted by a thick arm bound around her waist.

"You can't," Adrian said.

Shauna pushed against his arm. She grunted. "Watch me."

"He met her at the dungeon last night," Kimmy tattled. "He's the one who helped assault her."

Adrian banded his other arm around her. "This isn't the Kimmy you know."

"I'll say." She lunged forward, swiping with claws. Air *whooshed* between her fingers.

Kimmy leaned back. A millisecond of surprise crossed her features.

Missed by mere inches.

Kimmy held her fork with both hands like a mighty sword to defend herself. She yelled into the phone. "Help. 911, 911."

The inferno of anger inside Shauna raged up. She lunged again.

Adrian's voice spiked with irritation. "It's a trance!"

"Right." Shauna scoffed. And where does he keep the flying pigs? Maybe we can feed those to her next.

"No. It is." He confirmed. "She couldn't have come out of that sedative. No matter how desensitized."

Kimmy lifted her tiny makeshift pike with yet another chicken slice impaled upon it. "God has given me one face, and I make myself another…" She glanced to the chicken. "With some barbeque sauce!"

"See. There. She's not making sense," Adrian declared.

"You sedated her?" She gave him a long look.

"Maybe some *sweet-n-sour*!"

"Can't you give her something stronger?" Shauna asked.

Adrian's shoulder lifted with indifference.

Kimmy's actions seem to slow; she returned to the pan, poking and prodding the remaining meat, as if it were a primetime reality show. "Oh, you really did Shauna a service by giving her that shielding potion. It's the only thing that's kept her safe. That curse has been working hard to close its circle." She tipped her head in consideration. "I'm not saying she's a slut or anything, but the unlucky few who cross her path, they had a hard time keeping their hands to themselves."

The weight of Adrian's gaze settled over her, but Shauna dared not meet it head on.

"It's worse when she's squeaky clean." Kimmy continued. "Don't you think? No powder or lotion or makeup to dull the effect."

Kimmy lifted her tone. "Tell him, Shauna. This is the best part. Her body's constantly ready for it too."

"He knows," she muttered.

"About the ovulation part?"

Shauna's mouth unhinged with horror. "Kimmy!"

"Not only is she ready for it, she's running out of time."

"That's it." The words were scarcely audible under

Adrian's breath. He jerked open a nearby cabinet, retrieved a glass. Slammed it shut.

"Tick-tock goes the clock," Kimmy chanted. She followed his movements, confusion wrinkling her brow. "You're running out of time too, powder boy. She's going to run, the way you pushed her. Then she will die. She has to. It's the way of these things."

In no time, Adrian had a full glass of water and a look of determination that would have scared the most hardened of criminals back into the shadows. He unscrewed the cap from small vial he had retrieved from the spice rack.

"Aww, thanks I'm parched!" Kimmy held out her hands for the offering.

He tapped the vial until a tiny drop fell into the water. Before the vial's cap hit the ground, Adrian tossed the glass' contents into Kimmy's face.

She gasped and sputtered. Her hands reached to either side as if blindly looking for a towel. Shauna glanced left and right for something dry to toss her way, but before she could act, Kimmy slumped over.

Adrian crouched low and caught her around the waist before she somersaulted to the floor. He sidestepped, dragging Kimmy toward the living room. "Be right back."

"Okay." The word fell numb and distant as it rolled from her mouth. He might not be long, but the bile swirling a violent tide in her stomach said it wouldn't be soon enough.

She had to get out. Get some air. Before the full knowledge of everything she'd heard finally set in.

Then she'd lose her lunch *and* her mind.

****

Shauna plodded over sloppy, uneven ground on her way to the pond. The soggy conditions from earlier that morning had turned invasive and bitter with cold. The sun smoldered low behind the mountain ridge, tugging deep-blue shadows across the rolling landscape. Frost needled through the tiny holes of her sweater and numbed her toes.

She had slipped away to get dressed, but she hadn't chanced putting on an extra layer. The coat hung in the closet, and that meant crossing paths with Adrian again. She wasn't ready for that. It wouldn't take long, but she needed every second she could get. The gears around her seemed to be turning faster, as if trying desperately to make up for lost time, but Shauna's brain seemed more content to splat right where she stood and suction-cup itself in for the long haul.

Footprints of her youth had stamped this very bank in her childhood. Not so deeply set and weary as her current tracks. The prancing steps from nearly a decade ago held too much adventure and mayhem to sink so heavily.

How could she never share this place with her own children? The thought of a family seemed so far away, beyond possibility when it came to Richard. Even after all the carefully laid plans, it only felt like a distant dream.

Now, even the dream had been stolen.

Tears bent and wavered her view of the silent, ice-filmed pond like a carnival mirror. If she crossed to the other side, would she still find a footprint or two? She scanned the silent landscape of reeds, still water, and the encroaching dusk.

Of course not. The world had moved on without

her, even the silent pond held no trace of her past.

She trudged up the arched bridge that belt-buckled the pond. Her steps stopped short when the bridge's downside fell into view.

Two shadows emerged from a pale SUV parked several yards from the dirt road. One held back with his hand on his hip, while the other marched forward with hurried steps.

This was private property now. They didn't belong here.

She opened her mouth to speak, but her eyes and heart processed faster. A panicked gasp snared the words mid-throat.

"Miss Tamson," called the man holding back.

Squidlinski. Shauna's vision squinted. "*Hate* that tone." That meant the man coming toward her must be—

"We need to talk," Richard said.

"Why?" she demanded. "How'd you find me?" He knew nothing of her childhood.

"Your phone. We have a trace."

Knew it. Shauna clenched her teeth hard enough to send shock waves up her jaw.

"Listen, you're in some trouble." Richard hurried up the bridge toward her.

"We just want to talk," Squid persisted.

"No." Shauna back stepped the way she'd come, not daring to take her attention off Richard.

She expected the familiar, smug upturn of his mouth. She couldn't outrun him. But the more panic she let fuel her steps, the more dread seemed to weigh on his posture.

"Rich!" Squidlinski barked. Urgent warning trailed

in his voice.

Richard flashed a staying hand to the agent several yards behind, but he kept moving toward Shauna. "You might not trust me…"

"No shit!"

His hesitation flipped to an angry frown. "Better me than him. Come with me now, or I'll let agent Squidlinski have you."

The squid? Shauna snorted. She'd escaped him twice already. She'd fought past *both of them* before, she could do it again, right?

The squid stalked forward too, moving quickly to catch up.

Shauna's vision flicked in Adrian's direction.

It was only a microsecond.

One she never should have stolen.

Because when her attention returned, Richard struck. He wrapped both arms around her in a crushing grip. Shauna jerked and twisted; she rammed her elbow into his side. Richard dropped her fast, and he crumpled like a paper bag. She expected a yowl of pain, but it came out more of wheeze.

Free. Shauna raced back the way she'd come.

"Get her," Squid shouted. His thunderous steps boomed behind her on the old wooden boards. Closing in fast.

Squid snagged her sweater and yanked her back with brutal force. The neckline burned against her skin. Several strands of hair, caught in his fist, ripped from her scalp, as he whipped her in a tight circle. Her hip slammed into the bridge's handrail; the paint-flaked, wooden banister creaked and wobbled unsteadily, but Shauna clung to it.

"Let go!" Squid wrapped his arms around her and slammed his forearms down onto hers.

Spears of pain unclamped her hands and her wooden anchor slipped away.

Squid caught her arm. "Hands behind your back," he sneered. "You're under arrest."

Shauna spun and jerked her arm free, leaving him with the sleeve of her sweater.

She saw the gap and went for it. Ducking between the boards of the railing, Shauna flung herself over the bridge.

The sweater yanked over her head, and Shauna was free a mere second before she crashed sideways into the water.

Her muscles locked in protest the moment the cold slammed her. The weight of her waterlogged jeans pulled down with what seemed twice her bodyweight.

Up. Get up.

Shauna forced her kicks from a series of floppy gestures into some sort of useful locomotion. She broke to the surface with a gasp of sharp, mucky pond air. She fought the primal urge to fold her arms and legs in fetal position. She had to stay afloat in the tangle of duckweed and moss that tugged at her legs.

Panic...don't panic. With numb fingers, Shauna raked away the hair that plastered her forehead and hindered her line of sight. She twisted to take in her surroundings with flapping strokes. How could this not be ice? It's so cold!

"What are you waiting for? Go. She'll freeze in there," Richard said.

"Pond's not that big. She'll probably touch bottom."

Could she?

Shauna let the weight of her clothes pull her down, but a snare of alarm charged her back into fighting strokes the moment the water climbed up her neck. No, she couldn't reach it.

Squid's voice leered from the bridge directly above. "We know you're under there."

Her teeth rattled, and spades of pain and numbness shot up her arms and legs. Her back muscles spasmed in a feeble attempt to clutch the heat that fled her body.

"Come out," Richard called as he rounded the bridge to the bank. He neared the edge of the water, but wouldn't step in. "You can't stay in there forever."

"What do you want?" Her words shook. "Can't you leave me alone? Haven't you done enough?"

"I'm not trying to hurt you…" His words became hollow and distant. "Swim back before you freeze to death."

He'd let her too.

Chapter Twenty-One

"We just want to talk," Richard prompted again.

As he continued to reason with her, the words floated around in Shauna's brain, refusing to connect. All she could think of was the cold.

"I'm calling backup." Squidlinski turned and raced up the embankment with his head tipped to one side. The orders he panted quickly lost their meaning.

Shauna's flailing limbs inched her closer to the other side, her movements like stroking though quicksand. Richard's hammering footsteps over the bridge followed her across the pond again. Useless, she'd never make it out in time and manage to escape with these sluggish muscles. Not from one of them, let alone two.

She lunged for a nearby bridge post and wrapped both arms and legs around the massive wooden pole monkey style.

Shauna pulled in a lung full of air, stretching her tense ribs. She pushed out an ear-piercing scream. "Adrian!"

"Shut up," Richard hissed. "Come out now or freeze to death. Those are your only options." Richard's agitated steps paced tight, back and forth steps across the wooden planks above. He stuttered something urgent under his breath. His voice seemed to teeter on the edge of a breakdown, as though an ominous shadow had grown to life behind him, leaving him scurrying and desperate. "Shauna, come out. Honey, please come out."

Honey? Who was he playing up for now? Not her. He never called her that. "Leave," she countered.

His voice turned sinister. Quick and low. "I'm not. Not until I deal with you—"

Steady footfalls on the boards above cut his comment short.

Shauna set her gaze on planks, praying it would be Adrian. That he would step into view somewhere between the cracks. What else could make Richard so fearful?

Richard offered a helpless plea. "It's a suicide. We saw her go over. She hasn't come out."

The steps picked up urgency. A dark shadow snaked between gaps in the wooden planks above. It stopped at the bridge's highest point.

Please, Adrian. Please.

"Help," she breathed. But the cloud of warm air that escaped her chattering teeth carried away into nothing. The gasp for another breath overtook everything.

The numbness paralyzed her arms and hands. It seemed to turn them to slacked, strange appendages that were no longer her own. Her grip fell away, and her mind waded through a sluggish fog as she fought to react. She reached out again, for what should have felt like a massive post, slicked with frozen algae, but she felt...

Nothing.

Had she grabbed it? The question floated away in dreamy afterthought.

Did it matter?

Her vision darkened around the edges as the icy water climbed higher and her gasps for breath fought to stay on top of it. Shauna's own body weight tugged her down. The world above constricted to a pinhole point of wavering light, before it extinguished completely.

****

The man's words sped together with panic. "I don't know. She already went under."

Adrian's gaze raced across the pond as he threw off his coat. Fingers of icy slush stretched across the surface of the water, making ripples of movement difficult to track. He had to get in there, but he wouldn't last more than a few minutes. He couldn't search the entire fucking pond.

"She's already under," the man insisted.

"Where!" Adrian mounted the arched bridge with a desperate pace that rivaled the alarm pounding his ears. That's where the man's attention had been focused. Near the center. Just under the bridge. He'd just been talking to her. Why wasn't he helping? It couldn't be too late.

"Told you, man. She's a suicide. Let her go." A hand clawed onto Adrian's shoulder with a grip of desperation.

Adrian spun. The man's voice seemed familiar somehow, but not for long. Adrian slammed his fist into the man's nose. A nose that had recently been broken. The force rippled his features like flesh-toned Jell-O. An audible crack sounded against Adrian's knuckles.

The man's body sagged backward from the blow. He stumbled, and then crashed to the wooden bridge like a low-life sack of rocks.

Adrian ignored the flash of pain that jolted across his hand as he slammed both palms down on the railing and vaulted himself over. The next instant, a crash of water and the shock of cold swallowed him whole.

His feet touched down in slow motion, at the bottom of the uneven pond, and Adrian stretched his arms wide. His muscles tensed with shock. He fought his eyes open in the inky abyss, as he pushed his way through the stringy tangles of duckweed and moss.

He kicked to the right and spiraled outward from where he'd landed, pushing his lungs to the burning point, before he popped to the surface. In a single gasp, he took mental note of his bearings and plunged down again.

One second. Two. Three.

How much longer could Shauna last?

Every stroke went slower than before with his energy siphoned from every angle.

His mind roared with anger as he forced his muscles to keep stroking. Keep searching. She was here. Somewhere close. He had to find her.

Five seconds. Six.

Before Adrian could fully extend his next stroke, the backside of his arm brushed something solid.

He wanted cloth, hair, skin…anything discernible, but his frozen touch no longer registered with his brain. He clutched the weighted mass, drawing it closer to him.

There was no fight in it.

Adrian's stomach clenched. He yanked to the surface and a bellow of dismay escaped on his first breath.

Shauna, dear god!

What have you done?

Baby...What have you done?

Adrian side stroked to the nearest shore. A narrow sandbar piled under the edge of the bridge.

He rolled Shauna to her back and straddled her hips. Her milky blue completion and half-mast eyelids reminded him of an abandoned doll.

Don't think about it.

He laced his fingers together and shoved upward with the heel of his hand toward her diaphragm.

Water rolled from the narrow crevice of her waxy-grey lips with each blow.

Again. Again. The water kept coming.

Christ, it had to hurt. But Shauna didn't flinch. She didn't blink. Her glassy gaze stared down at him. The copper shine...gone.

No. She isn't. She can't.

When the water stopped flowing, Adrian adjusted the upward tilt of her jaw, and pushed a steady breath of air into her lungs. Her chest lifted and fell with ease.

Come on, baby. Breathe.

He pushed another lungful of air past her flaccid lips.

Breathe!

He felt for a pulse below the crevice of her jawline, but his damn fingers were so numb.

Fuck he couldn't tell!

He pressed an ear to the center of her chest and prayed.

The faint echo of a beat seemed too distant to be real.

Was it only in his mind?

If he could just reach in and pull it to the

surface…but he couldn't.

Adrian held his breath. If he could quiet the urgent drum of his own heart, he'd know for sure. The *pound, pound, pound* eclipsed everything else!

Precious seconds ticked away.

Adrian gritted his teeth together and turned his frustration inward. With a mighty exhale, he compressed the chemical balance within his own body. The inner filter of his mind sought out the life-sustaining potassium floating through his blood and shoved it down deep.

The pounding scuttled. Paused.

Precious seconds passed.

In an instant, the faint thud of Shauna's heart echoed in his ear.

Adrian relinquished the punishing grip on his insides and pulled in a shaky breath.

Her chest rose with a timid breath and flinched. Her features contorted in pain. Then her body erupted with a fit of watery coughs.

Adrian turned her to one side.

The coughing gave way to a series of heaves. She stole a quiet gasp before she vomited again.

The sound dampened from a sudden thunder of hurried footsteps that pounded on the wooden planks overhead. Adrian looked to shadows chasing along the wooden gaps in the bridge. Three men. At least. Maybe more.

How could they get here so quick?

They must be linked to that flat-faced douche bag on the bridge. The one who'd refused to help Shauna.

The one who…

And then it hit him. The broken nose. The voice.

The one who probably gave the order to assault her at the dungeon. Adrian's teeth scraped together. That son of a bitch!

The crowd got to the bastard still laid-out on the planks above, and stopped. "Is this the one?" The first man asked.

"No, it's a woman. She went into the water," another shouted.

"Did you see her come up?"

The shouting man paused, as if pushing a hand through his hair, his voice uncertain. "She was up when I left, hanging on one of the pilings."

"Any possibility she might've got out? I guess it's possible, given the condition of your friend here?"

The man's voice lowered with a bitter undertone. "I don't know what the hell happened to him, but *she* couldn't have done that."

"Well…let's get him to come to." A scuffle over the boards told Adrian they were trying to move the douche. Maybe get him to an upright position.

"That woman's a suspect in the Grigori fire from last night," the man insisted.

"Well…if she's gone under for this long, I'd say your case is closed, buddy."

A pause stretched overhead, as though the words from the first responder had blanketed the entire rescue team with a new perspective.

A loud crack split through the silence. The bridge's railing shuttered and a fine dusting of paint sprinkled from above. As though the man had punched it.

"Hang on, your guy is coming to," the responder said.

With any luck, they'd be focused in tight enough,

Adrian could probably slip away with Shauna unnoticed. He reached through the folds of his soggy denim pocket and pulled out a small plastic baggie of powder.

Or what used to be powder. He cringed. He'd used the shielding powder for years on Shauna. Even on himself when he needed to disappear from the public eye. Its potency could block out most everything: showers, perfume, hair dye—the harshest of girly chemicals. Hell, even Shauna's fire couldn't dull its power. But now it looked to have a power of its own. A funk—if you will.

The bag had been contaminated with microbial-infested pond water. Adrian pulled the baggie open and pinched out a slimy portion of goo. Tiny flagella flipped and jumped along the surface. The concoction's sulfurous fumes burned his sinuses and put his stomach on high alert—its contents ready to abandon ship.

He closed his eyes, willing himself to block out the new chemical puzzle that was busily piecing together in his mind. He pushed the gob to the inside of his cheek.

Adrian's gag reflux lurched in protest of the amoebic hoedown that ensued on his taste buds.

Forget holding it there to spit out later. Adrian forced down a swallow.

The cold lump slugged down his throat. Taking its time. He pulled in slow, steady breaths, willing himself to keep it down as he took another pinch and pushed it past Shauna's teeth.

He pulled back just in time for her teeth to snap shut. The corners of her mouth turned down. Distaste registered in the wrinkle of her brow, but she took it like a champ.

The shielding potion should still work. They wouldn't be invisible, but they'd be overlooked, and that was good enough for now.

Adrian shifted Shauna's limp frame into his arms and crept from under the bridge.

Chapter Twenty-Two

A slow caress traced the curve of Shauna's nose, followed by a playful tap on the very tip. Adrian's voice rumbled soft near her temple. "Feisty little…"

Without opening her eyes, Shauna pulled in a deep breath that stretched her aching lungs. "Mmm?"

He planted a soft kiss on her forehead. "You didn't take your pills."

"Mmmhmm," she protested, stretching her arms out butterfly-style.

His soft lower lip continued to play over her brow, and the warmth of his breath fanned her hair. "They're sitting. Right there. On the night stand."

Only two. She could skip two. He'd been feeding her antibiotics every few hours like clockwork, for daaaays! Surely her stomach could use a break from the constant bombardment.

At least he hadn't found them in a mass under her pillow. Like last time.

Shauna rolled to where Adrian stood next to the bed. His abs contracted to a series of hard planes and angles as she wrapped her arms around his waist and buried her face in his shirt. Perhaps she could appeal to his generous bedside manner.

Or distract him by other means.

Shauna grinned at his reluctant drop in posture.

"I'm not letting you get pneumonia."

Her words came out muffled, pressed to a thin layer of rapidly steaming cotton. "Lying here all day would give me pneumonia. What I need is exercise."

Adrian's tone lifted with faint amusement. "Exercise, huh…"

"Yep."

"Think you're ready for that? I don't want you to overdo it."

"No problem. I won't even get out of bed. If I get tired, we'll switch. Then *you* can be on top."

His abdomen bounced with a quiet snort. "Did Kimmy sneak you in more chocolate?" he paused. "Wait, you're trying to get out of taking your pills, aren't you?"

"A little."

Adrian's chest lifted and fell with a heavy sigh. "This. This is your downfall, shortcake." His tone eased to a somber note. "We try hard to break the curse. But you women try even harder. So damn stubborn." Tingles chased across her skull as a large, soothing hand sifted through the back of her hair. "The last thing I'd ever want is for you to kill yourself trying."

"She already did."

At the sound of Kimmy's voice, Shauna pulled far enough away to view the woman's heart-shaped face propped at the end of the bed. She hadn't even noticed her friend enter the room, or felt her plop, belly-down, at the end of the bed. She just appeared there, as if she was buried there hours ago, when Shauna had kicked all the blankets free.

Someone needed to put a bell on that girl.

Kimmy's cheeks were bunched and rosy from her hands propped on either side of her chin. Her head bobbed up and down with each word. "Until the paired hearts of young love cease to beat...your hearts stopped. The curse is lifted." She offered a hand in consideration. "Perhaps you're not both dead, but the rest of the world doesn't know that."

"They don't need to," Adrian emphasized.

Kimmy seemed to disregard his warning look as she crossed and uncrossed her ankles. "As self-appointed house hermit, and heir to your estates, the authorities have been keeping me informed. Pond's too frozen to keep searching for you guys. They'll be giving up the recovery mission tonight. Shauna's creepy agent will be forced to close his case."

"Your funerals are next Wednesday, by the way. Hope you like purple velvet cheetah print." She nodded to each of them. "Based on what you left at the scene, *your* sweater and *your* coat will be staring at that fabric for eternity."

"But what about O?" Adrian countered.

"He's got problems of his own." Kimmy looked pointedly to Shauna. "Seems your ex-fiancé had some major plans for our old house. It really is *the perfect picture of domestic life* on the outside. So plain, you'll look right past it, really. In fact, I'd wager that it's even a bit...what's that you call it? Over-lookable?"

"Shielded," Adrian offered. His tone fell pretty flat, but the mischievous glint in his eye told Shauna that he'd had—whether intentional or not—something to do with it and that he liked where it was going.

Any chance Shauna could get a good look at that figurative compass too? Perhaps an explanation for why the O was still along for the ride? "Can we back up a little—"

Kimmy closed her eyes. "Just a sec, this is where it gets good. You didn't know it, but your *little Richard* is a bit of a creepy, voyeuristic, masochist—oh, you know what I mean, a *weird-o* side to him."

Shauna's brow lifted in agreement. She sat back. "Actually that explains a lot."

"You. Have. No. Idea the extent of it. Seriously! He *did it* with O." Kimmy cringed. "Seriously. Who would tap that? He's like the Stay Puft Marshmallow Troll."

Shauna swallowed in distaste. "So that's where O comes in?"

Kimmy's face lit with enjoyment, and she flapped a coming along gesture with her hand. "Yeah, yeah, yeah, by the time the construction team left, the house had been fitted with bars, sound proofing, the works. Richard's got quite a knack for decorating too. Who knew?"

Shauna frowned. "Wow...oh-kay, but I still don't see—"

"Well, with O being the lone," she made air quotes, "*survivor* who knew about Richard's flaming fascination for other men, and his appearance at the dungeon, apparently, Richard decided it would be best to keep his dirty little secret under lock and key."

"Meaning O?"

"You got it. It didn't take much to lure him there. Just a *little* chocolate." She nodded to Adrian. "You're out by the way. Now O's under house arrest for the remainder of his life." She looked skyward. "I'd tell you how long that is, but I really don't want to jinx myself. Just know that he'll be kept busy, on a steady diet of bread, water, and really, *really* bad sex. And not bad as in good. It's bad—bad."

Shauna shook her head. "You're getting entirely too much pleasure out of this, you know that, right?"

Kimmy's eyes widened with innocence. She let her hands fall to the large mound of blankets. "Why shouldn't I? O's fate only improved when you two were at odds. It's *my* fate that gets better if you two lovebirds succeed. I happen to be the flip side of my brother's coin. That's all." She wrinkled her nose. "By the way, ain't karma a bitch?"

Shauna's brows synched in disbelief. "Your brother. You're really siblings? You and O?"

"Twins. Kind of a yin and yang," Adrian offered.

Kimmy tipped her head. Her lips stretched to a wicked grin. "Well, I think we were actually triplets, but judging by the size of O, he probably ate the other one." She pushed to her feet. "Long story short, you get a fresh start. With babies and everything."

Shauna's heart skipped a beat. "But what about the vasectomy?" She looked to Adrian.

"Hey, those things aren't fool proof," Kimmy exclaimed. "And you two will have a helluva good time shooting for the one-percent chance to spawn some little apotha-singies."

"Good. Now get out," Adrian said.

"Going," Kimmy called over her shoulder.

Adrian followed close behind until he came to the door and flipped the lock behind Kimmy with an audible click.

Shauna gave her best attempt at a stern look with both fists planted on her hips. "Adrian Sands, where'd all those manners go?" Not that she really wanted Kimmy to stay.

"I only use good manners with my own lady. Now, about that exercise…" His expression turned thoughtful.

His lady?

His? Shauna couldn't suppress her smile if she wanted to.

The mattress dipped under Adrian's weight as he crawled onto the bed fully clothed. He hovered over her, his knees firmly anchored to either side of her hips and his forearms framing her upper half. The warmth of his body pressing into her built an erratic flutter in her chest.

The touch of Adrian's lips came slow and content, teasing the perimeter of her mouth, until he puzzled their lips together and urged her mouth to open. She found herself straining closer, inviting his tongue's exploration with a coaxing brush of her palm along his stubbled jaw.

The press of his mouth grew firm with an urgency Shauna answered. Every dive and retreat she met and welcomed, as she pushed her fingers through the back of his hair. She closed her fist around the thick, close-cropped strands at the base of his neck. Just long enough to catch between her fingers. She tugged.

The deep rumble from Adrian's chest kicked off a blizzard of excitement in Shauna's belly. Desperate to hear that sound again, Shauna let her hand wander to the button of his jeans.

He closed a hand around her wrist and urged her hand away. "You first." The heated words tickled in the shell of her ear moments before his mouth descended to the crook of her neck. Tingles of delight chased down her body.

A tug at the band of her pajama bottoms, and Shauna's stomach clenched.

"If…you don't mind," he countered.

Did she? Shauna paused. It was no problem removing his pants, but hers? Now that's a different story. Not quite sure why, it just was. The flames-o-nuisance were a thing of the past, thanks to Adrian, but it left her feeling…unguarded.

Shauna went for his button again. Maybe if they did it together…

He urged her back and angled his head in opposition. "I lost my head last time. It was rude. Tonight, I show you how a true gentleman does it."

Oh…boy. Her pulse funneled south, all the while pounding out an urgent signal.

Adrian tugged her bottoms free and tossed them aside.

Shauna closed her eyes. The easy caress of his palm started at her knee and moved up to graze her inner thigh. His thumb began a deliberate massage that nearly reached the outer folds of her seam before he retreated again. Back down to her knee. Several rounds of this ensued, and each time Shauna's mind spun in a desperate chant as the warmth spread between her legs. *Closer, closer.* She squirmed.

Her legs eased further apart, and Shauna moaned. She remembered his touch. The way he'd toyed with her the first time. Oh, she'd been here before.

As if on cue, Adrian shifted lower. His moist breath met her inner thigh.

With his mouth? Not there. Too low. New territory. "Adrian!" she squealed in half-hearted protest.

"Mmm?" A seductive challenge darkened his gaze.

She opened her mouth, searching for a stall tactic. She could ask him to stop, but why would she do a silly thing like that?

His dark head lowered, and soft, warm kisses tickled across her exposed flesh.

"Umm…" Wasn't she upset at him for one reason or another?

His kisses continued unhindered, veering into dangerous proximity to the slick folds between her open legs.

Hadn't he betrayed her trust and stolen a rather sizable portion of her social life?

She released a nervous laugh. Was she really ready to forgive him so quickly? "You said gentleman." She shifted in attempt to cut-off his wandering mouth's destination.

"Yep, absolute gentleman," he agreed. He cupped his hands under her bottom, all the while dealing her a sinful, trust-me glance. "It's rude to make a meal of you without tasting first. Now be a proper lady and accept the compliment."

Forgiven.

Her head sunk deep against the pillow. She used both hands to cover the embarrassment heating her face. "Hardly proper for a lady to put herself in this position."

Adrian shifted to one side. The warmth of his palm under her left hip disappeared, but before she had the chance to wonder—*or secretly hope*—where it had gone, a feather-light caress chased over the sensitive petals of her vagina.

Any manner of objection fled her mind like dandelion seeds on the wind. Her thoughts swam as the caress deepened.

"In a moment, you're going to forget *all about* where you are or what position you're in."

Her voice came of the tail end of a heady pant. "What, another dose of your magic?"

"I don't know if I'd call it that." The faint line of stubble that framed his lips tickled over her bare mound. "It's more your magic than mine."

The moist heat of his mouth seemed to spiral in a steady rhythm of pleasure straight to the aching weight of her core. Feeding it, stoking it, as the pressure of his mouth deepened, and edged upward to her clit. Shauna couldn't keep her voice in check. The moment he introduced his first finger into her opening, her hitching cries dropped a full octave.

He stroked her, in and out, gradually adding a second finger as his mouth continued its torment. Her thighs clenched, and her hips rolled as she called out an intelligible chant at first, caught somewhere between pleading for him to continue and the fear of revealing exactly how much she liked it.

Her inner conflict fell helpless as she climbed to the crest of her orgasm with each perfectly measured flick of his tongue. Each thrust of his fingers.

He had to stop. At least slow down. "Please…" She squeezed her eyes tight and arched her back to what seemed an impossible angle. "I can't take much more!"

The wicked performance of his tongue eased away, leaving her swollen vagina dripping and bare to his scrutiny. His gaze caught hers. His jaw set tight, not so much in anger, but with a lurid challenge she hadn't recognized before. "Oh, you can take more," he countered. "We've only begun."

Shauna forced her anxious breathing to slow. What did that mean? The looming intimidation of Adrian's unknown sexual history floated through Shauna's mind. What if she really *couldn't* take everything he promised to deliver?

What if she wasn't ready for that? Whatever *that* was.

But Adrian didn't appear to be in the elaborating mood. He stood from the bed and fisted the hem of his shirt, then yanked it over his head. He tossed it aside and shoved off his jeans. The rustle of fabric became the only sound until he turned his fully erect profile to face her.

Her attention dropped below his waist level, to take in the straining reach of Adrian's—

A single word slammed into her mind.

Cock.

No other term could define it. That prominent tool, capable of both pleasure and pain, looked swollen with enough need to deliver a healthy portion of both.

Her thoughts must have registered somewhere on her face. Adrian's expression turned tender. "Change your mind?"

Caught in a vice of anticipation, Shauna couldn't squeeze out the words from her constricted chest. She shook her head.

He leveled his gaze. "How would you want it, pretty lady?"

She swallowed "Want—as in position?" People have this conversation?

Adrian's brows lifted, still waiting for an answer.

"I don't know…" She looked away. The heat that had radiated from every pore seemed to rush lightning quick to her face. "What's best? I'm willing to experiment." That last bit slipped out on a whim.

Is it possible to hunt whims down and blast them to a smoldering pile of ash? Adrian held medals as the reigning apothecary and the leading cultivator for underground sin.

And she wanted to play naughty with that?

Yeah, she kinda did.

"Best?" he countered. "That's up to you." He tugged at the hem on her shirt.

Shauna took the hint, and pulled the shirt over her head, thankful for the extra seconds of distraction. Guess it was Shauna's turn to bail off the elaboration train. All remaining whims were on mandatory lockdown. Cool air tingled across her bare chest.

So her severe lack of bedroom adventure might have peeked out a little. But the thought of Adrian teaching her a thing or two had her lower half feeling all *new kinds* of intrigued.

"Pleasing *you* pleases *me*." Adrian rounded the bed. "So forgive me if this sounds harsh, but for me? The *best* is when I get to see you come."

Shauna pressed her lips together to keep her jaw from dropping on its hinges. His tone flowed warm and open as afternoon sunlight, but his words and their meaning loomed deep in the shadows of seduction.

Adrian grasped the tangle of sheets from the bottom of the bed and ripped them away. The rumpled cotton material billowed and then tumbled to the floor, well out of reach. Nowhere to hide. Shauna's stomach tightened.

Adrian stretched out facing her. He cupped her shoulder and stroked the pad of his thumb down her

Kacey Mark

arm, as if coaxing her attention. The sexy lure of his voice tickled over the sensitive curve of her neck. "I asked you a question."

Shauna turned to greet his body and the image of their last encounter flashed through her mind. The way she rode against the firm expanse of his erection, and their hips grinding together in a mounting tempo.

The heady drumbeat of her pulse replied from deep in her core.

"I know you well enough now, Shauna. You *will* tell me." As if sensing her thoughts, Adrian wrapped his arms around her and rolled her on top. His expansive arms trapped her there, her wet core pressing against the length of his shaft. Her body ached to move, but he wouldn't permit it. Instead, he drew her forward, up the length of his torso until his mouth met the tight peak of her nipple.

When Adrian sucked it into his mouth, Shauna let a prolonged hum of appreciation for the delicate shards of pleasure and pain that shot through her breast.

Adrian rolled his hips until the mushroomed tip of his penis glided along her slick folds.

Shauna let her head ease back, and she sucked in a tight breath. "Oh…" Dear God, it felt good.

Adrian continued to administer the delicious friction with smooth, slow strokes. He gripped her hips with both hands and eased her lower half back and forth along the full length of him.

"Oh…I want that." Shauna clamped onto Adrian's massive shoulders, her nails scoring his heated flesh in a silent bid for more.

Adrian released her breast.

His strokes against the juncture between her legs

258

became more desperate, but without the distraction on her breast, she couldn't resist the heavy ache much longer. "I want it," she cried.

"What." He forced the back of his head deep against the pillow, and his eyes squeezed tight in what appeared to be a mix of pleasure and frustration. "Say it."

"Your cock!"

Just as quickly, his head lifted again. A gleam of determination darkened his stormy gaze. He gritted his teeth, and in one fluid movement, he angled his hips deeper. The full expanse of his erection slid inside to consume her. Shauna's moan of gratification spilled past her lips as Adrian eased back and thrust forward again.

She angled herself to meet him as their writhing bodies worked together, picking up speed. She plunged onto his swollen member again and again as they both strained for release.

The grunt that passed Adrian's lips seemed more agony than pleasure. In what seemed an act of pure desperation, he caged Shauna's hips with the expanse of both hands. Adrian guided her hips to move against him, forward and back, his shaft still fully embedded inside her.

Her slick body glided against his pelvis. She savored the brisk massage against her swollen clit, one that Shauna couldn't seem to get enough of. She planted both palms just above his shoulders, gaining leverage as she quickened her motions in a spellbound pursuit for release.

The mounting pressure that shot through her system seemed to build beyond her control. "My God."

It kept building. Building. Her tone sounded urgent, almost fearful to her own ears. "Oh my God, I'm gonna—"

"Come," he grunted.

With that final word, Shauna's release rushed over her. She cried out, and her muscles locked hard as granite, just as Adrian thrust deep and held. His roar of triumph chimed with hers.

Shauna collapsed on his chest.

In the distant shadow of her ragged breaths, Shauna caught his low murmur.

"Magic. Pure magic."

About the Author

Kacey Mark is a voracious reader and paranormal romance author who makes her home near the Wasatch Mountain range of northern Utah.

She loves writing eccentric characters and unpredictable plot turns.

She enjoys a good book that pulls her into its world and holds her captive until the very last page. But, then again, who doesn't love that?

She's often caught laughing at a book in the middle of a crowded room, and loves it when people wonder what she's up to.

She posts blogs weekly at
http://kaceymark.blogspot.com
You can catch her on Twitter
@Kacey_Mark
Facebook:
http://www.facebook.com/?sk=pages#!/pages/Kacey-Mark/218199808200456

Visit Kacey at
http://www.kaceymark.com

To chat with Kacey Mark and other Wild Rose Press authors of erotic romance, join us at www.groups.yahoo.com/group/thewilderroses.

Also Available

Prom Night in Purgatory
by
Kacey Mark

http://amzn.com/B00NLLPK6O

As a conduit to the afterlife, Baila Grey holds the record for most risks taken in a lifetime. And with her inability to land a single live boyfriend, she's ready to shoot that record sky high. Conjuring the ghost of Asher Landin, might be the best option for a finale.

Asher lives for his job—not that you could really call it living, he's dead. As a Collector, his gateway to the ever-changing world above only swings one way, and the morsels of life he gathers, his defense against insanity. Until he meets Baila and finds a new meaning to sanity. Asher needs to prove his ability to control not only the realm of purgatory, but his increasing urge to chase Baila around like a lunatic.

Asher and Baila can't deny the feelings they have for each other but can the living and the dead find a happy ever after together?

Also Read

Last Enchantment
Agents of CAT
by
L.M. Connelly

http://amzn.com/B010RX1VBG

An agent for CAT, the Central Agency for Talents, Tegan Gibbs was a powerful sorcerer until she was attacked and her virginity stolen along with her powers. Now she's a normal human being with a thirst for revenge. To discover and capture her attackers, she must work with the Earl of Derrington, the only man to ever stir the desires she so carefully kept tucked away. But he's an ancient vampire, and while once his equal, she now has nothing. Or so she thinks.

Oliver Derrington aches to bring Tegan back to life and into his bed. What starts as a rescue quickly turns into a passionate affair. They set fire to the night, but with the differences between them, Oliver fears his time with Tegan is limited. Yet, he'll fight to protect her—and to keep her.

Danger threatens from an unexpected quarter, and if they don't stop those responsible for stealing power from other Talents, they won't have a future—together or apart.

www.ingramcontent.com/pod-product-compliance
Lightning Source LLC
Chambersburg PA
CBHW070329260626
47160CB00003B/993